THE PROMISE

BY

SUMMER STORM

Countless hues of beautiful brown people, some in domestic uniforms, while others sported Brooks Brothers suits rushed home after a long week working for the man. No matter the hue or the uniform they all worked for the man. It was Friday the first and everyone seemed to be in the best of moods. A check on payday had a way of uplifting even the most downtrodden.

"Is that you Ms. Muhammad?" Hank said leaning over his broom.

"You know it ain't nobody but me Hank! Why you actin' all crazy?" The petite, little, Beauty of a butterball said smiling broadly.

"Cause every time I see you it seems like you just keep getting better and better looking. When was the last time I saw you?" Hank grinned. He had her attention now.

"Yesterday, you fool," she laughed as she stood waiting to hear today's pick-up line.

"I do believe you're right," Hank said looking as serious as always. And you know yesterday I asked myself. I said Hank that is one Beautiful woman. I wonder if she could get any better looking and then here you come today looking even better than you did yesterday. Lord knows God is good."

Cynthia grinned from ear-to-ear. She'd always had a soft spot in her heart for Hank. But as much as he flirted nowadays she wondered why he didn't just ask her out. Her thoughts were interrupted then by the two men in their mid-twenties that rushed by them.

"Nazar!" Cynthia shouted.

The young man's head spun around upon hearing the familiar voice.

"Hey sis. What's up?"

"No. Better yet what's up with you?"

Hank seeing the change in the woman who moments ago had been so upbeat went back to sweeping the sidewalk in front of his bodega.

It was obvious the woman loved her brother dearly and only wanted the best for him but she was no longer sure if her little brother wanted the same for himself anymore. If he'd only get himself together she thought.

"Ain't nothin' happenin' sis. I just been chillin' is all. Went down to the docks this morning to try and get some work but the cracker called everybody but me and Noah."

"Did you two go down there looking like that?"

Both young men dropped their heads.

"I wouldn't hire your asses either. Nazar I want you to go home right now and wash clothes, so you have a clean shirt and trousers for tomorrow. I don't know if you know or realize it but mama's not getting any younger and she's been carrying you ever since daddy died when it should be you carrying her. Damn Nazar. This is not you. What happened to the Nazar I used to know?"

Again, the two young men dropped their heads. Their guilt obvious.

"I don't know what to say sis. You're absolutely right."

"So, I can expect you home in an hour then?"

"Yes ma'am. I'll be there. Just let me run and handle this business."

He was sweating profusely now and beginning to get antsy. She knew in a minute or two he'd be on the verge of getting sick. She'd seen it all before and her heart went out to her younger brother for his pain.

"Go ahead and do you Nazar but be home in an hour," she said knowing full well that her words were now falling on deaf ears.

The two men shuffled away.

"Damn man. Does Cynthia ever give up? She's been crying that same tune for a while now," Nazar mused.t give up and

"No. She doesn't give up and I don't want her to. She doesn't give up because she knows another Nazar, a better Nazar. She knows the Nazar that was making Dean's list at City College on his way to becoming a Civil Rights lawyer. Do you hear me? A Civil Rights lawyer. That's the baby brother she loves and wants to see."

"I hear you Naz but tell me this? What happened to you that brought you down so low?"

"Life happened is what happened? And who the hell are you anyway? What are you supposed to be? My therapist or my shrink? You're gonna help me work things out?! Picture that. If that ain't the blind leading the blind," Nazar chuckled.

"I ain't mean nothin' my brother. I was just curious. You know Cynthia talks and treats me just like he treats you, so I figure I got a right to ask."

"C'mon man. Is you stupid bruh? I don't like seeing myself on this shit. Just think of what we gettin' ready to do and all the foul shit we done did for this shit. Sometimes it makes me wanna throw up in my mouth. Tell me something. What do you see when you look at this shit and the man you used to be?" Nazar asked."

"I try not to think about it."

"Maybe you should. This shit here don't do nothing but lead to an abbreviated life. This shit ain't gonna do nothin' but kill us or get us killed tryin' to get it. Eventually your number comes up."

"But not today baby. Today we hit O'Hara's Bar right after lunch time then we head uptown and hit Trip. I heard he's got that 'fire'. Say he's got that killa. Niggas on the block are callin' it that Whitney Houston. Say that shit is so good six or seven niggas o.d.-ed up on the concourse."

Nazar stared at his buddy and partner in crime and just shook his head. Nazar could remember the first time they'd gotten down as if it were yesterday. Daddy had passed away the week before. He'd been a Golden Glove contender and was defending his belt having won it the previous two years. Daddy had been his trainer, coach and his best friend. His father had been a pretty good middleweight contender in his own time taking then middleweight champ Emile Griffith to a fifteen-round split draw. And for the second time in his life he shocked the world by graduating Magna Cum Laude from Hofstra University with a degree in civil engineering. And still he found the time to drag every little lost soul and vagabond he found wasting time in the streets into the gym.

'A strong mind and body is the key to a full and wholesome life, he was always one to profess. And no one epitomized that more than his boy Nazar. He was proud of his Nazar. He was proud of all his kids but perhaps Naza more than all the others because he resembled him in both looks and temperament. And then when it appeared things couldn't get any better daddy died. Doctor's weren't so quick to come to a conclusion as to his cause of death since he'd just had his quarterly checkup the week before and appeared in excellence health. When all was said and done the doctor's agreed that there were heart problems due to his diabetes.

Still it hardly mattered what caused his death. The fact-of-the-matter was daddy was gone. To Nazar it meant that daddy was no longer in his corner. For as long as he'd known daddy had always been there for him in his time of need. Now, he was no longer there. Sur there was mom and his sister who loved him just as much as daddy did but when it came to that uncomfortable question that he couldn't quite seem to phrase it was always daddy that knew what it was that had him squirming on the edge of his chair. And where it seemed like a life-or-death situation to him it was nothing for his dad who only saw it as helping his son through his quest for manhood. Calm and resolved he'd tell Nazar a parable or recite a proverb and let Naz draw his own conclusions. He could see instantly if his son had gotten the gist of whatever it was that he was trying to convey. If not, he would start all over again with the patience of Job and try another approach and another until he too was fully convinced that his son understood and was at pace with the subject at hand. And perhaps unknowingly this was the apart he would miss most about his father's sudden departure from his world. His father was his teacher and he was the student eagerly grasping for knowledge in the ring and out.

To Nazar it hardly mattered what the cause of his father's death was. What most mattered to Nazar was the burning pain of not having his best friend in his corner anymore. And he was in pain. A pain like he had never known before and no matter what he did he could not extinguish this pain. It was a deep, excruciating pain; the kind of pain that would have called for group therapy if he'd been white and well-todo. But here in Harlem where resources still ran a little thin there were only two ways for a man of color to deal with the pain of such a loss. There were liquor stores on every block and can almost be said the same for the dope boys. If one had some very grievous pain, he could hit both the liquor store and the dope boys in a manner of minutes and be back up in the confines of his cozy little coffin.

"Sorry about your old man kid. Here take this," he said. "It's on me. It should take some of the grief away but don't count on it as a longtime fix. If you're not careful with it it'll suck you right on in and before you know it you'll have a bigger problem than the death of your old man. I'm telling you and this is real talk Naz but if it were anyone else but you I wouldn't have even considered doing this, but you've always been smarter and stronger than most of these niggas out here. I really and truly believes you a lot like me. I mean I fucks with it but I never let that shit fuck wit' me. You know what I'm sayin'? I respect the monster. You feel me?"

"I understand completely Trip. I ain't tryin' to drown myself in this shit. I just want to take a dip and test the waters."

"Ain't no change in the waters my brother. Like I said they'll pull you in, suck you dry and have you wonderin' 'What fuck just happened ten year later'.

Naz shook his head as he took the glassine envelope and shoved it in his pocket before thanking Trip and making his way home. The rest of the family were still at the repass. Nazar made his way to his room and glanced at the array of trophies he and his father had amassed over the years and he could feel his eyes welling with tears. It was all a bit too much. Who would take him, guide him the rest of the way? Nazar lay across his bed, his head in his hands as the tears rolled down his face until he was fast asleep. What seemed like hours later he was awakened by friends and family talking and doing their best to offer condolences.

Nazar got up, looked at himself in the mirror, pulling a piece of lint from his long black dreads, took a deep breath and made his way out among the crowd of wellwishers. There were people everywhere, in the hall, in the stairwell just standing, waiting to share their memories and condolences. The fact that so many people were affected by this man, his father, made him smile. Daddy with his infectious laugh and always a good word was always there in lieu of family problems. The world was daddy's family and he was just as involved in their triumphs as their failures but for both he was there. Nazar knew all too well accompanying his father on what seemed at the time worthless business. He commanded and demanded respect on the street and Nazar could not remember his father ever having lifted a hand in anger. And if you were a young boy caught hanging out looking like you had nothing to do and daddy saw you that was your ass.

"Whatcha doin' boy? Don't answer that 'cause you don't know what you're doin'. You're just hanging out waiting to be picked up by the police. Or you waitin' for some other loser that ain't doin' too much of nothin' either to come along and tell you how you can make some quick cash. At which time you begin your relationship with the police. You don't want to do that. I don't want to see that happen to you, so you be at the gym before I get there. You feel me?"

"Yes sir," the young man replied. But that was the point. They all knew him although they'd never met. They knew where the gym was although they'd never had any intention of going. But this man whose legend preceded his death was well known to them all simply for his work with the community. A devout Muslim he was if nothing else disciplined, diligent and driven. A hard man many a person decreed but a fair and good man who would give you the shirt off of his

14

own back all had to agree. And their agreement led to all of the people. Looking out of the window Nazar saw several of the street gangs from different sets milling around paying homage to his father. And again, his eyes welled with tears.

Nazar made his way amongst the crowd who had somehow forced their way into the living room. He was hoping to find among them a kind word, a memory to help him through his pain and anger and finding it all for naught he once again returned to his room full of melancholy and grief. There were no tears now as he lay across his bed. He feared he must have cried them all out but the pain, anger and the hurt still remained deeply embedded.

Desperate now he remembered the package his man Trip had given him. Digging in his pocket he grabbed the small envelope and poured the contents out onto the black lacquer dresser top drawing three lines in the white powder just as Trip had instructed.

"I usually break a package into half when I take a day just for me. White folks call them mental health days but anyway being that you're a newbie I'd break it into three and do one at breakfast, lunch and dinner. That should give you a break from the hurt I know you must be going through right through here."

Nazar bent over and drew in deeply finishing half the line and taking the rolled dollar and changing nostrils, he drew the other half of the line up his remaining nostril before sweeping the remainder of the powder back into the envelope and placing it in his drawer. Laying across his bed Nazar closed his eyes only to hear his father's voice.

"Son, you will never out brawl or outmuscle this fool. He's strong as a bull and there's no quit in him. What you have to do is to be smarter. For the next

16

three rounds you have to outthink him. What you have to ask yourself is what's the best way to Beat this man? Is it to brawl with him or out box him? Or how can I inflict the most amount of damage without incurring damage to myself? Should I brawl with him or box him? For the next three rounds you have to outthink him. You're on your own son."

Nazar could do little more than smile. He understood and was suddenly reassured. He'd use his footwork now, moving in and tattooing him with crisp jabs before moving out and setting angles for his next barrage of jabs that kept him backpedaling and offbalance. He was out of range now playing the role of the matador as the bull moved forward out of frustration and because he knew nothing else only to be peppered with a barrage of jabs again.

In between rounds his father said nothing. The next two rounds went much as this one had with Nazar gliding around the ring peppering his opponent until his opponent threw up his hands in frustration.

"Come on and fight me motherfucker," he yelled at Nazar who just smiled.

He knew he had him now but kept to his game plan until the other man dropped his hands out of frustration and Nazar who'd been studying his style or lack thereof moved in leading with a straight right jab followed by a vicious left hook that sent the man sprawling face down. He was out before he hit the canvas. After the fight was officially over, Nazar showered quickly. Leaving the facilities, it was his father and only his father who stood waiting for him.

"You took a large step tonight son."

"Does that mean that you're giving some serious to the prospect of me gong pro. That would really put a perfect end to a pretty good day pops."

"You make me smile Nazar,"

"Well, that's not quite the response I was
hoping for."

"Do you want me to be honest son?"

"Is there any other way to be?"

"Well, since we're being honest you know I
have had a considerable experience with up and coming
fighters and some can go pro at fifteen or sixteen and
have fairly successful careers. And you certainly have
the physical skills. There's no question about that but
your you're not a thinking fighter yet. That comes with
age and maturity and a few more years in the ring where
all of this becomes second nature to you. You're not
there yet. If that no-account excuse for a boxer had you
frustrated and totally off your game, then just imagine
what a fighter the equal of say a Pernell
Whitaker, Hector 'Macho' Camacho or even a Mark

19

Breland would do to your ass."

"Now tell me how you really feel pops," Nazar laughed.

"Seriously, though son, today you took a major step in the process. I made you accept the fact that you were in this, you and only you for the sake of you and yours. I gave you the motivation and freedom to take control of your life and your destiny. The changes you made in the ring today were made out of your motivation not to fail. For the first time you made to think and take control of your life and to come up with a strategy to help you to prevail."

Nazar broke out in a huge grin.

"Don't you see this was bigger than boxing son. This is what life is about. A parent's duty is to guide a child for as long as he can and then he must cut the apron strings and let them fly away on their own. I did that tonight. And all we can hope as good parents is that the training we've provided show up in their decisions and choices. Good choices lead to an easier life and the choice you made to box this boy tonight and keep your distance with the jab was a good choice, and a good decision. But what's more important is that this was your decision. You had no corner to lean on.

This was all on you. And once these decisions become second-nature then you'll be ready to go pro."

"I gotcha," Nazar said a smile now illuminating his face.

"Funny thing but the last couple of years that's all I wanted Nazar said dropping to his fighting stance before throwing a left and right that whistled.

"But pops thought I was a good two or three years from being legitimate middleweight."

"Okay. So, we put you on that fast track. Now who ya got training you now since your old man passed?"

"To be honest with you Trip I haven't been near the gym since pops passed away. I ain't even thought about it," Nazar lied.

"I get that. You're still going through the grieving process. Yeah, I get that. But you know that was your daddy's dream for you. And you're blessed enough to take it just as far as you want it to go."

"That's what you're not getting. Boxing was daddy's dream not mine."

"So, whatcha' sayin' Nazar? This could be your ticket out of this hell hole."

"You're right. I'm just sayin' I'm not sure what I want to do right through here. I'm not sure I even want to box anymore."

"I know Mr. Muhammad must be rolling over in his grave after all the time and energy he invested in your dumb ass. The odds have gotta be something like a million-to-one that has the God given talent that you have and one thing I know for sure is you sure as fuck don't turn your back on God's blessings. What the hell is wrong with you Nazar? Do you have any idea how much money you could make if you decided to go pro? I'll finance you and make sure your family eats while you train and go to school. Matter-of-fact and if you're willing to put the time and work in I'll set your first pro fight for a year from now. Until you decide what you want to do you can work for me and I'll make sure you keep some pocket change. In the meantime, I'll see if I can't bring Doug Le Gard and Joey Nema in. They're no Mr. Muhammad but they're said to be two of the best trainers in the city."

"Sounds mighty tempting. Just hope it's nothing too strenuous."

"No, nothing too strenuous. As you know I wear many hats in the community. I try to help those who fall on hard times from time-to-time. I lend them whatever they need to get by. Sometimes they forget. I need someone like you who's reputation precedes them to just show your face, so I can collect what's owed to me. You'd probably never have to lift a hand."

"Like I said the offer is tempting. Give me a couple of days to think about it."

"Okay. It's Wednesday. Let me know one way or the other by Friday. If we're going to do this there's no time to waste."

"Friday, it is Trip. I'll let you know something. Oh, and Trip,"

"What up Naz?"

By the time of his father's passing, Nazar was by all-accounts the best pound-for-pound boxer in the tri-state area having all the skills of a seasoned veteran. And although quiet and humble he'd amassed quite a following. Uptown and the Bronx where the folks proved quite knowledgeable when it came to pugilism the first person they chose to compare Nazar with was Hector Camacho. He was fast and quick and his slick defensive skills which electrified the crowds kept his name in the spotlight. There were never any unfavorable reviews and it was almost as if New York was waiting for Nazar 'One-Time' Muhammad to make the announcement that he was turning pro.

All thoughts of daddy were gone now. The pressures of carrying a 4.0 GPA and being first in his junior class were gone as well and for the first time in his life he knew how it felt to just sit back and relax.

The last conversation Nazar remembered having with his father was the one had with him in the corner demanding that he begin thinking for himself and become smart in his attempts to become independent. His father passed away the following day. Nazar now wondered if father had known he was dying.

Nazar always wondered why so many good, strong, bright young brothers had gotten into drugs. Good, strong brothers who could have very well college professors or a CEO for some Fortune 500 company given just a little direction and guidance. He no longer questioned. He understood now. He'd found the cure, the panacea, the remedy for all that ailed him and acted to fill the void of his father's passing.

Life was so simple now. No longer was he confronted with questions of his boxing career. Would he turn pro now that his old man was gone or would he adhere to his father's wishes of him remaining an amateur.

Life was so simple now. No longer did he have to answer questions about his quest to become a lawyer. Now his only concern was to not wake up writhing in pain, his stomach in knots, sweating profusely as he considered who had the best pain reliever for his affliction.

And although it had only been a couple of weeks since his father's passing no longer did Nazar think of his father or anything else for that matter. The thought of his father and his mother only brought about feelings of guilt and despair. His father had given him the foundation all little Black boys need to pursue any number of avenues but he'd eliminated these and all other options with his father's passing. Now little concerned him aside from his quest to get high.

It hadn't been bad at first. Daddy had left a little money to all of them. At first he went on with the same daily routine he'd grown accustomed to over the years. Get up at five a.m., put in his roadwork before coming home, showering and preparing for school.

Nazar rolled up the twenty Auntie had given him to help with his grief. Inhaling deeply Nazar sucked up half the line like a seasoned veteran before rubbing his nose and doing the same thing for the other nostril. It burned letting him know that the dope was good. Nazar locked the door before leaning back across his bed. Suddenly, filling nauseous he grabbed the tiny garbage can and let go of everything he'd consumed that day. And then it him. He was soaring, shadowboxing against a background of pastel blues and grays. His footwork had always been one of his strong suits and now he was dancing, gliding. Moving swiftly and gracefully he jabbed three sharp quick jabs followed by a left hook and an upper cut just like in the Mancini fight. He was too quick, too elusive for the slow-moving Italian. And there was daddy as always. He remembered the fight as if it was yesterday. He remembered hitting Mancini with everything he had in his arsenal. And although he was hitting that white boy with everything he had and knew he was ahead on all the scorecards the white boy was relentless walking through the barrage of punches Nazar threw as if they were nothing. At the end of the ninth Nazar was dead tired. He'd thrown his best shots and the young man across the ring seemed unfazed. And then he heard his father's words. 'Be smart son. Don't fight his fight.

Fight yours. You don't have to knock everyone out that you step into the ring with. Boxing is the art of acquiring points by touching your man without him touching you.' Nazar smiled. The dope had him now. He found himself talking to himself, coaching himself, motivating him to box this kid the final three rounds.

Stay out of his reach and just touch him when the opportunity presented himself. That was the key to victory. And Nazar followed it out to a tee. He was thinking in the ring now not looking for daddy's advice and approval. Yes, he was ready to turn pro. At least in his mind he was ready and who was there to oppose him. The only person who'd ever opposed his turning pro was pops and he was no longer here.

His skill level was on par with the best in his weight class. What Nazar's biggest problem came with his age. He was simply too immature, too emotional in the ring which in itself could be the difference between winning and losing. Someone say something about Naz's daddy and he would just start winging it. Daddy had warned him about this on more than one occasion to little avail. If a fighter showed up and wanted to brawl because he knew he was no match boxing Nazar Nazar would brawl with him knowing full well that this wasn't where his strength lay. It was that machismo thing mixed with that street thang where if you were challenged you couldn't back down. If you did you were a punk. And for all of Nazar's finer qualities he had difficulty breaking from that street mentality.

He knew he was way ahead on points but he'd had enough and for some reason Naz stepped out of the ring and went to the dressing room before the fight was over.

He'd gotten high to forget the reality of his father and the gym and here he was back in some gym, in some fight. There was after all, more to him than boxing. Or was there?

It had always been the same ever since he could remember but since daddy's passing he'd been able to slack off. Truth is boxing had never been high on his bucket list. It was more like he was fulfilling daddy's dream. But no longer did he feel compelled to spend his days in the gym letting some brute bang away at his mid-section.

For the first time in his life he had some free time after class to do whatever it was that nineteen-year old's did. The only thing wrong was that the mean streets had little or nothing to offer a young nineteen year-old Black man. But he didn't know that.

Mama and Cynthia understood his no longer wanting or needing to box since neither of them were big fans of the sport. But what they didn't understand that daddy did was that boxing was good if for no other reason than it kept Nazar and a few other young Black boys out of the streets.

Nazar remembered stopping by the dope spot every day even when he was boxing just to check out what was happening in the streets.

"If it ain't my nigga. Nazar 'One Time' Muhammad. What's up my nigga? You know I saw

34

your last fight against that bull-headed white boy that wouldn't take no for an answer. Nigga's face was a bloody mess and he just kept coming for more. See that's when I would've walked out and said you got it white boy. I mean *he wanted that fight*. I honestly thought you were going to punch yourself out. I think he thought so too but in the ninth you changed the game plan and hit him with the jab. And then you just kept hitting him with it. You went jab crazy. Stickin' and movin'. It was a Beautiful thing to watch and you ran away with the decision."

Trip, the local dope mogul who lived two floors underneath Nazar and his family was one of Nazar's biggest fans.

"No disrespect Nazar but since your pop's passing have you given any thought to who's going to train you now?"

"To be honest with you Trip I haven't even thought about it."

"I guess I can understand that with Mr. Muhammad's passing and all. You're still going through the whole grieving process. Yeah, I can understand that. But the sooner you can get back in there the easier it'll be. And you're too damn talented not to see it through. You know that was pop's dream for you. Ya gotta see it through Naz."

"That's just it though Trip. That was daddy's dream not mine,"

"I'm just saying. Just think about, Naz."

"You know I can remember when your pops would grab a bunch of us young hoppers and head us down to the gym. It was like he was herding cattle.
And when we'd get up to the Drew Hill Projects and we'd all get a little timid. You know scared like...
They had some hard-core fellas running the projects

back then. But your pops would always make it seem

like he had to to take the cut and we'd wind up in some

back alley where the straight thugs would be. It was a

dangerous place to be if you weren't part of that crew,

but pops always made it a point to come through there.

Them boys wasn't doin' nothin' but smokin' a lil weed

and shooin' craps but like I said if you wasn't family

you could seriously hurt. That was their own little piece

of Harlem real estate. Just like this is ours.

It was at this point that a rather disheveled

young man about Naz's age walked up.

Friday arrived sooner than he'd expected.

Classes had gone well, and he'd gotten an A on his

midterm assuring him an A for the course. He wanted

to celebrate but there was no one to celebrate with. The

closest person to him now was Cynthia and she

wouldn't be home until much later that evening. What

could he be doing? If daddy were alive there was no

question as to where he would be. In the gym. But no, he wasn't going there.

He knew Trip expected an answer and so after class he made it a point to head home. The decision as much as he hated to admit it was a no-brainer. He wasn't sure he wanted to box anymore, and it would be years before he had his own law practice and mommy and Cynthia were struggling to afford him now. Passing his building and cutting sharply into the alley he shook hands and dapped his boys. Many had taken the only road available to them and were engaged in one type of illegal activity. Yet to Naz these were his boyhood friends, his fam and he loved them and they him. Trip stood as he always did in the farthest recesses of the alley purposely. If you had beef with Trip chances were very good that you wouldn't make it through the dozens of soldiers to get close. Naz walked through unfettered.

"What's up baby?" Trip said grabbing the lighter man and embracing him tightly.

"You already know," Naz said smiling broadly.

"So, you're going to allow me to promote you?"

"Sounds like a plan moving forward."

Trip shouted and the whole alley came to a standstill. Then he hugged Naz.

"Man, Naz you don't know how much I appreciate this. This may be our way out. I mean for both of us. We may, thanks to you, finally be able to get out of this hellhole," he said grabbing and hugging Naz tightly.

By this time the two young men had walked the

better of twenty blocks when Noah's eyes suddenly lit up.

There was a bit more bounce in his step now as he

crossed over to the other side of the street and approached

a rather gruff and disheveled young man about his age.

The young man stood amidst a group of street thugs but

Noah was not afraid. It was almost as if the prodigal son

had returned as they welcomed him.

"My man Noah. Where you been my nigga? I ain't

seen you in a month of Sundays."

"I know," he said hugging several of the men.

"That's why I told my man Naz that we had to go uptown

and check on my nigga Dez. We walked a country mile

to see your punk asses."

"Must mean you got tired of that whacked,

watered down shit. Whatcha need my nigga?"

"First, I know if your shit is good? The

man known as Dez, obviously the leader of this small

posse turned to the small group and laughed.

"Nigga wants to know if the shit is good."

Everyone laughed.

"Don't come up here with no dumb shit nigga. If you come up here fuckin' with my product and you used to that shit from anybody but my man Trip this shit will have you in Harlem Hospital before the nights out. Trust me Black. You fuck with Trip?"

"You know that's my nigga but he's out. He's waiting for the re-up," Noah responded.

"Well, me and Trip been shopping together to get more quantity so you know the shit's as close to pure as you're going to find. And I ain't sayin' something nothin' about my my boy Trip's all about the paper so he may be cutting his but I leave the shit just the way it is and I got niggas and crackers coming from upstate, Connecticut and Jersey to get this shit. It's that fire my nigga. It's bangin' baby. My shit comes with a

42

money back guarantee baby. Now what can I do for you?"

"Let me get a twenty," Noah replied.

"I know you didn't take me through all that and all you want is a twenty. Nigga is you serious. Tell me Noah. How long has you been dabblin'?"

"Close to three years." Noah responded his embarrassment now showing.

"Three years. Which means you got to be spendin' close to a hundred a day just to maintain yo' habit. C'mon Noah. A twenty can't be nothin' more than a tease to you at this point." Dez said playfully as his boys moved in and out of the small circle catering to the needs of the constant flowing traffic.

All this talk was a bit much for Noah. And for what? This shit was getting personal and he really didn't need his business exposed like this in front of a listening public. He'd always been a very private person even when he'd been approached by coaches, talent scouts and other unsavory types.

Dez was trippin'. Any show of weakness on the street was nothin' more than an invitation to every piranha lurking in the shadows. And asking him how long he's been using in front of these ruthless, cutthroat motherfuckers who sold the shit and looked down on the users could only lead to an eventual Beat down or worse. These same niggas who knew his weaknesses for the dope they sold would use this to exploit the weakness that had now become his tragic life.

Noah was angry now and though just a skeleton of who he had been a couple of years ago he was still close to the two hundred pounds he'd been when he led

Hamilton to the city finals. Close to six three he was better than average with his hands and could very well have pursued a career in the ring had he so chosen.

"I don't give a fuck how long I've been using I ain't never let no one disrespect me or mine and today would be no different he thought to himself as fingers dug into the palms of his hands and became fists. No, this was utter disrespect and simply could not be tolerated. He had to handle his business and he had to handle it now.'

"Yo Dez I'm not sure I quite understand the point you was tryna make about the twenty. I came up here to do some business. Either you 'bout makin' this cheddar or you ain't but all that shit about how long I been usin' ain't nobody's business and I don't appreciate you puttin' my business out here in the street."

Nazar who had been standing by watching saw Noah closing the distance between himself and the shorter man he'd come to know as Dez. Nazar was aware of the move and didn't know how much Noah had retained but when they were younger they'd trained together under Naz's father's watchful eye. Noah was gifted, athletically speaking bettering him on a number of occasions in the ring but inevitably chose basketball.

"It's just safer," he laughed. And being that he was so blessed and gifted the transition from a Golden Gloves contender to a first team All-American point guard was no problem. Naz looked at his friend now and wondered what had caused him to drift so far from home.

Now here he was about to take on five hardened thugs knowing full well that they were strapped and not afraid to use them. And all because he felt he'd been disrespected. How many brothers had died because they too had felt disrespected in some way.

"Noah," Naz said just loud enough to get his friend's attention yet quiet enough not to add to the growing friction between the two men. Although he could understand Noah's annoyance about being put on front street by Dez the fact remained that there were five of them out here in the streets selling dope with little or nothing to lose. And for that reason, Naz wasn't too fond of the situation he now found himself in.

"Noah here's the twenty I owe you. Almost forgot."

"I know you!" One of Dez's lieutenants shouted out. "Man, I kept staring at you saying I know this kid. You're that boxer I saw win the Golden Gloves last year ain't you?"

Naz dropped his head somewhat embarrassed.

"Man, you don't wanna fuck with this kid," he said to everyone and no one in particular. "I saw him

Beat the fuck out of this white boy from Long Island.

White boy came in there with all this hype and left on a

stretcher. You him ain't you?"

Naz had to smile. Glad now that the kid

recognized him defusing the situation he handed Noah

the twenty. Noah's face brightened immediately and

Dez always the businessman and not wanting to lose a

loyal customer noticing how far he'd pushed Noah

suddenly became almost apologetic.

"Yo bruh, I apologize if you think I was trying

to disrespect you. You should know me better than that

Noah. How far we go back? Like elementary bruh and

we always been cool. Sorry if you took it that way. I

was only playin' with you bruh," he said reaching to

shake hands and make amends. "We good, bruh?"

"We're good," Noah said but anyone knowing

him knew he was easy to anger and not so quickly to let

things go. "Now about that forty."

48

"I gotcha. Look go up to apartment 2C. That's one of my spots. And leave those females alone. They're working."

"Whatcha tell 'em Dez?" one of his boys laughed.

"Got to. Every time a nigga goes up there he wants to fuck with one of the girls. That shit ain't happenin' while they on the clock. You feel me but you two go on up and tell them I said to let you in. I'll be up in a minute. Just chill. I'm gonna hook you up."

Noah was smiling now as he ascended the two flights to the tiny flat at the end of the long, narrow hallway. The smell of stale urine was strong but neither man noticed so intent were they on getting lifted. An armed body guard stood outside the door.

"What up Noah?" the large man said nodding at

Noah out of respect for who he'd been. Noah ad not only been a high school standout, but he'd been a playground legend as well and this is where most brothers knew him from. Some of his playground moves are still being compared to "Tiny" Archibald. This afforded with not only street credibility but even more importantly respect.

"Oh shit. Nazy Mhammad," he said turning and looking at the other man. "Trey do you know who this is?"

"Nah, bruh."

"This here is Nazy Muhammad the best welterweight and middle weight in the Tri-State area. He's the two-time Golden Glove champion and will be a three-time champ if he doesn't decide to go pro. I'm telling you the boy is nice. You got to go see him. This here is my man. We grew up in the same housing project. We used to walk to school together every day. Back then he was a skinny little dude and I used to have to look out for him. But no more. He can take care of himself nowadays. How you been Nazy. Man, it's been awhile he said hugging Nazar tightly. "How you been?"

"I'm good. How you been Big Man?"

"Chillin'. Trying to stay as low key as possible and under the radar. Hey man I'm sorry to hear about pops. He was a good man. No. he was a very good man. He used to keep me runnin' though. He either had me runnin' to school or if he saw me just hanging out he'd run my ass to the gym and then had me run some more. Mr. Muhammad was a good man."

A big fan of his childhood friend he turned once again to the young man by his side.

"Trey, I don't know whether you realize it or not but you're standing in the presence of royalty. This man right here hasn't lost a fight since he was fourteen.

Remember this name, Prince Nazar Muhammad, the
best pound for pound boxer in New York City for the
last five years. Am I lyin' Noah?"

"You right Murph.," Noah smiled.

"I know. I grew up with 'em. We got older
and went our separate and all, but these are my boys.
I'd give my right arm for either of 'em. Now the best I
can do is follow their careers in the papers. I don't
know if you know it or not, but this man could have
easily jumped from high school to the NBA. His junior
year in high school he was the best guard in the nation.
Do you hear me? The nation. And that was as a junior.
I just hope y'all ain't come here to do what I think you
came to do."

"Whatever they came to do is none of yo'
goddamn business. I pay you to guard the door Murph.

That's it. Guard the goddamn door. They feedin' us and you tellin' them not to shop with us. What the fuck is wrong with you? You takin' the bottle outta my baby's mouth."

"You don't understand Dez, man. I grew up with these brothers. They ain't your run of the mill niggas. These my boys. They like family. We like brothers."

"And that's all well and good Murph but your friends didn't come to see you. They came to see me to do business and you fuckin' wit' my business. Now step off.," Dez said disregarding and thoroughly disrespecting the larger man. Murph moved aside hugging his boys as they went inside. Despite his boss' stern admonishment he still looked at the young men now entering the apartment with a disapproving eye.

Passing the kitchen, it was hard not to notice the two bare, buxom, bronze Beauties who appeared to be wearing only thongs. They appeared coy perhaps bashful glancing quickly before laboring on. Nazar focused on the shorter of the two who blushed dimples when their eyes met.

Nazar was enamored but then thought of the next time he'd see her. He probably wouldn't even notice her walking around like a zombie. Yes, in a couple of hours she would see another side of him a side even he didn't want to see. How would she look at him then? What would she think?

"Is you comin' man," Dez shouted at Nazar.

Nazar went through the door of the tiny bedroom. The room was gaudily decorated with red, black and purple velvet wallpaper.

Dez saw Nazar's face and laughed out loud.

"Don't say nothin'. The apartment belongs to an old woman. She lets me get it every now and then

54

when she needs a little extra cash. You fellas want something to drink?"

"You must have been reading my mind," Noah smiled.

"I'll send Mia in with the drinks while I fix you your package."

"Sounds good to me," Noah commented. He was fidgeting now, and it was clear that if Dez didn't return soon he'd be sick.

Dez was gone now and despite Noah trying to make conversation it was obvious that he was on the brink. It had been hours since Noah had had a taste and his jones was beginning to come down on him. His mouth and eyes began twitching spasmodically.

"That girl ain't brought those drinks yet?" Dez said irritated now. Nazar had two things on his mind. He wondered which woman Mia was and could only

55

hope it was the one with the dimples. He wondered if
Noah could hold on without throwing up his insides and
wearing out their welcome. Dez noticing Noah's
condition drew a sizeable line on the table in front of
Noah.

"Hit that. That should hold you off 'til I weigh
this package for you. Damn! Where the hell is that
girl?"

Dez left again slamming the door hard behind
him.

"What the fuck is he doing Naz? We been here
for over an hour and still ain't been served. Poor
customer service if you ask me," Noah chuckled in an
effort to mask his growing discomfort. Noah then
began picking at the festering sores on his arm. This
was a bit much for Nazar who began questioning
himself as to why he was even there. He thought of

Murph's eye of disapproval and rose to step out the door when the door swung open and the cute little shorty stepped in with a tray of cold drinks.

"Lemonade, beer or maybe something a little stronger. I have Hennessey."

"That's fine honey. You can leave the bottle right here."

Nazar who was already standing held out his hand.

"Nazar."

"Monica. You're that boxer, aren't you?"

"I guess I am. You're a boxing fan?" Nazar asked incredulously.

"What are you trying to say. That girls can't be boxing fans... Matter-of fact I saw you fight that Puerto Rican kid from the Bronx in your last fight. What's his name? Hector."

"Hector Valdez."

"Yeah that's him. I remember you hit him with this pretty combination in the sixth and I knew it was over then. I remember it like it was yesterday. You hit him with a hard jab that stunned him and then followed it with a right cross and then the left hook. It was beautiful. You let him hang around for a couple more rounds but he was done after that combination."

"Wow," Nazar shouted excitedly. "I can't believe you've actually seen me fight."

"Yes. I have but I didn't actually go to see you fight. My girlfriend begged me to go to see her cousin who was on the undercard."

"Oh, so that's why the sudden interest in 'the sweet science'?

"Wow. My dad's the only person I've heard to refer to it as that."

58

"Oh, so your daddy is the real fight fan?"

"Why is it so impossible to believe that a female can like boxing? You do realize there are women boxers, nowadays don't you? But anyway, to answer your question, yes, my father is a huge fight fan. He did a little boxing before he left PR and came here and was working in the gym up by Prospect and fell in love with this kid who came in to play around. My dad took him at nine years old and trained him till he was champ. You probably know him as Hector Camacho. I think I was seven or eight when he started taking me to the fights. By the time I was nine I knew the difference between a right cross and a right uppercut. And I've seen 'em and met them all. Breland, Tyson, Camacho. Those were the days but to tell you the truth I haven't seen anyone with your quickness or hand speed since Camacho."

"And that's not only in the ring. From what I hear he's got some moves outside the ring as well too little cousin," Dez said as he entered the room.
"Monica are you working or just standing around shooting the shit with Nazar?"

"Shooting the shit," she said turning back to Naz. "But any way my daddy trained Camacho. You may have heard of him. Tito Medina."

"Get out of here. Everyone that knows boxing knows Tito Medina. Tito Medina's a legend. That's all I heard when I was growing up. 'If Medina was in his corner the boy wouldn't have lost that fight.'"

They both laughed.

"Say Monica let's hook up some time and talk more."

"I'd like that. Give your number to Dez and I'll get it from him later.

"Will do," Nazar sad smiling broadly.

"Okay sweetie. Do you think I can handle my business now?" Dez interjected.

"Certainly, Dez and by the way I'm leaving now. Gotta take mama to the doctor's. Trina's coming in early to take my place."

"Not a problem as long as you 've got all the bases covered. Tell Aunt Mimi that she's in my prayers."

Once the door closed Dez turned to his customers and slammed a clear cellophane bag on the table directly in front of them.

"What's that?" Noah inquired.

"You tell me?"

"Looks like an eighty."

"You've got a good eye Noah. That's what I'm giving you for your forty dollars and that shit's as pure as you'll get. Niggas out here in these streets is calling it that Whitney Houston so be careful with it. Every night some nigga from right around the way is going to the hospital or the morgue offa this shit. So, don't get stupid offa this shit and think you're bigger than this shit. You're not. Do you hear me Noah?"

Noah was already cooking it up but lifted his head just long enough to acknowledge Dez.

"Take your time and enjoy. Ain't no rush. You can lock the door but no one's gonna bother you. You know what? Just to make sure there are no accidents."

Measuring carefully Dez was soon at work cooking, adding a taste here and there before pulling the plunger back and passing the needle to Noah who had to find a vein before settling on his foot.

Taking a fresh needle from the box of syringes he drew up the other half of what was in the spoon.

"Need me to hit you off Naz?"

"Nah Dez. I don't bang. I just sniff."

"Man, that's a waste of good dope. Let me hit you off one time so you can get the full effect of the dope. You playin'. Just lean back and close your eyes."

Nazar hardly felt the needle puncture his skin. That was the last thing he remembered. And the he was gone. He was out of the realm of the common every day folks who were most if not all of the people he knew. He was untouchable now. He was moving now, dancing to the beat of the heavy bass in his head. Jab, jab, duck and come up throwing. Yes, a furious flurry of devastating body punches that made him drop his hands and then… He was soaring now above the clouds and now he understood why his heroes like Joplin, Hendrix, Miles, Coltrane, Parker, James had chosen this avenue of self-destruction. Somehow the mundane monotony of living or better yet existing just wasn' t enough. They sought more. Just as in their music they took it to another level which many refer to as genius. They simply sought more than what was allotted. Nazar was rushing through time now. He wondered if this defined who he was and why he constantly sought more. They said he was in another league. They'd referred to his genius in the ring. He wondered.

Both men sniffed the lines left for them. Noah grabbed his stomach and reached for the garbage.

"Damn this shit is good," Noah muttered.

Nazar had to concur. He was boxing again. His opponent was a muscular Croatian who was slow afoot and lumbering but had a long list of consecutive knockouts to his credit.

"Stay away from this guy. All I want you to do this fight is dance and keep your distance. I need you to be smart. With the power, he has all this guy needs to do is catch you once."

Nazar never saw the man's face. He was like all his opponents. Faceless. And like all of his opponents Nazar made quick work of him. Jab, jab. Step away. Double jab, and a stiff upper cut caught the plodding boxer coming forward. The Croatian seemed unfazed and was still coming forward putting pressure on Nazar. The Croatian plodded forward throwing looping left hands intent on taking Naz out with one thunderous landing. But Nazar was already aware and deftly slid to the right just as the man was throwing it. Ducking into a traditional boxing stance Nazar countered with a vicious upper cut that may have very well ended the fight there if Nazar hadn't followed with a chopping left hook. The Croatian prospect went down in a heap. Eight, nine, ten... It was over.

Nazar couldn't remember feeling any better than he was feeling right now. Dez wasn't lying. *He had been playing.* This was how it was supposed to be done.

This was the way it was supposed to feel all the time.

Glancing his watch, he wondered where the time had gone. Noah was still out and it was already after eight. Looking at the table Nazar picked up the glassine envelope. Except for the tiny amount they'd done most of the dope was still there. He considered leaving Noah half then reconsidered and put the remainder in his pocket.

There was no Dez now, no voluptuous little half-naked girls to catch his eye. All that remained was that ugly red, purple and black wallpaper suggesting and elderly Southern Black woman. He wondered if he ventured into her bedroom or living room if he wouldn't find the three portraits Southern Blacks loved so much. There was first and foremost the white Jesus followed by Martin Luther the king and of course President John Kennedy to complete the triad.

Stepped into the night air was refreshing bringing Nazar out of his self-induced slumber.

Business had picked up tenfold since Naz's arrival earlier. It was almost like Christmas at Macy's. And Dez and his boys were handling business like seasoned veterans always keeping an eye out for sheisty customers trying to run some game or the occasional pretty young girl who tried to parlay the only thing she had. Seeing him Dez did not miss a beat hugging a woman tightly and with a deft hand sliding the package into her pocket. They were smooth and cool in a world he was slowly getting to know although he wasn't all that sure he wanted to.

"I see Rip Van Winkle is up," Dez said loud enough for anyone within earshot to hear. "How'd you like that?"

Nazar couldn't understand how anyone could be so loud and uncouth. And the way he treated those closest to him made Naz's flesh crawl. Dez had quickly grown into someone Nazar never wanted to run across again in his lifetime.

"Listen, Dez. Is there any way I can get a set of works?"

"No problem. Give me a sec. I got you."

"Oh and let me give you my number to give to your cousin."

"Bruh, you don't remember giving it to me earlier? She already picked it up. I told her to give you a call around nine."

"Thanks, Dez. Good lookin' out," Naz said hugging the shorter man. "Now about those works."

"In your pocket."

Damn. The boy was good at his craft. Nazar had to smile.

"You be safe Dez."

"Always and a word to the wise son. You have a world of a future awaiting you son. Don't throw it away with that shit. You just dabblin' now so you have a choice. Don't throw your life away like Noah did. Boy should be in the NBA, but he made a bad choice. Don't do that. And I'm gonna tell you something else bruh. My little cousin finds out you fuckin' with that shit and she's gone. Just a word to the wise son."

"I gotcha. Good lookin' out man," Nazar said sincerely. He was shocked to find there was a heart behind all of Dez's false bravado.

Nazar raced down the crowded street. It was 8:15. If he hurried he could still have time to take a shower before she called. He felt dirty. The ugliness of the purple, black and red wallpaper coupled with a man sticking him with a needle full of poison and Noah unconsciously picking the scabs from his arms while he slobbered on himself so much the front of his shirt was wet. It was all so ugly and dirty now. And he longed for a shower to wash himself clean of all of today's transactions and transgressions. He'd gone somewhere today he would have never dreamed of going. Could it be his father's sudden death? Whatever it was he was slippin' into a world he never would have considered if his father were still alive.

Pulling his collar up to protect himself from the cold autumn wind he made short work of the twenty or so blocks that stood before him. The warm heat comforted him as he stepped into the foyer of the small apartment.

"Is that my Nazar?"

"Yes ma'am."

"How was your day son?" she said kissing him on the cheek.

"Good ma. I can't complain."

"That's right as long as you got up out of bed this morning you're blessed," she said before slumping into her favorite chair.

"How are you doing ma?"

"A little tired but otherwise good."

He hated to see his mother like this. She worked so hard cleaning and cooking that by the time she got home she had little left for her own family. If he'd just gone pro when he wanted to they would have been on easy street and mama wouldn't suffer so trying to keep a roof over his head. But daddy had objected saying he wasn't quite ready.

'Give it a year or two Naz. Be patient son. You're still young and you still have things to work on.'

Those were his father's words but then he had supplied another income. There was no other income to speak of since daddy's passing but there were still three mouths to feed.

His older sister worked Cynthia but that didn't help him with the guilt he was already feeling. Two women struggling to take care of him a grown man. Dismissing the thought, he turned to his mother.

"Ma. I met a girl."

"Oh, really."

"Yeah. She's really cute and that's not even the best thing about her."

"So, what's the best thing about her Nazar?"

"She's the daughter of Tito Medina."

"And I'm supposed to know who that is."

"Absolutely unless you were living somewhere else when we ate dinner. That's all daddy would talk about. I think daddy modeled himself after the man. Tino Medina is boxing royalty. In your husband's opinion he was the best trainer and cut man in the city." "Is that right and you met his daughter? And because she's the daughter of this famous man that makes her even more attractive to you. Is that what I'm hearing? Explain it to me again. I don't think I understand."

Nazar laughed.

"No, ma. That's not what I'm saying. What I'm saying is that because he's her father she knows boxing. I mean she *knows* boxing."

"This girl knows boxing?"

"That's what I said and she just about cursed me out. Probably would have if she cursed."

"A nice girl. Well, that's good. You should bring her by. I'd like to meet her."

"Yeah. I'm gonna bring her by just as soon I can take her out for a cup of coffee."

"Is that a hint."

"No, you do too much for me already ma."

"Let me jump in the shower and see if I can't get some studying in before she calls."

"Okay honey. Cynthia left your dinner in the oven. She made your favorite."

"Baked ziti? I'll never make weight with her doing the cooking," Nazar chuckled.

Nazar checked his watch before jumping in the shower. It was 8:45 giving him all of fifteen minutes before Monica's call. At five of nine Nazar sat on the edge of his bed lotioning his face and hands with the new Jay-Z album setting the tone. He was up and alive and feeling good overall. And at precisely nine the phone rang. He liked this girl already.

"Naz here."

"Hey Naz. This is Monica. I met you up at Dez's today."

"I know who it is. I was hoping you would call. So, what's up with you miss lady?"

"Well, as soon as I get off the phone with you

I'm going to start studying for this econ exam I have on Wednesday."

"Oh, so you're in school?"

"Yeah, I'm a senior at Fordham in the Bronx."

"What's your major?"

"Accounting."

"That's good. I'm gonna need a good accountant in the very near future."

"You can be my very first client," she laughed. There was a quiet silence. "Nazar can I ask you a question?"

"Sure. Anything. Just ask."

"What were you doing at my cousin's today?"

"That's a bit personal. Don't you think?"

"Well, I know why your boy Noah comes through."

"That's Noah not Nazar. But, if you must know Noah was on his way up to see Dez and he thought that Dez might be able to help promote me and help me get a manager. I'm considering going pro. I mean there's little more that I can do in the amateurs. If I go to the Golden Gloves it can only hurt me. I'm already three times Golden Gloves champ but if I were to lose it would only hurt me in going pro and a fourth Golden Gloves champ wouldn't really add to the resume. So, you see it's a lose lose proposition. The only reason I haven't gone pro is because my father who was also my trainer didn't think I was ready."

"And you think you're ready?"

"I have to be. With my father gone things have been incredibly hard on my mother and my sister. They keep telling me to finish school, but I've always done both and nothing would change."

"I feel you. You had me scared me there for a minute. I thought you may have been dabbling." "You've got to be kidding me Monica."

"I see athletes like Noah do it every day. They think they're bigger than it is and the next thing you know they're hooked."

"Well, you got the wrong one here baby."

"I'm so glad to hear that but what you told me scares me almost as bad than you messin' with that narcotic."

"And what's that?"

"The mere fact that you would even consider letting my cousin in your camp for any reason is frightening. Don't get me wrong I love my cousin and appreciate the fact that he lets me work for him during a rough time in my life, but he's mean and evil to the core.

You saw the way he spoke to me today. And he treats all of us like that. He's just nasty to the core. Trust me you don't want to be beholding to him."

"Thanks for the heads up but I gathered the same thoughts after seeing the way he treated my boys Murph and Noah."

"Oh, you know Murph?"

"Yeah, Murph and I grew up together. He used to take care of me when I was younger."

"He's nothing but a big ol' teddy bear. The boy ain't got a mean bone in his body and Dez treats him like shit."

"Trust me. Dez had no idea why I was there other than to bankroll and babysit my boy Noah."

"So, tell me. What is this about you looking for a manager and promoter? Don't you have a Golden Gloves championship to defend in a couple of months. Are you even in the gym."

"No. Just can't get motivated. I lost my trainer and manager about a month ago when my father died."

"Oh, I didn't know. I'm so sorry."

"Not half as sorry as I am. He thought I was two or three years from turning pro but like I said with him gone my mother and sister Cynthia are killing themselves just to make ends meet so I have no choice but to turn pro now. You know when I lost my father I lost my best friend as well. He was the only trainer I've ever had, and I've been searching but it's going to be difficult to replace him."

"Well, search no more. I'm going to need you in the gym tomorrow. You go to Monroe's up by the armory, don't you?"

"Yes."

"Then I'll need you there by three, so I can see what I'm working with."

Nazar laughed. What was she saying? He didn't really know her and couldn't imagine what she had planned but at least it was a way to see her. He didn't have any money to take her out so sure he would meet her at the gym at three.

"Listen Monica. I could talk to you all night, but I've got a test in the morning and still have some studying to do."

"Oh, that is just so sexy. A man that has his priorities in order. Go ahead and handle your business baby. I'll see you at three."

The phone went dead before he had a chance to say goodbye.

'So much for formalities,' Nazar said smiling and muttering to himself before picking up his textbook on American History. It was two o'clock in the morning before Nazar felt comfortable enough to put both textbook and index cards on the night table beside his bed.

At six he was up and dressed in his warmest jogging outfit.

"Glad to see you back on the grind," his sister Cyntia remarked.

Grabbing her he leaned over kissing her on her forehead before pinching her arm. The woman shrieked in pain before trying to slap Nazar who deftly ducked the oncoming blow.

"Love you Cyn," he said grinning broadly and heading out the door. "Oh, and last night's dinner was bangin'."

The plump but very attractive thirty-five-yearold woman smiled broadly. Oh, how she loved that boy.

Nazar never imagined what a mere month layoff could do but after only a mile into his five-mile run he was drained and exhausted. His legs felt like lead and he had had to go somewhere deep inside to summon the fortitude to finish the five-mile stretch. Returning home he showered quickly, grabbed a croissant, his backpack and the envelope with his name printed neatly on it.

Opening the envelope as he headed down the stairs he read the note. It was always the same. Still, it felt good knowing that his older sister, Cynthia had devoted her life to making his better.

Nazy,

Daddy used to always say. Keep a little change

in your pocket. So, here's a little

change. Only wish

it could have been more. Have

a blessed day lil'   brother and may God

keep you safe.

Cynthia

Enclosed was always a crisp ten-

dollar bill. Sometimes there was a twenty but that was

rare and even more so now since daddy had died.

Still, it hardly mattered what she left him. What

mattered was that she loved him and was one of the few

people that stood by him win, lose, or draw.

But today for some reason he felt like himself; almost the way he felt when daddy was alive and in his corner. It was almost as if his father had come back and reincarnated himself in this five-foot two little dynamo who seemed not only interested in his career but his well-being as well.

He sat in the large lecture hall and tried to give his full concentration to the chubby, balding middle-aged professor going on about something or another, but his mind kept seeing visions of Monica standing in the kitchen with nothing other than panties and a facemask on.

The test hadn't been nearly as hard as he thought it would be and he felt

pretty sure he'd aced it. He'd planned and was on schedule to graduate early but with his turning pro he'd need the summer to work on and perfect his craft.

That's what he decided as of last night.

The clock in the lecture hall seemed to be stuck at two-twenty-five.

Nazar sat on the edge of his seat cringing as he waited for the short, balding man to dismiss the class. Finally.

Nazar was changed and jumping rope by five of three. Little had changed in the Uptown Gym other than the fact that daddy's booming, baritone voice was now absent. There were a couple of new rising stars in the gym. Nazar knew of them but had yet to meet them personally or professionally. One kid Nazar took particular notice of was a kid in his weight class who had come out of nowhere to knock out twenty three in a row in running through most of New York's top amateurs. Nazar knew it was just a matter of time before the two were paired to see who the reigning king of New York was.

Shortly thereafter Nazar found himself in the ring found himself sparring with a hard-hitting Haitian middleweight who must have outweighed Nazar by a good fifteen to twenty pounds. The Haitian had an upcoming bout against another up and coming contender who was considered a slick boxer and Nazar being the closest thing was asked to go a few rounds. Everyone seemed impressed at how well Naz danced and boxed keeping his distance from the hard-hitting Haitian. Occasionally the Haitian would catch Nazar with a looping left that shivered Nazar to his core but call it ring savvy or just his boxing instincts Nazar would clinch in an attempt to clear his head. When the cobwebs cleared Nazar was once again on his bicycle boxing, jabbing and staying clear of the thunderous bombs his Haitian counterpart was so intent on throwing.

"Cut off the ring," his cornermen shouted but Nazar was too elusive, too evasive, too slick for the Haitian who plodded on steadfast as Nazar danced, jabbing occasionally, to close out the round. Nazar felt good. It had been a little more than a month since he'd been in the ring, but his skills hadn't abandoned him. The second round was similar to the first with Nazar boxing skillfully and staying just out of reach and no matter how much his corner pleaded with the Haitian fighter he had no more success than he had cutting off the ring than he had had in the first round.

And then a hush fell over the gym as the door open and the foot two bombshell walked in. Dressed in low rider jeans and heels the petite woman strode to Nazar's corner and had a seat on one of the few empty seats to be found.

"When he throws the jab I want you to counter with an overhand right. C'mon baby! That should be automatic. That's boxing 101 baby. I thought you told me you boxed. You can't score going backwards. I want you to box. I don't want you to mix it up with him. Just touch him. Do you hear me? Circle him. Jab. Double jab then get the hell out of there."

Naz had to smile as Monica slid the mouthpiece in his mouth and slapped him on the butt as the third round was about to start.

"C'mon baby. Jab Nazar. Good. Again. This time double it up so you can throw your combinations. C'mon baby. Remember everything begins and ends with the jab. That's it. Again. Beautiful!"

And though all eyes were on her now for her boxing acumen she saw no one but her boxer. The round ended, and Monica smiled. "You're doing beautifully," she said grabbing the mouthpiece out and giving him a sip of water before pouring the remainder of ice cold water down his back making him sit squarely up on his stool.

"Listen. I want you to double up on your jab. Do that and you can follow with your combos. Remember everything follows the jab. And you've got a nice clean, crisp, stinging jab. He doesn't like it at all. It really is a thing of beauty. You just have to let it go. Do you hear me baby? Let the jab go. It all starts with the jab," she repeated as she rinsed the mouthpiece and slid it back in his mouth.

"C'mon Nazar. Shoot the jab," Monica yelled one high-heeled leg up on the stool her jeans straining to hold all of her in was certainly a sight to behold. The entire gym seemed fixated on the tiny woman who had taken over Naza's corner. Some because she was fine, but most were boxing fans and this lil' woman obviously a student of the sweet science had Naz boxing as well as he ever had. What had been a fight quickly turned into a rout under her tutelage.

"Time," yelled the dark-skinned older man.

Monica threw Nazar a towel. Nazar smiled proudly.

"Let me grab a quick shower. I'll be out in ten," he said smiling broadly now as he headed towards the locker room. It was eight o'clock by the time the two exited the gym and hit the streets. Fall was coming and there was a nip n the air but neither felt it.

"You really had me fooled," Nazar said.

"How's that?"

Nazar looked at the young woman by his side and smiled broadly.

"When I met you yesterday you appeared all shy and coy. I saw someone totally different in the gym today."

Monica dropped her head. She knew exactly what he was saying and had to smile herself.

"What are you saying Mr. Muhammad?"

"Oh, don't call me that. I start looking for my father when you do that. But seriously I almost didn't recognize you."

"I hope that's not a bad thing. It's just that I've always been a daddy's girl and being that he stayed in the gym I guess that's where I grew up."

"In the gym?"

"Yeah. And I guess that's where I feel most comfortable."

"I see. And you know your stuff too. A couple of the fellas came up to me after and asked me who the chick was with all the skills. So, tell me something why with all your boxing skills are you up there at the spot risking everything?"

"C'mon Naz. In all honesty how many females have you seen in the corner since you've been boxing?" Naz took a couple of minutes to think back.

"Exactly. We're just not represented or considered in any official capacity except to go walk buck naked between rounds holding the placard indicating what round is coming up. So, being that my mom got a new job putting her in the next tax bracket, so they cut off my financial aid. Being that as it may we're still poor and there aren't a whole lot of companies knockin' down the door looking for an accounting major with no experience, so I ended up working for Dez."

"When do you graduate?"

"After this semester I'll be a senior."

"So, you still have a year left to do at the spot?"

"Lord God I hope not. Like I said I've been everywhere and no one's really looking for a college student with no experience."

"Well, in that case, we'd better see about getting you out of there. You do know that if the police run up in there you can kiss that college education and your future goodbye, don't you?"

"I think about it every day. But it's not only that. I hate the fact that I'm selling poison and helping to ruin someone's life. But anyway, how do you propose to get me out of there?"

"Well, as soon as I talk to my man Trip and let him know I'm not happy with the trainer and cornerman he's gotten and can bring you on board for less than he's paying the two he'll jump at the chance to bring you on board. I just brought him on as my promoter and manager but He's only managing my affairs until I can find a manager that I know and trust and has my best interest at heart. I'm not saying that he doesn't have my best interest at heart but he's new to the game and has no idea of what it takes to manage."

"Who is he and why did you choose him to promote and manage you?"

"He's one of my boyhood friends, just someone I grew up with. He runs the neighborhood. You know the local drug kingpin from around the way. You may know him. He and Dez do a lot of business from what I understand. His name's Trip." Monica shook her head.

"No, I sure don't. Was he at the gym today?"
"Nah, but his eyes and ears were. I'm sure he's already heard about this fine female in my corner. I can almost guarantee that. He's got feelers all over the neighborhood."

Monica had to smile.

"Well, that is good news but if I put all my eggs in one basket and depend on you having a successful pro career I'll probably be doing five-to-ten in some woman's prison upstate," she said only half teasing the six two Nazar walking by her side.

Nazar was suddenly somber.

"And what was wrong with my performance. Kid couldn't touch me. I was dancing, moving, sticking him with the jab. I would have knocked him out, but his trainer asked me to go easy on him, so I wouldn't ruin his confidence on the eve of his fight." Nazar said leading Monica up the stairs of the brownstone. Turning the key, he showed her into the parlor.

"Ma, Sin," he shouted just as soon as he had her seated.

"Go ahead. You were saying."

"I was saying that the fighter I saw today is not the same fighter I saw fight Hector Valdez a few months ago. And this pug I saw today wasn't even in the same league as Hector."

Handing Naz her parka the young woman made herself right at home in the sparsely decorated brownstone.

"I admit I wasn't as sharp, but I haven't been in the gym in more than a month. It's gonna take a lil time to take off some of the ring rust."

"I get that but that's no excuse for forgetting one of the fundamentals of boxing," she said crossing her leg and folding her hands in her lap.

"What did I forget?"

"That the best defense is a good offense and a good offense begins and depends on keeping your jab in your opponent's face to keep him off-balance. Once you do that it opens up everything. But for some reason you refuse to use the jab today, so you had a hard time keeping him off of you. That's why he caught you with those haymakers."

"And what would you propose I do instead?"

"My daddy always said that the art of the 'sweet science' is to stick-and-move. That is to hit and not get hit so it's important that you as a boxer to use your footwork and move and jab, pick up points and then move away. And that way you can not only prolong your career but not wind up with your brains scrambled when it's all over and it's time to sit back and relax with your kids and grandkids. I'm telling you that's what adds to the longevity of any fighter. Look at Bernard Hopkins out of Philly. He's still fighting and has all his capabilities and he's close to fifty. And do you know why?"

" No. Why?" Nazar asked incredulously. He knew that every word the young woman before him was saying was true but enjoyed picking her brain and hearing her speak and was really curious to how much knowledge she really possessed when it came to the 'sweet science'.

"Because he's as good a defensive fighter as you'll find. You know another great defensive fighter that never got the recognition he deserved?"

"Who's that?"

"Pernell Whitaker."

"I've heard of him but never seen him fight."

"What! You can't be serious. You've never heard of 'Sweetpea'? He may be the prettiest fighter I've ever seen. And you've got the skills to be just as good if not better."

"You really think so?"

"I know so."

"You two seemed to be in such a spirited conversation I hated to interrupt."

"Hey ma," Nazar said hugging his mother. "This is Monica, the person I was telling you about. Monica, my mother, Mrs. Muhammad."

"Nice to meet you Ms. Muhammad," Monica said standing and walking over and hugging the older woman who was as surprised as Nazar was.

"Same here," Mrs. Muhammad said winking at her son. "Now I see why Natz is so taken by you. If I didn't know any better, I would have sworn I would have sworn Naz was in here talking to his father. Yes, I can see what his attraction is now."

"Yes, I can see too," Naz's sister Cynthia said eyeing the younger woman up-and-down.

"Monica, this is my sister Cynthia."

"You are a cute little thing."

"Nice to meet you Cynthia," Monica said grabbing the woman's extended hand and pulling her close before hugging her. Nazar and his mom's eyes locked for a moment and both smiled. Cynthia's usually hard demeanor melted under Monica's embrace.

"You're a pretty lil' thang and I heard what you were telling him about using the jab and you're absolutely right. I don't know what lil' brother doesn't get. Daddy was forever telling him the same thing. His best and easiest fights have always been when he has the jab working but there are times when he forgets he has beautiful boxing skills and wants to revert to being a slugger. I don't know what that's about. Some ol' machismo shit I guess."

"Cynthia the language," Ms. Muhammad said.

"Sorry ma. But it's the same thing daddy used to tell him all the time.

Monica smiled at the pudgy, little, caramel woman.

"Monica is it?"

"Yes ma'am."

"Well, Monica between the two of us I think we may just be able to mold this knucklehead into a title contender."

"You really think so?"

"I do. I really do and I'm so glad Nazar finally has someone in his corner in and out of the ring."

Monica breathed a deep sigh of relief.

"Well, with you guys in his corner the sky's the limit but listen I've heard so much about you I just had to stop by and meet you but it's getting late and my dad's probably having a seizure cause I'm not home already. It was nice meeting y'all and I will be checking in to let you know how he's doing from timeto-time if that's alright with you?"

"Alright? You'd better young lady," Ms. Muhammad said hugging Monica.

It was Cynthia who now stepped up and grabbed Monica.

"I'm so glad Nazy finally has someone in his corner," Cynthia said hugging Monica.

Monica smiled before turning to Naz.

"I really need to be getting home."

"Okay. Let me grab your coat."

"I hope you're figurin' on stayin' around chile. This is the first time I've seen him look like himself since my husband passed."

"I hope so too but that's up to Nazar," Monica said smiling as she slipped her parka on.

"Again, it was so nice meeting you both and I hope to see you soon."

Nazar and Monica walked the first few blocks in silence with Nazar throwing combinations into the crisp, cool fall air before Monica broke the silence.

"You know I was just thinking that that guy you were sparring with wasn't in your league, but you allowed him to make a fight of it."

"Yeah, you're right," he said now rubbing his right side where the Haitian had delivered some devastating body blows.

"Okay so if you know that then for the next three or four weeks we're going to concentrate on you throwing nothing but your jab and your defense."

"And that's it?"

"That's it. And something called ring generalship. I want you to be able to win even when you have off nights simply because you control the fight because you're the aggressor. I want you always coming forward behind the jab keeping the pressure on you opponent until he simply withers under the pressure."

"Sort of like this?" Nazar said grabbing Monica and pinning her arms to her sides and placing his mouth on hers before letting her go.

"Yes, something like that but I think if you did that in the ring against your opponent you'd get a few sideways glances," she said smiling.

Back at home now Nazar took the steps two at a time before bursting into the living room where his mother and sister were sitting watching television.

"Well what do you think?"

"I like he her. She's cute as a button but is down to earth and doesn't seem stuck on herself," his mother commented nonchalantly.

"She's no dummy. I'll give her that.

I like her. You can tell when someone comes from a good

family. She's warm and manner able. I think she'll be

good for you lil' brother."

"She must be okay if your sister likes

her. You know Sin doesn't like many people," his

mother smiled.

Content with their take on Monica

Nazar retreated to his room where he lay across his bed

a larger than life smile across his face, staring at the

ceiling. He considered sniffing a line to enhance the

way he was feeling right now but declined knowing that

the heroin paled in comparison to the way Monica

made him feel. He liked her and wondered if there was

any truth to love at first sight. He didn't know. Was it

her bubbly personality or the fact that they just had so

much in common? Lord knows she was fine as hell

with her cute little dimples. And she had let him kiss

her, so it was obvious she felt something for him as

well. Or could it be her knowledge of the sport he loved so well. Whatever it was he was happy and that he hadn't been in quite some time. Even when daddy was alive he hadn't felt this good.

At 6 a.m. he was up and out the door. He was sore but the run this morning was so much easier. His mind was in the right place. The fire was back, and he had something to prove. There was a spring, a bounce in his step that he lacked yesterday. He was motivated. And that motivation came in the form of a five two dynamo named Monica.

An hour later Nazar was home. Showering quickly and throwing on his jogging suit, he picked up his cell phone and sprinted the four blocks to the gym. It was Saturday and he wanted to get as much work in as he could before she got there. Maybe he hadn't been as impressive as he could but the things she said stuck in his mind and he promised to be more effective today.

He felt good and stood outside the gym in an attempt to gather himself. Taking out the new Samsung he punched in the number.

"Good morning. And who do I have the pleasure of speaking to on this beautiful Saturday morning?" the bubbly voice answered.

"You already know. You are certainly bubbly this morning."

"That's my job. I'm supposed to be bubbly. Hopefully I can bring something positive to whoever I run into today. It's my job to uplift someone, anyone I talk to. That's just apart of trying to make this world a better place. Gotta do my part to make sure whoever I encounter has a better day.

What's up? Now what is it that I can do for you sir?"

"I feel ya. I was wondering if you had some free time today and could come down and watch me train? Maybe give me some pointers you know that sort of thing."

"I wish I could. There's nothing more that I would like to do but I need to work all I can to get this money together."

"I hear you. Okay. I can't argue with that. Let me talk to my sponsor and see what I can put together to get you in here."

"You do that, and I'll see if I can't stop by after I get off. What time do you finish up?"

"I'm trying to get in all the work I can, so I guess I'll be there 'til around 9 tonight?"

"Alright. Like I said I've got to put this work in. I'll give you a call later and let you know one way or another. Talk to you later."

Nazar left the locker room and entered the gym not half as enthusiastic as he'd been but steadfast just the same. At eight o'clock convinced that she wasn't coming he packed his gear up and headed home. Nazar wondered how he'd occupy his time on this Saturday night. He had nothing to do until it was time to hit the gym again. He knew Monica wouldn't be able to join him with her work obligations. She'd already told him that she would be a no-show. He'd already dismissed the two men Trip had suggested for his corner. After meeting and talking to both he knew that although men were proficient in their craft neither had a personal stake in his development as a boxer or a person. No, he'd found his trainer and manager. Now if he could find Trip he knew he could work things out.

112

He knew finding Trip wouldn't be hard on a Saturday night. Nazar walked along 8th up 'til 116th before he saw his boyhood friend directing traffic.

"Trip. What's up baby?"

"Same ol' same ol'. Just tryna keep the lights on. Hold on. Naz. Do you see this motherfucker?" Trip said seeing something he didn't like with one of his workers.

Nigga is you stupid or what? You gotta niggas in back of you tryna get some. You settin' yo' self up for a fall. Put yo' self-up against the wall that way nobody can do no sheisty shit behind yo' back."

"But I know you right behind me too Trip," the young man said smiling.

"One day I'm gonna step away and you gonna be on your own. Always practice good habits youngun'."

"Yes sir."

Nazar thought back to Dez and how he treated his workers. There was no comparison. And that's why Dez got so much love out here in the streets.

"You were sayin'?" Trip said still holding Nazar's hands in his own.

"Oh! Yeah, yeah, yeah."

"Fellas tell me you're back in the gym and had a really good workout. But what they wouldn't tell me is why you let go the two of the best cornermen in all the five boroughs. It wasn't easy getting them you know? And they didn't come cheap either."

"I understand. What were they costing you?"

"Close to four grand a month. You know what that adds up to? That's close to fifty g's a year. And that ain't no drop in the bucket. That's one too many night out here in these streets. I ain't greedy. I ain't tryna stay out here in these streets forever. Some niggas like this shit. I don't and so far, I've been lucky or blessed but eventually your number comes up. And the longer you're out here the more likely your numbers gonna come up. Me. I'm tryna retire and go live on a ranch with some horses with a large porch that I can go sit out on and sip my coffee and smoke my cigarette. Now if I can only get you to not fire the best cornermen in the city I might just get to that front porch a little quicker. So, I know you Nazar and you don't do anything without having though it out first. So, what's up?"

115

"You trust me Trip?"

"You already know. What's up?"

"Then give me thirty-five and let me hire my own trainer and cut man."

"Let me think about it."

"What's to think about? You know I need both if I'm to be on this fast track to that pro money." Nazar was in the street now with the same boy he'd grown and though he and Trip had taken different roads to their own success he knew Trip as if it he were his own brother.

"Besides she's already started training me and it almost feels like pop's is in my corner. I mean the girl is the straight skinny. I mean she really knows her shit."

"Oh, that must be the chick everyone's been talking about. They say she's real knowledgeable when it comes to boxing. They tell me she's fine too."

"All that and she's good too Trip. If you can get away for an hour or two come and see her work. She'll be there tonight after six."

"See what I can do," Naz grabbed his boy and pulled him to him.

"See you tonight Trip," Naz said before wheeling around and pulling out his cell.

"Monica, I need for you to be here at the gym by six."

"Excuse me sir but don't you mean you'd like?"

"No, I mean I need you here by six."

Monica hesitated. She hadn't heard this tone in his voice before. He sounded as if he were desperate almost as if someone was holding him hostage. Whatever it was it was important, and if was that important to him she would be there for him.

At a quarter of six Monica strode into the gym up by the armory on St. Nick's in heels and jeans turning every head in the place. Pulling her hair back into a pony tail she threw her duffel bag into Nazar's corner and waved for him to follow her.

"Check the men's room for me."

"It's empty."

Monica ducked in and was out seconds later having changed into a sweatshirt that read 'NO PAIN NO GAIN'.

"Oh goodness. Am I in trouble?" Naz

smiled at the tiny woman who looked to be all business now.

"You know I sat down and had a talk with daddy last night about, you and he was telling me that it wasn't uncommon for a boxer who finds out they have a little power to forget that the jab and their boxing abilities are what got them in the first place," Monica said as she took her time lacing up his gloves. "What happens is they knockout an opponent or two and suddenly think they are knockout punchers and go in throwing caution to the wind looking for the knockout punch that electrifies the crowd. That is not boxing. They say Camacho was like that. He got a little too caught up in his own hype and so my daddy developed this jacket which only gives you the use of one arm. The only way you can fend off an opponent is with the use of the jab and your footwork. Your footwork will keep you out of harm's way. This will

119

not only help your offense it will improve your defense ten-fold," she said slipping it on and tightening so it pinned his other arm to his body.

"You're not serious,"

"You'll be fine Naz. Just keep the jab out there and stick-and-move."

The bell rang, and Monica forced the mouthpiece in the mouth of the one-armed fighter. Naz's opponent on this day was an older boxer with a ton of experience under his belt. He was a crafty old fighter who Monica had specifically picked after watching him go a few rounds with that new up-and coming welterweight now sharing the gym. What Monica most liked about the savvy, older fighter was that he was quite adept at cutting off the ring and going to the body. If Nazar were to survive he would have to double and triple up on the jab just to keep the savvy, old fighter off of him.

Nazar met the older fighter in the middle of the ring where they touched gloves. Nazar's opponent led with a lethal body shot that made Nazar double over at which time the older fighter connected with two crisp, chopping right hands.

"Get off the ropes. That's it. Move, now jab. Good. Now double it up. No. no. no. Nazar you have to keep movin'. Don't run. Just move. Angles baby. Move to that place you can get your jab. That's it baby. Dance. Jab. Turn him. That's it," she shouted. The bell rang, and it was obvious Nazar was visibly shaken.

"How do you expect me to keep this guy off of me? One armed fighters don't win many fights."

"You're doing fine. You'll get more comfortable as time goes on. Just keep turning him and keep your jab in his face. Double and triple it but keep it in his face. If it's in his face, then he's off-balance. He becomes a defensive fighter and a defensive fighter can't hurt you. Just keep throwing your jab. No lazy jabs. I want crisp sharp jabs. Do you hear me Nazar?" Monica shouted loudly enough for everyone in attendance to hear.

The two older men in charge of the other fighter couldn't help but laugh.

"She tellin' him right though," one of the men mused. Nazar met the other fighter in the center of the ring. Angry now that he was at a disadvantage he threw three quick, stinging jabs snapping the other fighters head back. Before he could recover Nazar circled to his left catching the older man with another three hard jabs to the temple.

"That's it baby. Stick-and-move.
That's all you have to do."

The crafty veteran recovered and did
his best to cut off the ring and pin the younger man
against the ropes but Nazar was up on his toes now if
not ducking and weaving, avoiding the vets looping
punches.

"Beautiful baby! That's it! You're
boxing now. That's it baby. That's the sweet science
at it's best!" She said commending him on his ring
generalship. "You're beating him, controlling the pace,
outpointing him easily and it's all behind the jab.
That's Beautiful! That's what I'm talking about baby.
Now let's work the body. Don't abandon the head but
you work the body and his hands are gonna come down
leavin' the head open. You feel me?"

Naz shook his head.

As the rounds went on Monica's tone changed and the praise flew. And the more she praised him the better he boxed. It was a match made in heaven.

Trip sat three rows back. When the sparring session had ended he made his way to the ring.

"You don't see that too often. You're drawing crowds to see you spar. Or perhaps to see the little lady in your corner. She's very good."

"Oh, my bad. Trip this is Monica. Monica meet one of my oldest and dearest friends. Monica this is Trip. So, what did you think?"

"I think you made a good choice. I think we can go with that."

Nazar jumped and shouted as if he'd won an Olympic Gold medal.

"Thanks Trip. You made a real good choice. It's gonna pay off. Trust me."

"I hope so. Listen, I gotta get back to work. You look good Naz. Keep up the good work Blackman," Trip said hugging Naz. "See you around the way my brother."

"Who was that?" Monica asked. "Whoever he was he certainly made your day."

"And if he made my day then he made yours as well."

"I'm not sure I understand."

"You will. Let me grab a quick shower."

"Fifteen minutes later Nazar

125

emerged from the locker in a New York Knicks warmup and a fresh pair of Nike Air Force Ones looking just as smooth as he wanted. Trip had given him his monthly stipend and he'd given momma six hundred of it to help her catch up on some unpaid bills. With the two hundred he had left he'd treated himself to the warm up suit and sneakers.

"And where do you think you're going tonight?"

"Hadn't planned anything other than walking the prettiest little girl in all of Manhattan home."

"Not sure I know who that is but can I tag along."

"Wouldn't have it any other way. You ready?"

The two walked out into the cold, brisk,
fall autumn air.

"So, tell me. Who was that guy?
You two seemed to be really close but he doesn't seem like
you. You know what I'm saying? It's hard to explain."

"I think I understand. You are
trying to draw a connection between Trip and I because
of my demeanor and his. I guess in a lot of ways Trip
appears hard and intimidating. I think that's the way a
lot of people see him. I don't see him like that. Trip
lived on the floor below me all my life and I guess
because we're the same age we became friends. A lot of
times because of the way his house was he stayed with
us. It was crazy. One week everything was cool then
the next week his mother would be shooting at his
stepfather. The lady from DSS used to come out so
often she stopped filling out any paperwork she'd just
sce my dad in the crowd and wave at him asking him if

he were going to take him. Too make a long story he's probably the closest thing I have to a brother. He and Dez are partners. They do the same thing with one difference. Everyone loves Trip. He gets much love out here in the streets. And you know why?"

"No. Why?"

"Because he knows how to treat people. He doesn't demean you because you may be down on your luck. No, he'll come back with something posiive and uplifting if not give the fiend a taste."

"Hard for me to say anything positive about a drug dealer."

"Even if that same drug dealer just agreed to your being my trainer and cut man at thirty-five large a year," Nazar shouted.

"Get the hell out of here! Are you serious," Monica screamed.

"Well, that is minus the ten per cent cut for your manager and agent who really had to go to war to get this deal done."

"Whatever you need sweetie pie." She said jumping on his neck.

"Did you really arrange to get me thirty-five g's Naz. Oh my God! That's real money. I mean that's a good starting salary in any field. Especially with no experience, no resume. He must believe in you as much as I do. Does he know boxing?"

"He was in the gym a lot growing up. If daddy caught him or anyone else just hanging out they spent time in the gym. He knows boxing, but he didn't come to see me today. He came to see you

today. That's why I was so adamant about you being

here. He wanted to see if all the hype was true. He'd

heard about you long before today."

"So, you had him come."

"I did."

"And why didn't you forewarn me?"

"Because you're very good at what
you do naturally. I didn't want or need you to change
in any way."

"Oh my God! I can't believe this.
I'm thinking he's blessed me again. I really do. I think
he's blessed me with you."

"Jury's still out on that one. Listen I have a few dollars, let's go somewhere and celebrate. It's about time someone starts making some money as much work as we put in."

"Tomorrow. I promise. I'm exhausted. I don't know if I'm comin' down with something or if I'm just exhausted from running or just the news. You don't know how much this helps. This will enable me to get out of that house and get my own place. Oh my God I'll finally be able to breathe. Can u imagine eleven people in a three bedroom,"

"I don't think I even have the capacity to imagine eleven people in three rooms."

"Well, it'll be ten shortly. Do you have any idea as to when I start getting paid but I'm sure you're going to go with Trip and I to sign papers with a lawyer? Any dealings with Trip and there's a

131

lawyer involved. He does his best to keep his nose

clean. If you have one or your father has one you may

want to have him represent you although Trip will give

you a fair deal. Right now, he's feeling pretty good

about this deal because he's paying you considerably

less than what he was paying those other two jokers but

with a few wins your salary will go up accordingly."

"How much more were they

making?"

"It doesn't matter. First of all,

you're an unknown commodity, second of all, you're a

woman in a man's arena so to be receiving a salary at

all is a blessing so what I got you is a godsend. You

feel me?"

"Oh no, you don't have to tell me. I

was just curious as to how you manipulated him into

giving you thirty-five grand sight unseen."

"Trust me. It wasn't sight unseen. I'm his investment so he keeps tabs. He knows when I'm in the gym and when I'm slacking off. When he wants specifically to know how I'm doing he'll get in touch with a couple of trainers with differing views and draw his own conclusions and from time-to-time he'll show up and see for himself. Rarely if ever does he comment leaving most of the opinions and strategy to those more knowledgeable. Thirty-five grands a lot even for him so I invited him down personally to check on his investment. I would think it's a career change that you couldn't pass up. And it gets you out of the spot."

"You don't have to convince me sweetie. I know I've been blessed," she said grabbing his hand and squeezing it tightly. They walked the remaining six or seven blocks to Monica's deep in thought. She was making plans. Her first priority was to escape the dirt and grime of the people who plagued the good citizens and made all their lives a living hell.

Outside of her building Dez and a few of his boys were posted up.

"How's cuz been working out for you Cap'n?"

"She couldn't be any better. Just what the doctor ordered pardner," Naz grinned.

"And what did you expect? She comes from elite stock. Damn girl's close to being royalty," Dez said grabbing and hugging Naz. "They tell me you've stated putting the work in and are looking sharp again. Even heard that she's got you boxing with one arm tied behind your back to improve your jab and your footwork. They are even telling me that you knocked out this kid with one hand tied behind your back. Is that true?"

Naz dropped his head almost in acknowledgement.

"Damn. I sure would have liked to have been there to see that one," he shouted. "True story?"

"Real talk," Naz lied grinning the whole while.

Monica threw him a sideways glance condemning the lie.

"I'm going to head up. It's apartment 12C, the one with the wreath on the door."

"I'll be right up,"

"So, Naz from what Mia tells me you're considering turning pro?"

"Yeah, I'm considering it but then I've been considering it for the last five or six years. If I win this year's Golden Gloves that'll be the perfect jump off."

"But you've already won two. You don't need that as a jump off. I'm just sayin'. Anyway, when you need someone to invest in you that'll have your best interest at heart come and see me. We'll make this a family thing."

"Thanks, Dez. I appreciate the offer. I'll let you know."

On the elevator up to Monica's apartment Nazar considered Dez's offer for a split second before dismissing it. There was just something about Dez or maybe it was him. Whatever it was he just didn't like the kid.

Spotting the enormous wreath that covered the entire door Naz rang the doorbell before knocking lightly.

A scantily clad woman not much older than Monica answered the door.

"Hi. I'm Nazar, Monica's friend."

"Oh. You're that boxer guy Monica's head over heels with."

"I didn't know that. Thanks for the heads up."

"Oh. Did I say too much? Lil' sister's gonna kill me if I let the cat out the bag but there's one thing she didn't lie about."

"And what's that?"

"That you're cute as you wanna be. I'm Cicely, Monica's older sister. And have daddy and Mia tell it you're the second coming."

"I don't know about all that but one day I may just be a contender with your sister's help."

"I think you're far too modest Mr. Nazar. From what I hear you're a fabulous fighter. Me. I'm more of the lover myself," she said smiling and winking mischievously at Nazar. Nazar didn't know what to make of the woman's flirtations. Hadn't he made it plain that he was there to see Monica?

As if on cue and sensing Nazar's uncomfortableness Monica appeared.

"Mom, dad this is Nazar. At he same time an army of children all vied for the stranger's attention. This is Nazar the fighter I was telling you about," Monica said grabbing Nazar's hand and pulling him into the living room. Grown women, each more attractive than the next walked up and kissed him on the cheek while the army of children continued to vie for his attention.

The house which smelled of arroz con pollo was warm, the inhabitants down'-to-earth and Nazar was easily comfortable.

Exiting the apartment an hour or so later with Monica by his side Nazar breathed a deep sigh of relief.

"You okay sweetie? I know they can be a bit much," she said seeing how unnerved the children had Nazar. "I guess it's safe to say you're not ready for a family of your own yet," Monica grinned. "Now maybe you can understand what I was telling you about needing my space."

"One thing's for sure. There's no lack of love or sense of family," Nazar mused as he tried to collect himself. One little girl insisted on feeding him mouthfuls of macaroni and cheese at dinner while another was adamant about telling him about each one of her twenty-six classmates and their daily behavior while still another little boy finding out Nazar was a boxer insisted on throwing every conceivable punch at Nazar's head with an occasional one landing every so often.

"Do all of you stay there," Nazar asked dumbfounded.

"All except Cicely. She has her own

place downtown, but you might as well say she stays there too. She's there more than she is home. If I had my own place, I'd be damned if I stayed there. That's for sure."

"Did you see the roaches? I know you did. How could you miss them, and we have rats too. The air don't work in the summer and the heat don't work in the winter. I love my family dearly but when I get outta there I ain't goin' back."

"Stop that. Stop looking back. And never hate on a foundation like yours. You come from a beautiful family that loves you. Their imprint on you makes you who you are today. And now you've been blessed with the opportunity to find a place of your own. So, stop looking back at the negative side of things."

"I guess you're right. You know you're good for me. I tend to be overly critical. I think I'm a perfectionist."

"No problem there. I'm not a real big fan of underachievers. They don't really motivate me."

"I'm a handful."

"I was born with two," Nazar said holding out both of his hands for to see.

"Oh my God! How he has blessed me. And now he's blessed me with you," Monica said hugging Nazar.

"Funny thing, I had similar thoughts about you just this morning," he said smiling deeply from within.

"I have a feeling that if we work

together that even the moon and the stars are possible," Monica whispered just loud enough for him to hear. Her profession of love was all Nazar needed. And the best part of it all was that she was in his corner.

The days passed and fall soon turned into winter and it wasn't long before Monica she entered the gym and pulled Nazar into the office.

"I don't know if you've heard but Hector Valdes is turning pro in April. That's the rumor anyway. That's four months from now and gives me just enough time to tailor a fight plan to beat him. I mean that is if you're inclined to turn pro in the next month or so."

"I can see my improvement, but do you really think I'm ready?"

"You told me you thought you

were ready when I met you. Now six months later you're doubting yourself? I think I'm working backwards. Are you losing confidence in your abilities?"

"Not at all. I'm just curious as to where *you* think I am in my progression?"

"I do. I really do and I also think that beating the top local boys will pack the Barkley Center. After you claim the top spot in the city and become a household name you'll be able to choose your opponents. We just need you on the undercard of the next big fight. What do you think?"

"If you say I'm ready then I'm ready."

"Okay. Then meet me at my place. I want to go over some fight films I managed to pull together."

144

"Give me a time."

"How's six, six-thirty sound?"

Monica had procured a small apartment down in SoHo for little or nothing and had done a masterful job of decorating it with rich, lush earth tones that blended well and gave the place a soothing ambience. Monica had given his own key and he often went there for some solace and some peace of mind. Between their schedules they hardly saw each other if it wasn't in the gym. She'd made it plain that as much as she loved him they would not engage in sexual activity. Having little or no choice in the matter he agreed and only counted the day they were joined in marriage.

Nazar spent the night there on several occasions but never, not once had he taken the liberties of entering her bedroom. And today would be no different although he felt the heat rise within him anytime she was near. If it was one thing he'd come to know about her it was that she was both loyal and faithful. She loved, and she loved hard. He remembered on one occasion when he'd feigned being angry with her. She'd gone into seclusion and it was three days before she would even speak to him or anyone else. When it was over she politely informed him that this would never happen again. Drama wasn't a part of her agenda and just as he was on the fast track to his own fame and fortune she too similarly had an agenda of her own, but it did not include self-inflicted bumps and bruises. Either he was on board and they would ride it out together or they could end it now.

That was the first and last time they'd had what even came close to a disagreement. The mere thought of not waking up to her cheerful voice was enough to put a damper on his day and he hated the thought of not seeing her for long periods of time. Yes, she had

146

become an integral part of his life. She completed him and deferred much of the press nowadays with her flippant but poignant remarks on everything from 'the sweet art' to our current president's state-of-mind. The fact that he'd won the Golden Gloves twice prior to their meeting was of little consequence now. In their eyes, she was the creator, the mastermind behind this latest welterweight sensation. And their sparring sessions had to be rescheduled for late evenings because of the sheer numbers of reporters coming to see the little lady work. Ring magazine even went so far as to do a feature article on the bronze bombshell as they now referred to her. Monica took it all in stride, smiling for the cameras and always providing some good copy yet remaining humble and deflecting all attention away from her fighter so he could concentrate on one thing only. The fight.

Kissing her softly, deeply, passionately Nazar was convinced by this time that this was the woman he wanted to spend the rest of his life with. She had quickly gone from eye-candy to friend and confidante. And after talking to mama and Sin he was convinced that his instincts were good that he'd be making a wise choice in asking for her hand in marriage, but he would wait. He'd wait 'til they declared him champion and that very night when he was being declared king of the world he would declare her his queen and fall to his knees and ask her for her hand in marriage. Yes, that's what he would do. That was the plan. Kissing her softly Monica was completely oblivious to the transactions taking place that so involved her.

There was no question about her feelings towards him and most of the boxers and hanger ons in and around the gym respected that. There were a few who refused to acknowledge the relationship, but Monica would sidestep them and let them down with as much tact as possible but on one occasion there was one particularly overzealous man who like Nazar was simply overwhelmed by the little dynamo so after pretending to watch Nazar work out for more than a week or so he made his move. He was new to the gym and ever since rumors had gotten out that Nazar was contemplating turning pro more and more people had frequented the gym and even more when it became known that the legendary Tito Martinez was the father of the little lady in this new welterweight phenoms ascent to the championship. Those that truly knew New York boxing knew that Naz was not new.

In any case, and after one particular vigorous sparring session in which Monica had him wear the jacket and concentrate on his jab which by the way he had gotten quite adept at keeping his opponents off -balance with. So proficient had he gotten that even wearing the jacket he broke his opponent's nose with a stinging jab in the seventh which halted the affair. There was no love lost between the two men who had fought in the streets earlier in their lives. Words were spoken before, during and after the fight with the crowd splitting in back of their fighter. Nazar's followers outnumbered his opponents two-to-one but parties were ready when Monica stepped to the center of the ring and picked up the megaphone.

"Stop the dumb shit!" she shouted. "We all Black people here. We gotta stop fighting and hurting each other over dumb shit. It was a good fight.

Both men are warriors. Give them a hand and let's get on with our business as Black folk."

And slowly they began clapping and heading their respective ways. The stranger watched all of this disregarding everything else and became even more adamant in his mind that he was going to have this woman.

"I'll be out in fifteen," Nazar winked at Monica who was throwing dirty towels in a duffel bag.

"Excuse me miss but I have a proposition for you if you have a minute."

"Fifteen. You have fifteen."

The stranger smiled. He liked her. She was strong, vibrant, confident.

"The truth is I've been watching you for the better part of a week now and I've come to realize that you could be the face of the Tank Gym.

I'm sure you've heard of us. In any case, we have four or five top prospects ready to take that next step and no one

151

of near your caliber to take them there. I think you could."

"I'm flattered and yes I know the Tank Gym but I have my hands full now."

"You could keep your clients here but when people see your face, we want them to associate it with the Tank Gym. And we haven't even started talking money yet. I can promise you or put it in writing right now that we can double your current salary for doing the same thing you're doing right now with no interference from any of us. You run your camp the way you see best for twice the money and you'll be affecting twice the amount of lives," the man's voiced raised to a desperate pitch now drawing the attention of ringsiders.

"Like I said before Mr. I didn't get your name?"

152

"Irish Mickey O'Rourke."

"Well, Mr. O'Rourke like I said I have one fighter and with everything else going on in my life my plate is full. I couldn't do it if I wanted to although your offer is quite enticing. Thanks anyway," Monica said picking up the last of the towels when the man seemed to rush her. No one understood the man's move but he never had a chance to lay a finger on her and she had everything she could do to stop the men from beating the little Irish man to a pulp. By the time she had the crowd calmed down Nazar appeared and once he heard what had just transpired he too lost his mind and now it was the other men who had to restrain him.

"What was on your mind man? You might have had a chance with anyone else here in the gym, but you picked the princess. Have you lost your mind?"

"I need her. She's the difference between us going under or surviving. I offered her twice the money and the bitch turned me down."

"I should slap you but I'm not going to lower myself to your level," the bouncer and former heavyweight contender replied. "You may be unaware of this, but everybody don't do what they do for money. Some folks do it solely for the love of what they do. She wouldn't be the same with any other boxer. This is her boxer. Do you feel me?"

The little Irish man pondered the bouncer's words. He'd neglected to consider the woman's reply but then who would turn down twice the money for doing the same damn thing they were doing now. It made no sense and now look what he'd gone and gotten himself into. It must have made them niggas feel good them finally getting to hold a white boy for the police.

Nazar's mother, Mrs. Muhammad hearing the news called Monica directly to check on her. When Nazar decided to take the fall semester off to concentrate on boxing after his mother and Cynthia pleaded with him not to Monica received a call.

"Not to worry Ms. Muhammad. Nazar will be enrolled in classes this fall." And a text that read, 'I got this sister. Don't give it a second thought.' The funny thing was she never addressed the subject directly. She simply said one day after training and a week before his pro debut would he think she'd be smothering him if she transferred to John Jay, so they could take some classes together. She had to admit she hadn't seen him this excited since they first met. To Nazar it was a good sign. It meant that she wanted to spend more time with him outside of the gym. Because of him she now had her cute, little, loft and could now attend school. And she included him in

155

everything. Together they were inseparable and loving every minute of it. If he had a little too much wine or it got to be a bit too late he knew he could always crash, there. It was always on the couch. Oh, he was trying more and more but she remained firm in brushing him off.

"You know one-day last week I was hangin' out with my thirteen-year-old niece and I asked her if she had a boyfriend. And this is what she told me. She said. 'Aunt Mia, I'm just now learning to control what happens in my own life. I can't and don't have time to try and control mine and be a part of his too.' "I don't know if that makes sense to you, but I understand completely. I need to get my own life to the point where I like it and am comfortable with it before I can offer myself in my entirety to you. My success is dependent on you. Everyone tells me I'm pulling double duty, so your rep stays intact."

"How's that? What's double-duty?"

"You know. I'm your trainer and inhouse pussy included."

"Get out of here. Who thinks that?" You're trippin' now Monica."

"C'mon Nazar. You can't be that naive. Half the gym comes to watch me to train you because they know I can coach. The other half comes to watch my ass. You watch. In due time, someone's gonna challenge you for not only the king of the gym but they're also gonna challenge you for me. You watch and see."

"Where did all these negative thoughts come from and why are you bringing them up when things are going so well? That's what I don't get. Mama always says that the tongue is a sword. Think

157

and it will be. So please don't think any more negative thoughts baby," Nazar whispered.

"Let's just stay focused on our goal. Let's think about sipping coffee on the front porch of our farm during the winter while the deer scamper in the snow in the front yard. Let's think happy thoughts m'love."

"I'm sorry. You're right. It's just that I'm not immune to the rumors and chatter in the gym. I hear things."

"I know. That's why I suggest going to the Poconos for training camp."

"But that way would have been way too expensive."

"You pay to rid yourself of the distractions such as these though. You wouldn't have had to hear that idle gym chatter."

"True. I guess I just have to refocus and reassess the whole situation. Pops, over there, told me you've probably never experienced anything like this before?"

"What's that baby?"

"Having a trainer that's as fine as me," she said smiling broadly. "Seriously though I have a plan for my life and when I do decide to lay down with a man that man will be my husband. I look around at all my girlfriends that have two and three kids because they were in love but they didn't hold the man accountable and check the resume now their doing the whole parenting thing alone and most of these niggas ain't even in a position to take care of their kids. That ain't for me. I gotta check the resume. And then he has to put the time in and at least pretend that he's interested in something else other than my sex. And if he chooses to hang around because he simply likes me as a person then maybe we can talk commitment. Then once we have committed we can talk sex. And that's my plan."

"I hear you but let me ask you this sweetie. Haven't I done or at least attempted to do everything you've asked me to do since I met you?"

"You have,"

"And there's no doubt that I love you."

"No, there isn't but you need to stop right there. I love you as well and have devoted the last six months to your career and your success but you're out of your cotton-picking mind if you think I'm going to give up what I've cherished all my life because someone riding a wonderful wave of good fortune asks me too. Don't work like that here. In my mind it will happen when it happens and when it's supposed to and from what I've been told I'll feel a certain *ZING!* That says that's it. That's the ticket."

"And you're telling me that you've never felt like that when we're together?"

"Oh no, I'm not saying that at all. I'd be lying if I said I didn't feel anything or get that *ZING* every then and again but then I just turn it off when I say 'we have so much to do and so far, to go that we don't have time for anything else and I refocus to the task at hand whether it be winning the championship or graduating on time. I just have to push us away for now. Besides it's so important that we are truly friends first. Don't you think so?"

Nazar shook his head in agreement although he still had other ideas about the friendship and how he could help it evolve.

161

"And I think we're at a real good place right now," she said smiling and blowing Nazar a kiss. "Besides you're only twenty-one. And although I may be your flavor of the week you may very well change your mind in a month. That's just what young men do. They see something one day that they just can't live without. The next day they see something new."

Nazar dropped his head. One of the reasons he enjoyed boxing was that it gave him an outlet. It was almost like therapy for him and hard to get him into any in depth conversation. Monica should have realized this by now. She'd known him long enough to know. And though he'd long ago disengaged from the whole topic she hadn't realized he was simply feeding her enough to keep her going. He loved to hear her talk and her own unique and twisted views on things.

"C'mon Monica. Have my eyes ever strayed in the six months that I've known you?"

"No. I can't say that they have. That's because you're still curious and it's my job to keep myself new so as to keep you curious. How am I doing so far? Seriously, though and not to change the subject but do you realize there's only a week before the fight?"

"How could I not? Every conversation either begins or ends with something about the fight."

"And well it should. Don't know whether you're aware of it but you're a boxer and not just any boxer you're considered the best pound-for-pound boxer in the city. And after a stellar amateur career all eyes are on you making your pro debut. You're the talk of the town. They're all focused on the fight and the sad part about it is you don't seem as focused on the fight as any of them and they don't have to be focused. You do."

"I know you're not accusing me of not focusing on the fight. Because I don't have or take your demeanor does not mean I'm not focused. I'm focused. But I'm not consumed by this fight. There are other things in my life. I wonder how my mother's holding up and how soon will it be 'til I make enough where she won't have to work at all. I can actually see her aging before me. Then when I finish worrying about that I wonder if the owner of the little bodega that's always flirting with my sister is serious about Sin or if he's just tryna hit it for the hell of it and how she would be really hurt. I wonder how I did on my history exam and if I'm going to make dean's list. I wonder if Monica and I are going to ever be ae able to sit down and relax and talk about something other than work. You see there are other things in my life besides boxing

164

and I have to give them time as well, but you don't have to worry I can multi-task and you will never see anyone more focused than me when I step into the ring on Saturday."

The days that led up to the fight were a blur. He'd never trained so hard in his life but the last few days was more strategizing than anything. And the last few days Monica had him damn near go blind from watching film after film after film.

"You see how wide and sweeping he throws the overhand right? He telegraphs it every time he throws it. When you see him throw it or start to throw it I want you to slide right, counter it with the jab and then double up with the left hook. You can even step inside and throw the upper cut but I want you to be on the inside if you throw the uppercut. Bada bip.

Bada Boom. You feel me?"

"I feel you," Nazar said smiling.as he watched Monica now so immersed in the film. It was true. Monica watched old fight films the way other women watched the Notebook. And before he knew it it was fight night. Unlike other fighters Nazar never grew uptight or nervous. To Nazar it was just another day at the office. In the locker room before the fight everything was surprisingly quiet with everyone seemingly locked into their own thoughts. He'd unofficially made Monica his manager after she'd arranged the fight found out what up and coming boxers got as debut money and made sure Nazar's got double that.

When the lights had dimmed in the Garden Nazar found himself alone with Monica. Even when his dad was alive there were always four or five people in the dressing room before the fight. Monica, however seemed perfectly at peace with the two of them there. She remained quiet and reserved.

"No last-minute instructions?" Nazar asked in an attempt to break the silence.

"If you don't know it now there's nothing I can do, I have nothing to say because you have trained hard and know what it is we have to do once we step into the ring. You asked me once if you were ready. Nazar I have never seen a fighter so ready,"

"Five minutes," came the warning. Nazar and Monica made their way towards the ring. But before they could make it to the door a knock came. And though he'd never met him Nazar knew exactly who the tall, handsome, man was when he stepped through the door.

"Daddy! I didn't think you were going to make it."

"You asked me to be, here didn't you?"

"Yeah. But…"

"There are no 'buts'. How are you holding up young fella?"

Nazar stuck out his hand in awe of the legend now in front of him.

"I knew your father. He was a god man. I'm truly sorry for your loss."

"Thank you, sir."

"You two ready"

No sooner had he asked than there was a knock at the door.

"Fighters you have five minutes."

"Let's go," Mr. Medina said grabbing an old,beat up duffel bag that had seen better days Monica grabbed Nazar's hand squeezing tightly.

"You okay sweetie?"

"I'm good."

"You nervous."

"I wouldn't say nervous. Excited yes. But no I'm not nervous."

"Hope you don't mind me binging my father in. He volunteered, and I couldn't say no. He's the finest cut man in the business."

"I don't mind. I just wish you'd gotten someone who knew a little something about boxing, so I'd have a chance," Nazar laughed.

"Oh no you didn't," she said laughing and punching him in the arm. Climbing the steps of the ring Nazar glanced the front row where he saw Trip. Nazar turned around immediately and went back down the stairs to where Trip was sitting. The men hugged each other.

"I want you to go out there and beat this motherfucker's ass Naz," Trip said whispering in Nazar's ear.

"Thanks for the opportunity Trip. I wouldn't be here if it wasn't for you. I love you man."

"Then make me proud and go out and beat this motherfucker's ass."

The two held each other a bit longer before Nazar made his way to the ring where he made it a point to dance around the ring, showboating before electrifying the crowd with the Ali shuffle all. He was throwing jabs and combinations that were a thing of beauty. Looking out over the crowd he noticed Dez and his crew sitting a few rows back. And of course, there was Trip sitting there like a proud father.

Hector stepped into the ring like a seasoned veteran. Poised and ready he had a good camp and was in great shape. A small contingent of cheers rose up from his followers. It had been less than a year since the two's last encounter, but Hector was now considerably, bigger, and stronger. At least he appeared to be. Nazar smiled. 'Bulk up. Convince yourself you are stronger. But you will not touch me. I am too fast, too quick for you.' Nazar told himself as he circled the ring. He was ready.

"Looks like Hector's been working out. He's bulked up. Trying to gain some power," Monica mused. "Not smart. All that did was make him slower and easier to hit. They want him to be a boxer slash slugger, ready for the clinches. He's perfect. What I want you to do is the same thing we work on every day in the gym. The very same thing we work on every day

171

in the gym. Do you hear me? The man in front of you is nothing more than another sparring partner. Only difference is he's got more trinkets on his shorts than they do. Feel him out the first couple of rounds. Study him and use the jab to keep him at a distance. Once we study him and see his shortcomings we can go to work. Mow you see an opportunity you make quick work of him. Just remember it all begins and ends with the jab. Keep it in his face. And keep your head moving. Duck and weave then stick and move."

The bell rang, and Hector came out like a raging bull intent on erasing the two previous losses to Naz. Nazar caught off guard grabbed the larger, stronger man hoping to clinch but Hector refused to allow that pinning Naz against the ropes and pounding him with vicious body shots until the bell sounded.

"He's strong. Hits a lot harder than he used to," Naz said breathing deeply.

"Ya gotta stay off the ropes," Monica said coolly, calmly hoping to relax her fighter.

"You don't have to tell me that, boss."

"Okay. Do as I tell you and he'll never lay a glove on you."

"Stop being stupid, Naz," was a voice from the crowd he knew well. Do what your corner tells you and stop playing into his hands. Nigga can't box with you. Listen to your corner man," Trip yelled.

Naz nodded his acknowledgement.

"I need you to box him Naz sweetie. Hit him with a jab followed by two or three more then get on your bicycle and get out of there. Only stop long enough to get off a couple of more stinging jabs and then move. Hit and run just like we practiced. Now come here. Naz went over to the young woman who

held her hands up for Naz to bend over and kiss her.

"Well, this is somewhat different,"

the color commentary man told the world. We don't

usually see too much kissing in the corner Roy."

"No. I guess you don't but then you

don't see too many trainers and their boxers engaged

to be married either."

"Whatever's going on in that corner

it must be working. The kid was undefeated in his

amateur career."

"Okay well let's sit back and watch

and see how it goes in his pro debut. That first round was

a little shaky for Nazar."

"Yes, it was. Hector is clearly the

bigger and physically stronger man. Let's see how the extra weights hurts or helps Hector in the ring as we start round two."

Impressed by his own new-found success Hector charged across the ring just as he'd done in Round 1 but this time Nazar caug-ht Hector coming in with a high, stiff jab that caught Hector flush on the temple and stopped him in his tracks. Sidestepping him Nazar shot two more to the man's chest which froze him once again and left him huffing and puffing like an angry bull about to charge. Naz continued this for the rest of the round leaving Hector frustrated.

"That's it baby. Stick-and-move. That's it baby. Keep the jab in his face. That's it baby. Now double it. Triple it baby. That's it baby. You're boxing beautifully," Monica screamed at the end of the round. "You're boxing him beautifully, Nazar but

175

Hector's scary. He gets lucky and you're outta there

so, what I want is for you to start following up behind the jab. I want you to start sitting down on your punches. I want you to start following up on the jab with the left hook and overhand right. When you're on the inside use the uppercut. Let's end this and go home now. I'm starting to get a little hungry," she said grinning at Nazar.

Nazar was well in command by the fourth round but Hector refused to go anywhere doing just enough to hang around. On his feet and charging across the ring at the beginning of the fifth round came Hector only to be met with a stiff jab that stunned him momentarily and long enough for Nazar's chopping right to send him to the campus. Up at the count of six it was clear that Hector was frustrated.

Nothing he had chosen to do was working. It was just like his other fights against Naz. He couldn't hit him because he was elusive. Tonight, was no different.

Now on his feet and seemingly unscathed by the flash knockdown Hector screamed.

"Stop running and fight motherfucker." Before Nazar could follow up on Hector's request the bell rang.

"Don't listen to that shit Nazar. He wants you to brawl with him. Right now, it's a shutout. You couldn't be boxing any better. And the knockdown? Right out of Tyson's bag of tricks. You look good. You really do. Now what I want you to do is show him some of that two-fisted love. Jab. Then jab some more and watch those combinations open up for you. I want you to let it go. Unload everything you've got on him without punching yourself out. Let's get him out of there."

The bell sounded and Nazar was on his toes and dancing beautifully. He was jabbing now. A single followed by a double and a triple had Hector reeling. Nazar knew he had him now. An uppercut followed by a left hook and the referee was pushing Nazar to a neutral corner. The bell sounded saving Hector.

"You hurt him. So, you know you can take him out but remember there's nothing more dangerous than a wounded animal and Hector is hurt. Don't be careless. Keep your hands up and work the body. Box him Nazar. Box him."

Nazar met Hector in the middle of the ring. He held his ground and was now building points on the scorer's scorecards by doing nothing more than hitting with quick, sharp, stinging jabs and then moving just beyond his reach. It was a beautiful strategy and those that knew the 'sweet art' cheered at Nazar's every flurry. As the round came to a close Nazar measured the slower moving man with a jab before catching him with a crushing upper cut. And still Hector did not go down.

"Let's go back to boxing him Naz." Monica said taking his mouthpiece out and giving him water. "We're six rounds in baby and you're looking good. Boy's got a chin like iron. You've hit him with everything, but the kitchen sink so don't worry about the knockout. You're way up on the scorecards so just keep doing what you're doing. Box him and keep your hands up."

Naz had other things in mind though. He'd seen a chink in Hector's armor at the end of the last round. Each time Hector would throw a jab he would

179

drop his hands to his side. Making himself clearly the aggressor Naz waited for Hector to throw his jab then he hit Hector with a left right combination that made the larger man wince and take a step backward. Nazar noticing he was shaken was all over him now throwing a barrage of uppercuts and left hooks until Hector crumpled under the onslaught.

"You saw something?" Monica said keeping her composure as best she could. "You saw something?"

"I did. He would throw the jab and then drop his hands," he said grabbing her and swinging her in the air.

"Ah, baby we did it!" she creamed hugging him tightly.

Mr. Medina was in the ring now cheering and hugging his daughter and Nazar as if he'd just found the crown jewels

"You ought a beautiful fight Nazar," The older man said shaking his hand and grabbing his shoulder at the same time.

"Thank you, sir," Nazar replied grinning that the man they referred to as a 'legend' had paid him a compliment.

"And you my daughter had a wonderful fight plan. That's the way you fight a slugger/brawler. You box him and that's what you did. Congratulations Mia," he said hugging his daughter tightly.

And then there was Trip who seldom smiled entering the ring, the grin of a proud father pasted on his face.

"Congratulations. Good debut kid.

Come see me tomorrow. We need to talk."

Nazar nodded.

"Beautiful baby. You fought a smart and

you looked good doing it. We've got some minor things

to work on but we can save all of that for tomorrow.

Tonight, we celebrate your first pro win. I mean if that's

what you'd like to do."

"Depends on what you have planned

for me tomorrow."

"Nothing physical or strenuous for the

next couple of weeks. Your body needs to rest and

recuperate. Then we get back to the gym to prepare for

your next fight which will be in three months."

This caught Nazar's attention.

"You have someone in mind?"

"I don't want to commit to any one

opponent right through here.

There are way too many up-and-coming prospects, but

we need more than just a hot prospect. We need

someone highly marketable, so we can start selling you

as a brand, as a product so we need someone that

shimmers in their own light. Once you beat* him

you'll be the new hot commodity, the new drawing

card. This is where boxing takes a backseat to the

business aspect.

Sweetie, boxing is not about the best man winning. It's

about choosing your opponent's carefully. I'm not

looking for opponents whose sole intent is leaving you

permanently brain damaged. No, what I'm looking for

are fighters who are challenging and game but not

difficult opponents. We want a fighter having a

tremendous upside when it comes to selling tickets but

usually on the downside of their careers. That's how

you'll gain experience, gain exposure and climb in the

rankings. Then when you're in contention is real the real wars begin. So, don't look at it as padding your wins. I'm just trying to keep my fighter and my man healthy and safe. What he doesn't know it but I have plans for him once this whole boxing thing is just a memory."

"Great fight young man," Mr. Medina said grabbing and hugging Naz. "You fought a very, smart fight. You'll go a long way if you keep boxing the way you did tonight."

"Thank you, Mr. Medina. That means a lot coming from you."

"Well, let me let you kids go. I guess y'all are heading out to celebrate?"

"No sir. Actually, if you have a few minutes to let me grab a quick shower we can all go together."

"You two don't want to go out and grab something to eat?" Monica said surprised at Nazar's response.

"No. I'm good. I think I'm going to head home and just head to bed. I'm beat."

"You sure you're okay Naz? Daddy can you give me a minute to speak to Nazar alone?" "Take all the time you want. It's your mom's night out with the girls. I promised her I'd babysit so I'd better get out of here."

"Okay daddy," Monica said before turning to Nazr. "What's wrong dude?"

"Nothing baby. I'm good."

"You're lying to me Nazar. You're coming off the biggest win of your young life and you're not showing any emotion at all. What's up?"

"Same thing I heard before the fight if you recall. You told me that because I didn't show any emotion then I wasn't focused. Was I focused? Did I fight a better fight than even you could have imagined?"

"You did," Monica conceded.

"Then give me some credit. Everyone doesn't show emotion in the same way and it's always been my instinct to go home and think the whole thing out before commenting about it."

"I thought that was one of the reasons I was in your life. I thought we could lean on each other when the difficult times came along. That's one of the good things about having a partner."

"Just thinking about your business plan baby. I was thinking about the things I hoped to achieve."

"And what's at the end of your rainbow baby?"

"That's simple. You're what's at the end of my rainbow. I see how you have everything organized, planned and now you're orchestrating our lives. I appreciate the time, caring and devotion you're investing in me but what concerns me is nowhere in your planning did my opinion come into play."

"I just assumed when you asked me to manage you that this is what I was supposed to do. Nothing's written in stone. I was just throwing out some ideas. I thought this is what you wanted."

"What I want is to have a say, a voice in what happens in my career. Let me tell you something sweetheart. I've only been managed by one person in my life."

"Your father?"

"Yes. So, I'm not had a lot of experience in what a manager does other than line up fights in the best interest of his fighter. But if I can say something, draw one correlation it's that you two have almost identical management styles."

"I'm not sure if I should take that as a compliment or condemnation."

Nazar had to laugh.

"Listen I love you and my father but both of you have the uncanny ability of being controlling almost suffocating at times. And despite both of you having my best interest at heart did it ever occur to you that if you consider me a smart fighter then given the opportunity that may carry over into life itself. When my father passed away I was crushed but in a strange sort of weird way, but I was relieved in a sense too. For the first time in my life I felt free and in control of my own life, my own destiny. You feel me?"

"I'm listening. I'm learning you Mr. Muhammad. Continue," Monica said resting her head on his shoulder and pulling her collar to brace herself from the cold, winter wind coming off the Hudson.

"When I met you, I hadn't been in the gym for a good month and wasn't sure I was going to box again. Inside I knew I would simply because it brings order and discipline to my life, but I sat out because I could. Suddenly it was my choice to make.

You feel me?'

"And you see me as limiting your freedom of choice in much the same way your father did. Is that it?"

"I think that's the reason you're in

189

my corner to begin with. You two think so much alike but neither of you had the ability to slow down enough to ask me what I want for myself."

"Guilty as charged, I'm afraid," Monica said squeezing Nazar's hand in her own. "You're absolutely right and I apologize. I overstepped my boundaries. I guess I was just being selfish. All I saw was us crossing the finish line."

"And ain't nothin' wrong with that except you gotta keep in mind that there are two of us in this relationship and both of us should have a say in how their life plays out."

"I hear you baby and again I am so sorry but let me ask you this. What would have been so different than the path I chose for you?"

"Seriously?" Nazar said smiling.

"Real talk."

"This could be our first argument but my biggest problem with you is that I love you to death and although you think you're responsible for my welfare I don't feel the love. I feel more like a prized bull before the state fair. And all I do these days is try not to disappoint. Do you know who I most fear when I get into the ring nowadays?"

"No, who?"

"The only opponent I have when I enter the ring is my fear of disappointing you. But you hardly seem to notice because everything is proceeding as planned. It almost as if I've taken the liberties of falling in love with a woman that's fallen in love with a dream of championships and not the man."

"That's not true at all Nazar! Boxing is not my first priority. You are. Why can't we commit

191

to our future together and continue this crazy ride together as one? What's wrong with just staying committed to our craft and each other?"

Those were the words Nazar yearned to hear. He knew this is how she felt but he still felt as if something was missing. It didn't help that she held him at arm's distance behind closed doors but as close as they were it still felt as if there was something between them.

They were back in her loft now after walking the mile or so from the Garden. Grabbing a couple of glasses and a bottle of Chablis Monica poured the wine.

"So, what are you saying Mr. Muhammad?" Monica sat directly across from the weary fighter.

"To make a long story short, I think the void I'm feeling when it comes to you can only be filled by you agreeing to be my wife."

Monica put her glass down on the living room table before placing her head in her hands. She sat like this for a few minutes before seemingly regaining her composure.

"Nazar."

"Yes, dear."

"I think you should leave. This has all been a bit much. Don't get me wrong with our first win and now this it's been one heck of a day. I think I'm just gonna marinate in it. Good night Naz." Nazar who was undone by this

sudden change of events grabbed his paperboy cap and made his way to the door.

"Oh, and Nazar."

Nazar stopped turning to face the woman who controlled his every waking thought and still remained an enigma to him.

"The answer to your question is yes I will marry you," she said smiling before closing the front door of the brownstone.

The win in the ring felt good but nothing compared to this. After six months all his hard labor had finally begun to pay off not only in the ring but out of the ring as well. And the one hundred and twenty-five-thousand-dollar purse Monica managed to get would put mama and Sin on easy street and pay for their wedding. No. Naz couldn't see how life could be any better.

Sitting in her bedroom, sipping a glass of Zinfandel, curtains pulled, lights dimmed, with

Booker T blasting Green Onions Monica was having similar thoughts. The man she loved had asked her to marry him. No. Life couldn't get any better. Smiling, Monica only wondered what had taken so long. After all, and although she'd stayed focused solely on advancing his boxing career at times she still wondered that as aggressive as he could be in the ring why he was so passive and submissive when it came to her. Perhaps the lopsided win had given him the confidence to step up to the plate. She couldn't be sure but whatever caused the sudden change in temperament she was certainly glad for it.

In the months following it had been difficult trying to separate herself from being trainer, manager, lover and partner. At times it had been difficult just holding back her emotions. There were times she wanted to just grab him and hold him for just being one of the good guys. At other times and before fights he'd come into the ring his well-toned

bronze colored skin glistening with every muscle taut

and firm. These were the times she wanted him most

and often felt herself getting moist from the heat she

was exhibiting just being in his presence. Ever since

their first meeting he had that certain something that

literally made her loins quiver. The French refer to it as

'gene se qua' for that certain type of charm one

possessed. Whatever it was it had only grown stronger

since their initial meeting. She had everything she

could do not to act or speak on how she was feeling.

There was no one to go to talk about how she was

feeling. Nazar was the only person she really confided

in. By no means could she be ever be considered

brazen or forward. She liked to think of herself moore

as classy, traditional in a sense. And because she held

her chin up and made it a point to keep to herself most

of the other females in her neighborhood saw her as just

another little, cute, bougie, chick stuck on herself.

Monica had no airs about herself but had too much going on in her own life to get caught up in the streets. Those that knew her knew her to be cordial and down to earth. Those that knew her knew that. And yet this man that she had spent virtually every waking hour with for the past six months was telling her that he was unsure of her intentions.

Monica picked up the phone. She had to tell daddy. But then she had to call Cicely first. If she didn't she'd never hear the end of it. Having second thoughts Monica put the phone down and reached for the bottle of wine. Tonight, she wasn't calling anyone. Tonight, she was going to savor a dream come true.

Monica loved Nazar and tonight he let her know that he too loved her and was committed to spending the rest of his days with her. It was a beautiful thought that etched a warm smile on her face and in her heart.

The sudden vibration on the bedside table shook Monica from her daydream.

"Yes, dear. Figured you'd be asleep by now considering the day you had. You won your pro debut in splendid, style then you proposed marriage to a wonderful young lady. I'd say that makes for a pretty full day."

"It does. I think I'm more emotionally drained than I am physically. Was actually thinking about going out and putting in a couple of miles just to clear my head. But before I did that I just wanted to make sure I was right about one thing."

"And what would that be?"

"You did agree to marry me tonight?"

"That I did my love. Was that all you needed?"

"Yes. That's all sweetheart. You made my day. Goodnight."

Monica hung up the phone grinning broadly before jumping off the bed and shouting for all the world to hear.

"Yes, Lord. Yes." She was excited. Where would she find the time to arrange a wedding with managing and promoting his career alongside with trying to graduate this spring? Just the thought of it was fatiguing.

And where most parents worried about the impending dangers of those mean Bronx streets on a daily basis. Mr. Medina never had that to worry about that. At least not where his youngest daughter Mia was concerned. What he did have to worry about was the same thing he had to worry about in himself. She'd inherited it and it was something he was still grappling with at fifty-nine. You see at fifty-nine he was driven

almost to the degree of compulsiveness. Over the years

he'd made it work for him and he was quite proud of

the fact that he'd never done an illegal thing but worked

hard to take care of his nine children. The fact that he

was a world renown trainer mattered little to him.

What made him most proud were his children. But it

was this same obsessive-compulsive behavior that had

driven Mia to exhaustion and near death once before.

Monica's annual doctor's visit was

tomorrow and though she hated to go to the doctor's

med seeking she knew she had to get him to prescribe

something to slow all of this down right through here.

She could almost feel an anxiety attack getting into

position to start countdown.

"And where is daddy? I told him my

doctor's appointment is at nine. It's eight fifty-five

now and it's a fifteen-minute drive."

"Calmese! Calmes!" her mother yelled.

"Yes. Mama's right. Calm down. It's Saturday morning. Does everyone have to get up because you do baby sister?"

The door opened and entered the fifty-nine-year-old Mr. Medina fresh from his morning walk.

"Morning to you Mrs. Medina and to all my children. Where's my baby daughter? Are you ready to go?"

An hour later, coming out of the tall, stone-faced building it was obvious the visit had not been a good one. His arm draped around his youngest daughter's shoulders one couldn't be sure who was holding who up. It wasn't easy trying to overlook the anguish now etched on his daughter's tear-stained face.

"And this too shall pass my

daughter. C'mon Mia, we've been here before. With the
Lord's help along with your will and determination this
is only a minor bump in the road. You're in total control
of this disease."

"I hear you daddy. And you're right.
You're absolutely right. I guess I'm crying because
there's always something. Everything I think that things
are finally working out and taking a turn for the better
something like this pops up."

"I believe they call that life."

Monica forced a smile at her father's
attempt to lighten the subject.

"Can you drop me off at school
daddy?"

The two rode downtown in virtual silence. When they arrived, Monica turned to her father and hugged him.

"Thanks daddy."

"No problem sweetheart but let me ask you this. Are you going to tell Naz?"

"I will but I want to wait until he settles in a little better. He's got an awful lot on his plate right through here. I don't want to just pile on."

"He's a big boy. I think he can handle it. I think it best you be up front and honest about what's going on. Just my opinion. Love you Mia."

"Love you too daddy and thanks for the support."

"No worries and relax Mia.

Relax."

"I will daddy," Mia said as she blended into the sea of college students.

Months followed blending one spectacular win into another until the winning and success inside and outside of the ring became a blur. Naz had six wins under his belt and had yet to be challenged. But instead of Monica's life growing easier and less stressful as the doctors had recommended she'd suddenly found herself elevated to celebrity status in the wake of Nazar's success. Suddenly she was a star in her own right most notably for being the 'brains behind the boxer'. At first she embellished the new found attention, the reporters and the stories of her humble beginnings under the tutelage of the legendary Tito Martinez molder of the great Hector Camacho. But when they had to increase security at the gym ad she had to sneak in through the back entrance of her building to avoid reporters it all became a bit too much. She alrcady had constraints on much of what she was trying to do and after a while she found them to be mere leeches, stretching and distorting much of what she had to say in order to serve some ulterior motive or just to sell a few more tabloids. She'd had more than enough on her plate as it was.

Together they'd planned on a small wedding but Monica recognized that the more publicity would only help foster Naz's career so despite her many trepidations she invited the press.

Nazar, on the other hand, was beginning to blossom with the added exposure never failing to sign an autograph or agreeing to a reporter's request for an interview.

"Did you read what Lupica wrote about you in the Post?" Monica shouted before throwing the paper down in disgust.

"Yeah. I glanced it."

"He's saying that you're not as good as they're saying and that most of your fights have been against boxer's way past their prime and journeymen." "Well, he didn't lie, did he?" Nazar

smiled.

"He didn't lie? Why Benitez was a world champion in three weight classes. His ring savvy and experience took you the distance."

"That's true and he's in his forties. Think I would have been able to stay with him when he was in his prime? C'mon Monica. Lupica's one of the fairest writers there is and if that's the way he saw it then that's probably the way it is. Why are you so worried about one article anyway? Wasn't it you who told me that any publicity is good publicity?"

"So, none of this bothers you?"

"Not in the least. In fact, I was thinking about throwing out some storied rumors about our love life just to get things sort of simmering and get some more publicity."

"What love life? You sure wouldn't get anyone to buy that story," Monica laughed. "But anyway, back to Lupica. He's been following boxing for as long as I can remember and if anyone knows he sure know that you're a legitimate boxer. So, why is he writing this garbage? I only wish I'd never invited him to the wedding now.

Nazar laughed.

"I don't know why you let the little things get to you. But anyway, let me get out of here. I'm supposed to meet Trip at eleven."

"Okay, sweetheart. You be safe. I have a doctor's appointment at one thirty. I'll see you at the gym around three."

"That sounds like a plan. Didn't you just go to the doctor's a couple of weeks ago?"

"Yeah. It's nothing to worry about. It's just a follow up."

"If you say so. Wet dreams my love," he said kissing her on the forehead before grabbing his Kangol cap and heading for the door.

Thirty minutes later he was back uptown in the Harlem neighborhood he called home. Walking past his building he turned into the alley. Figures stood in small circles. An outsider making an errant turn or looking for directions could easily be beaten or robbed for no apparent reason other than they were lost. It was a whole different vibe

though when Naz stepped into the alley.

"Yo Naz! What's up baby?"

Came the greetings as Naz made his way through the

alley to the back where Trip stood surrounded by his

top lieutenants.

"What up Blackman?" Trip

said grabbing Naz and squeezing him tightly. "You

okay my brother?"

"Never felt better."

"Heard you two are thinking about

tying the knot."

"Looks that way."

"Well, all due respect my

brother. From the little I know of Monica I don't think

you could have made a better choice. She has two

qualities rarely found in people these days. She loves

you and she's loyal," Trip said grinning and handing

Naz a large envelope.

"What's this?"

"I took a little side bet on

your last fight. This is your cut. I gave Monica's to her

father to give to her."

"Appreciate that."

"No, bruh. I appreciate you.

You certainly know how to put some money in a niggas

pocket. I just wish you had a fight every day. I'd be

swimming in cash if that were the case."

"*Damn.* And I really thought

you cared about a brother."

"I do. Believe me I do

especially when he's feeding me. But on the real Naz,

I just started talking to the Garcia camp and they seem

interested in getting you two together."

"You're talkin'

welterweight champ Danny 'The Destroyer' Garcia?"

"The very same."

"Damn Trip. I don't

know. Do you think I'm ready for that? Did you talk to

Monica about this?"

"Absolutely. She was

the one who told me to go for it. She even went so far as

to guarantee that you'd be in the best shape of your life

for the fight. Funny thing is I believe her."

"Is that right?"

"Yes. Told me

she'd have you ready in six months although a year would be better. Me. Myself. I think you're ready now, but she seems to think you need at least two more warm up fights and who am I to disagree with her wen she's brought you this far."

"True dat. Glad I stopped by to find out what's on my agenda."

"Ah, stop it Naz. Monica and I are looking out for your best interests."

"I understand that Trip. And I'm grateful. It's just that she and I just had this discussion.

I ain't mad atcha. I just want to be included in the future especially since it concerns me."

"I feel you and I'll keep that in mind but don't go hard on her. She was just trying to do the right thing."

Nazar broke his usual ritual and refused to call her that night. A championship fight in less than six months and she hadn't even mentioned it.

The following day Nazar hit the gym after classes with a chip on his shoulder and few words for anyone. He took his anger and frustration out in the ring. Mr. Medina was in his corner sounding just like his daughter.

"Jab Nazar. Everything begins and ends with the jab."

Nazar had come to love the older man, almost as much as loved Monica but today he wasn't feeling them or anyone else for that matter. He was finished working the speed and heavy bags. Mr. Medina had been working with him for the last couple of months trying to increase his power. And since he didn't feel like sparring and couldn't be reckoned with Mr. Medina let the young man have his way.

"Tone baby. I ain't seen you in a minute. What's up baby? I ain't seen you since we graduated."

"I know. It's been hectic."

"Tell me. Did you ever get up wi' ol' girl you was always chasing in high school?"

"Married her a week after graduation. Damn! It has been a minute. Hell, Naz. I have six daughters. I've got two sets of twins a two-year-old and a three-month-old."

"*Damn!* You've been busy.

Tone laughed.

"Guess you could say that but I don't have any regrets. I'm crazy about my girls. They give me a reason for living. Remember how crazy I used to be?"

"I remember Miss DeWitt turned to write on the blackboard and you jumped out her second story window. Boy, if you could have seen her face. That shit was epic."

"Yeah, well my wife and girls put and end to all the dumb shit. Now all I do is go to work and go home. Not much of a life but I love it."

"So, what are you doing here, Tone?"

"With six girls and a wife one job ain't getting it so I pick up a little change here and there sparring around the different gyms."

"Now that I think of it you were a pretty good boxer in high school. Did you keep up with it?"

"Nah, I guess once we moved downtown and out of your pop's jurisdiction I kinda got away from it. By the way I'm sorry to hear about pop's passing. He was a good man. He stayed in my ass. I think your cornerman's calling you."

"Tell me something Tone. What do they pay you guys for sparring?"

"Most of the gyms pay between twenty and thirty dollars a round unless you run into a contender with an upcoming fight who needs the work such as yourself then I gets upwards of forty dollars a round."

Mr. Medina interrupted the reunion brusquely.

"That girl ain't coming in raisin' hell at me 'cause you ain't training. Now get into your respective corners and remember no punches to the head."

The bell rang, and the two men met in the center of the ring each jabbing tentatively feeling each other out. Before the round ended Monica was in her fighter's corner.

"How's he doing daddy?" she said kissing her father on his balding pate.

"He looks good," Mr. Medina said before striking the bell. Again, the two men met in the center of the ring but this time it was different. Seeing Monica Nazar's whole demeanor changed.

"Hey baby," she shouted waving at him. Choosing not to answer he dug a hard left to Tony's midsection that made the father of six wince. Shooting two more lefts to the very same place made Tony take a knee.

After a minute or two Tony was up. Touching gloves, the two proceeded but it was soon evident that even though Tony had Naz by a good ten pounds he was clearly overmatched. After a thunderous body attack followed by a left hook to the temple. Tony was out before he hit the canvas.

"What the hell are you doing Naz? What the hell was that? That was a sucker move. You know there's no going to the head in sparring," Monica yelled.

"My bad. I thought it was 'protect yourself at all times,' Naz mumbled loud enough for her to hear before shooting her an evil look and heading for the showers. It bothered him that he'd just had this conversation with her and, yet he was still the third party to know what was going on when it concerned his life. It was true that he'd agreed to both she and Trip to manage his affairs, but he shouldn't have to hear about his life second hand. She'd told him she'd understood. Yet here it was again raising its ugly head. Perhaps he was making too much of it but how hard could it be to include him in the decision when it was his life on the line? Was that really too much to ask from his trainer, his manager, his woman?

"Where are you going Nazar? You still have an hour left."

The slam of the locker room door was her only response.

"What the hell is wrong with him? This isn't like him," Monica said turning to her father who was still helping Tony regain his faculties.

"I don't know. The two were talking like old friends. I had to break them up. I don't know. I thought they were friends but come to think of it Nazar's been unusually quiet since he's been here like something's on his mind. But everything was cool 'til you walked in."

"Oh, Lord. What have I done now?" Monica said reaching for her phone.

Dialing Nazar she was surprised when the call went straight to voice mail.

"Nazar. I think we need to talk. Stop by. I should be home by seven."

Monica was feeling more and more fatigued each day. And now this. Dr. Ali warned her about trying to keep up with her current schedule and advised her to slow it down and contemplate dropping something until she'd at least regained her strength and was feeling better. But Monica couldn't conceive a viable plan for dropping anything at present. She'd considered letting Cicely and mama plan her wedding but when she considered Cicely's penchant for the color purple and mama's Puerto Rican obsession she rejected the Puerto Rican Prince fetish that would surely cloudy her wedding for all of New York City's elite.

She surely couldn't just stop working with Nazar. They were so close now. Just a couple of fights away. And in just a couple of months she would be finished with school for now and at least have a degree in accounting which she sorely needed now that she was actively managing Nazar. She tried explaining this to Dr. Ali who'd been her doctor and therapist since she was a child and he'd responded.

"If you keep going the way young lady you may not have the chance to do any of them. Monica sweetheart I really can't help you help if you're not willing to help yourself." The implications were clear enough. Still, she knew no other way and what was it that daddy used to say? It's mind over matter. If you don't mind, then it don't matter and that's what she used as her daily mantra, but it wasn't working today and all of a sudden, she felt a real fondness for her bed. Your illness has remained dormant or in remission for most of your life. But if anything will inflame or incite the disease it's stress. And your stress is frankly and in direct correlation to your lifestyle. You simply have too much on your plate for one person. Frankly, you have too much on your plate on your plate for two people," Dr. Ali smiled as he tried to bring some levity to the whole situation. Monica was like a daughter to him, but she was strong-willed, always had been and all he could do was advise and let her know in no uncertain terms what the risks were. Listen. I don't have sickle cell anemia but if I tried to simulate your schedule I too would be suffering from exhaustion and fatigue.

Seriously speaking, my child, if you don't slow it down I'm going to be visiting you up at Saint Luke's if it doesn't mean the end of you. I know you think you're young and invincible, but you can't outrun this thing. The faster you run the more it takes over. What I'm telling you Monica is that you can't out run this disease."

It didn't take Monica long to shower and find her bed. Not long after she put her head on her pillow was she sound asleep and probably would have slept straight through the night if it hadn't been the steady staccato she heard. Rubbing the sleep from her eyes she wondered who it could possibly be. And then she remembered telling Nazar to stop by. She really wasn't ready for any drama and wondered if she couldn't just offer him the couch and save the conversation for the morning. As soon as she saw his face she knew that wouldn't be possible.

"You okay, Naz?"

224

"I would be if I didn't bump into people in the street telling me that I have an upcoming fight with Danny Garcia in a couple of months and once again I'm the last to know about it. I believe I asked you to keep me involved in all things involving me."

"Listen. I am so tired of your bullshit. You asked me to both train and manage your career. You also asked Trip to manage you. We are doing no more than you asked us to do. Discussing upcoming bouts and fighters is what we do? You gave us that responsibility. Now you don't want us to discuss it without your presence. No. What we do is discuss it and when we've come up with a decent proposal then we run it past you, so you can sign off on it. That's what we manager's do. So, stop crying and get off your high horse. This is how the game is played baby. You're in the big leagues now."

Naz was left speechless and long after the little lady had said her piece Naz remained standing there wondering what had just happened. Monica was sleep by the time he found his favorite comforter and lay down on the couch.

When he awoke it was too the smell of homemade biscuits, bacon, baked apples with cinnamon and hot coffee.

"Good morning sweetie. You hungry?"

"Starved," he said grabbing Monica and kissing her on her forehead.

"Grab a plate and help yourself," she said grabbing a cup of coffee for herself and having a seat at the table.

"Let me ask you something Naz. Are you afraid of Mendoza?"

226

"What? Are you serious? Why would you ask me something like that? You know I beat him three times as an amateur."

"Because when we talk of contenders and prospects you never mention Mendoza."

"Because he's a scrub. He's street. If I had paid attention to that punk all of the Bronx and Manhattan would have been at war with Brooklyn. That's the way he rolls. He thinks he's some Mafia godfather, a balla. He won a couple of fights and it went to his head. He started believing his own hype. I don't like him. Never had. That's why I don't enter him in conversations with respected and respectable boxers."

"Well, that's good to hear. May just give you the incentive to close his mouth once and for all. I just hadn't heard you mention him and the fights only a couple of days away. I was just hoping you weren't overlooking him."

Nazar's face grew into a large grin.

"I don't know if you realize it or not, but you do this before every fight. What is it? Your own emotional status. Do you get butterflies? Suffering from nervous anxiety? That's it isn't it? You're scared to death. So, when you think you've done all you can possibly do you you try to get inside my head and find out what I'm thinking," Naz laughed. "How's that working for you?"

"Just trying to cover all the bases. You're so closemouthed about things I deem important."

"Such as?"

"Your opponents. Your upcoming fights."

"I look at them all the same. I never try to figure an opponent which doesn't mean I don't study their weaknesses and tendencies, but I spend less time on them than I do myself. You see if I'm the best I can be then that's all I can do. And if I'm at the best I can be then chances are I'll win the fight. If I've done everything I can do in preparing for a fight and lose then there was nothing I can do. I was at my best. So, far though no one's been able to beat my best."

"All that's well and good but that was then, and this is now. Since you've fought him he's gone to Kronk Gym and trained with the late-great Emmanuel Stewart. I'm telling you he's a different fighter than the fighter you fought three times in the amateurs. I watched both his amateur fights and his pro fights and I'm telling you he's a different fighter. The boy's good. The oddsmakers have him a two-to-one favorite so instead of coming in here chastising me what you need to be focusing on is Mendoza. If you don't there will be no championship."

Monica said brushing by him and giving him a chance to process. Reflecting on what she'd said he had to admit she was right. And where he'd always assembled his own pre-game fight data it had never been worth much or gone too far in depth with all that. What if Mendoza was a different fighter. After all, it had been years since he'd fought him. His thoughts were suddenly shattered by the sound of glass shattering.

Naz jumped up from the dining room table and raced to the kitchen. Arriving in the kitchen seconds later, he found Monica lying face down. How many bodies had he seen in this position? Many of whom had come to arrive in this position because of a right cross or a left hook from him. They had not mattered to him, but this was different. This was his girl and there was no reason for this sudden collapse. Unconscious he did not panic.

Instead Naz turned her head, took her pulse and monitored her breathing before checking her airways making sure that they were not blocked. He then picked up the tiny cell and called an ambulance before calling Mr. Medina. Agreeing to meet at Saint Lukes, Naz did not attempt to move her but only placed a pillow under her head to make sure she was comfortable before packing her an overnight bag just in case she was admitted to the hospital. And although her breathing was shallow and uneven Naz hoped it was no more than a fainting spell at worst. An hour later sitting in the lobby of Harlem Hospital he was joined by

Mr. Medina.

"How's she doing? What happened?"

Naz repeated the morning happenings and Mr. Medina took it all in and was surprisingly not overcome by his daughter's situation confusing Nazar who knew how much the man now sitting to his right loved his daughter. Funny thing was the more they talked the more Nazar got the feeling that Mr. Medina had been through all of this before but then with eight or nine kids it was quite possible that Mr. Medina had been through all of this before. Even so it was all a little eerie that Mr. Medina was a s calm and relaxed as he was.

Nazar recounted all he could recall and again Mr. Medina seemed fine with his recollection. And then he did his best to bring Naz up-to-date on Monica's health issues without saying too much.

"Naz, in the time I've come to know you. I've come to love you like a son. But I don't get involved in my children's personal affairs so I'm going to leave it up to Mia to tell you what's going on with her physically. I hope you understand."

A few minutes later a nurse came to them.

"Are you the party here for Ms. Medina?"

"Yes ma'am," Nazar said.

"At the present time the doctor is only permitting immediate family. Are you immediate family?"

"Yes ma'am. I'm his father and this is her older brother. What room is she in?" Mr. Medina lied.

"Room 302. Would you like me to show you the way?"

"No. We're good. Thank you for all your help," Mr. Medina said smiling at the pretty young nurse.

The two headed for the elevator. Mr. Medina stopped Nazar before entering the room.

"I don't know if Monica's told you or not, but she's been going to the doctors for the past month or so but in my opinion it's basically a waste of time because she ignores everything they tell her. I'm sure by now you recognize how stubborn and muleheaded she is. Talk to her Nazar. You've got to get her to slow down."

Naza shook his head. He wasn't sure he could do anything. He had to see where her head was at first.

"Tell me something sir. What are the doctor's telling her?"

"You know how driven she is. And now with the wedding and all she simply has too much on her plate. We've all told her that she needs to let something go. She refuses to let her mother and sisters help. And the doctors have told her on more than one occasion to slow down. They even warned of something like this happening. On her last visit with Dr. Ali he said she was suffering from extreme exhaustion and fatigue. Between you and me she's just doing too much but the doctor and I are unable to make her see that."

"Why didn't you tell me sir?"

"She didn't want anything to interfere with your upcoming fight and like I said I don't like to interfere in my children's lives once they are adults. And she promised me she would take care of it. But come on Naz you had to wonder how she could go to school full-time, come and train you and then go home and plan a wedding 'til the wee hours of the morning."

"Honestly, I never gave it a thought but with your help we're going to fix all that right now."

"Just tell me what I can do to help son. I'm at my wits end."

"Well if you can train me for the next two months I'd certainly appreciate it."

"Mia's not going to be too happy with this latest development."

"She has no choice. She's banned from the gym until I get clearance from her doctors that she's fit enough to return to the gym."

"Sounds good to me. Let's see how she takes it."

The older man seemed to have aged in front of Naz. Still, there was something Mr. Medina seemed to be holding back.

"No worries Mr. Medina. I'll handle it."

A big, burly, Black nurse with an infectious smile approached the two men.

"Mr. Muhammad, I assume?"

"Yes ma'am."

"A Ms. Medina told me to look for the best-looking man in the waiting room. Glad I didn't have to walk that far. Anyway, she's requesting your presence."

"Thank you, ma'am." Nazar said as the nurse looked him up and down for the third time.

Nazar walked into the room and was visibly shaken. Monica who was always appeared so strong and vibrant now seemed helpless. Intravenous tubes ran from both arms and Naz felt his eyes welling up with tears.

"Come here sweetheart," Monica said grinning. "My two favorite men. A girl can't ask for much more than that. Come here daddy."

Mr. Medina smiled kissing his youngest on the forehead.

"How's my baby feeling?"

"I'm fine. I just wish the doctors would release me. I'm supposed to meet the caterers at twelve."

"See that's the problem Mia.

You need to rest. Dr. Ali said you're running yourself to death. You're suffering from dehydration and exhaustion. You have got to slow it down. But listen Naz has something he'd like to tell you so I'm going to run down to the cafeteria. You two want anything?"

Both of them shook their heads no.

"I don't believe you'll be meeting with anyone today sweetie. I don't know if the doctor's told you or not but you're suffering from severe exhaustion and dehydration. And that's nothing to play with. You're to remain here under bedrest for the next two weeks."

"And how am I supposed to do that. You know we have the Mendoza fight Saturday after next."

Hearing this Naz quickly regained his composure. Moving to her side Naz bent all of his six three frame down and kissed her forehead before taking her hands in his.

"Uh oh. You look serious. What is it?"

"You're not doing the fight Monica. I've asked your father to be in my corner for this one."

"But we've worked so hard to get here."

"There are no buts. You're my manager but I'm managing this one. And you're off this fight. The doctor's say you've run yourself ragged. I can't believe you're dehydrated but anyway until I get further notice on your condition you are no longer my manager. Besides I think I like your father better anyway. He doesn't yell quite as much," he said

240

causing both she and Mr. Medina who was back now and munching on an apple turnover to smile.

"Seriously though, when the doctors say that you're fit and ready to return you can resume where you left off."

Monica in desperation turned to her father.

"But daddy," was all she could muster hoping. Almost pleading that he would come to her aid.

"Sounds like a good plan to me son," Mr. Mendoza said purposely ignoring his daughter's plea.

"Listen sweetheart. I

haven't been home since this morning. I'm going to run home and take a quick shower. I'll be back. Would you like me to pick you up anything?"

"A job. I think I've just been fired."

Both men laughed before kissing her and making their way to the door.

Nazar now spent the majority of his days between the gym and the hospital. Monica was chomping at the bit to be released but both Naz and the doctor both agreed that the best way to limit her movement was to keep her in the hospital under strict bedrest. Monica had other plans refusing to be shut completely down and after three days she had Nazar bring her laptop which she promptly hooked up the hospital TV.

"These are Mendoza's last three fights.

Tell me what you see."

It was obvious to everyone that the rest had done her good, but everyone agreed that another three or four days wouldn't hurt. Monica was having none of that. demanding that the nurse take the intravenous out and allow her to sign out. All they were doing was padding the bill and she didn't have it to give them for continually pricking and poking her night and day and feeding her bad food. No. It was time for her to go. The form read "Against Medical Advice' and with her signature Monica was once again a free woman.

Nazar and Mr. Medina spoke with the doctors. All agreed that she was fit enough to leave, and the extra time was just for precautionary methods. As far as Monica was concerned it didn't matter what they discussed. It was time to go.

Nazar tried to feign anger at her decision but had a difficult time being angry at the fiery, little, five two bomb shell as she threw her heels and jeans on. She was moving at the speed-of-light now. To even think that the three men standing there could slow her down once she'd made the decision to leave was a little naïve on their part. Now as he waved down a cab the sudden realization that he alone would be responsible for her health tore at him.

"Baby, I'm going to move in tomorrow," Nazar said staring out the cab window at the deserted, lower-Manhattan streets.

"Are you asking or telling me." She said grinning coyly.

"I'm telling you," he was surprised to hear himself say and was even more surprised when there was no response.

"You know you're sleeping in the guest room."

"Whatever," Nazar replied in disgust. Nazar had long ago accepted the fact that she held her virginity intact and was proud of her mental and physical fortitude, but it was on days like this when she insisted on parading around in a body-suit, skin tight jeans and heels that were the hardest for him to take.

She was smiling broadly now.

"I want you to know that I'm aware of what you and daddy are trying to do. You're basically trying to put me under house arrest. And now you want to move in and act as warden. You two are funny but I do appreciate your concern and love you both," she said grabbing Nazar's hand and placing her head on his shoulder.

Nazar was glowing on the inside. It was good to have her back. This tiny little woman completed him, making him feel whole once again.

"But what you don't realize is that I refuse to just sit around so now that I have my best friend around on a full-time basis we can watch unlimited tape of Mendoza 24/7," she laughed knowing how much Naz hated watching tape.

"You just don't know how to relax do you? I may just have to put you in restraints," he said grabbing her in a bear hug. Giggling, Monica did not try to break his hold but lay in his arms contentedly.

"You know I graduate next week. Without school and being able to train you what's left? And I'm not one of those people we talk about so often who sit around waiting for good fortune to come their way. Well I'm not one of those people. You have to get out there and make good fortune happen to you. You feel me?"

"Yes, sweetie I've come to pretty much understand that about you. But after this fight I'm taking you on vacation. I was thinking someplace warm. How's Jamaica sound?"

"Sounds wonderful but why don't we wait until after the championship fight and coupled with our wedding we can call it our honeymoon?" Monica raised up and kissed her man lightly on the lips.

"Even better," Naz agreed.

"Listen. I've got to go and finish studying for my last exam. Did you hear that? My last exam. I can't believe it. Four long years are finally over. Thank God," kissing him deeply Monica left him sitting there on fire.

"Baby," pleaded Nazar but it was all to no

avail.

"Not tonight but soon baby," she said

smiling before turning and heading down the long,

narrow, hallway to her bedroom

The days passed quickly and before he knew it it was fight night. At seven-thirty that evening Monica headed uptown on the subway to the Garden. On this particular night Mendoza was supposedly at his best but Nazar was better. At exactly forty-one seconds of the first round Nazar 'One-Time' Muhammad dropped Hector Mendoza with a chopping right hand. The crowd which was overwhelmingly in his favor went crazy almost as if he'd hit the go-ahead home run in the seventh game of the World Series. It was pandemonium in the Garden. Mr. Medina was on him first.

"We did it son just the way we planned it. And you shut that loud mouth up. You are on your way."

Trip was just as excited although Trip's victory centered on other things.

"We made a bundle here tonight, baby. Do you hear me? A bundle but we'll talk later," he said smiling before kissing Naz on both cheeks and trying to escape the bedlam that was now the ring.

Seeing Monica surrounded by the growing swell of reporters he motioned for her to join him in the ring as he awaited the official decision. Hugging her tightly he looked her in the eyes.

"How'd we do baby?" Nazar said grabbing and hugging Monica tightly.

"You're still dropping your right. You get in there with a seasoned fighter, one of those wily old vets and he's gonna pick up on that right away and that's going to be your downfall. You've gotta learn to keep your hands up man."

Nazar grinned broadly and hugged ever her even more tightly. Win or lose she kept the same demeanor and far as as she was concerned there was always room for improvement. If there was one thing he understood about her it was that she was a perfectionist and that his best would never be quite good enough and, so he accepted this and kept plodding away at his craft.

Nazar couldn't help but love this woman. While the Garden cheered wildly over the devastating knockout Monica was looking to shore up any weaknesses which could lead to his eventual defeat.

Fact was, she was already planning for the next fight.

"Gotta give you credit though your jab was crisp and sharp. It was a sight to behold. And you weren't pawing with it. It had snap and pop on it. It set up the right hand perfectly," she said matter-of-factly.

Naz grinned.

"I know. I was there, remember?"

"Oh hush, smarty. C'mon let's get outta here."

"What did you have in mind?" He muttered sheepishly while Mr. Medina cut the gloves off his hands.

"Don't worry about it. Just shower and get dressed with the quickness. I've got a surprise for you."

Nazar's eyebrows rose in mock anticipation.

"Don't let your mind play tricks on you. You're not getting any of this 'til it's time and now is not the time."

Nazar dropped his head in mock disappointment.

"I'll be right there bay. But you know I've go to do this press conference first. Shouldn't take more than ten or fifteen minutes.

By now, if there was one thing Nazar loved even more than his heroics in the ring and that was helping to redefine the image of the boxer in the new millennium. He loved the fact that his voice, his ideas, his approach were all helping to usher in this new era in boxing. No longer was the boxer looked at as just a driven young man trying to escape his

surroundings. He was no longer just trying to escape
the urban ghettoes, or the squalid living conditions of

Mexico with its dirt floors and implore able living

conditions. No longer was he trying to escape a war-

torn Sarajevo and trying to rescue his family from the

refugee camps. No the new boxer arose from Detroit

and was a banker. He was from Argentina and held

down a full-time job as an elementary school teacher.

This new aged boxer like Nazar was going to school, to

college, to become a lawyer. Boxing had never been a

means to an end but had always remained simply a

means to put some order to a lifestyle that somehow

demanded it. But it had never been an escape. It was

just a way of instilling some discipline in his life.

That's what boxing had meant to him. These were the

new boxers. No longer was it just another dumb pug

trying his best to answer questions from the press in a

complete and coherent sentence. No, Naz was intent,

determined to reinvent the stereotype. Humble and soft-spoken his usual shy and reserved demeanor was suddenly transformed when the bright lights were turned on him.

"Nazar. Nazar," they shouted.

"Second row red tie," Nazar pointed.

"Nazar. With all the hype and fanfare about how great Hector was did you ever think it would have been this easy?"

"I never take any boxer for granted despite what the press says. My trainer prepares me for every fight the same. We never take anyone for granted."

"Next question?"

"Tell me 'One-Time' who do you want to fight next? Do you have a particular fighter that you want as a tune up fight or are you ready for a championship fight now?"

"That's a good question but I don't really concern myself with those things. I have a great management team that handles all that. My job is simply to be ready to go when they say it's time."

"So, what you're saying is it doesn't matter who you fight next?"

"What are you trying to do Teddy? Are you trying to pick a fight? I don't want to fight you Teddy. You look like you've been working out since I last saw you," Nazar said to a room full of laughter.

"Seriously speaking though, it doesn't matter much who I fight next. This is what I signed up for and to be honest and without trying to sound overly confident it really doesn't matter since I do believe

myself to be the best pound-for-pound fighter in my
division."

"So, what you're saying is that you're
ready for Danny Garcia and a chance at the belt?"
"What kind of question is that? I just

beat the number one contender where else is there for me
to go? Of course, I'd like a shot the belt. Don't you
think after my performance tonight I deserve one?"

As if on cue Mr. Medina jumped in and
grabbed the microphone.

"On behalf of Team Nazar we'd like to
thank you ladies and gentlemen."

Showering quickly Naz found Monica in
the lobby engaged in what appeared to be a pretty intense
conversation with one of the members of Mendoza's
camp.

"No problem Caesar. Let me run it by Nazar and I'll get back to you. I've got your card."

"All right. Get back and let me know either way," he said making his leave.

"What was that all about?"

"Wants to open a gym. Says he's got a few good prospects that are just languishing where they are. Told me to talk to you to see if you might be interested in helping to train a few of his prospects. We'd also have a percentage of the gym. Told me to talk to you to see if you'd consider having a sit down to talk more."

"He had you there why didn't he ask you if you were interested?"

"I've known Caesar a long time. He's cool people but he's ol' school in that he's real traditional and it's only respectful for him to talk to the man in the relationship. You feel me? In his eyes you're the power. I'm just a minority partner. That's just the way some men see women or don't see them." Nazar laughed as Monica threw three quick jabs his way.

"*Whoa! Slow down girl!* You know I'm sore," he laughed.

"Cause you keep dropping your right hand trying to be pretty," Monica joked.

"Ah, c'mon girl you know I'm pretty when I dance. Ain't nobody prettier in the ring than me. I see you watching me girl," Nazar said dancing now.

"And to think those idiot reporters think you're sweet and humble. If they only knew,"

Monica said laughing and still flicking jabs at the dancing Naz.

Inside the apartment Nazar wrapped his arms around Monica kissing her deeply, passionately before abruptly pushing her away.

"What the hell was that?" Monica said looking at him for some kind of explanation. "Damn you! You're killing me baby," his eyes filled with fever and frustration.

"What's wrong?"

"You must have ice water in your veins and the discipline of Job. Me. Well I'm only human and I've just got to have you, lay with you, sleep with you, make love to you."

"Oh, stop whining and kiss me so I can tell you all about your surprise."

"In that case, I guess I can suffer through this or better yet we can go into your room and rehearse for the honeymoon."

Monica laughed out loud.

"Guess that's one of the reasons I love you so much. You keep me laughing. If it's not your constant pursuit of my forbidden fruit or the way you jump around in a boxing ring and think you're dancing. I remember when I first saw you I was like 'Why they trying to teach this poor kid with Tourette's how to fight."

Not being able to contain herself Monica fell over on the couch in laughter. "Whew!" she said gasping for air. "That was a good one if I do say so myself," Monica said impressed by her own attempts at humor.

Naz feigned hurt but was smiling on the inside at his shorty's spirit and feistiness. She was a handful when she was happy and feelin' herself and that's where she was tonight and the place Nazar loved her most.

A quiet fell over the room as each drifted into their own thoughts. There were no uncomfortable silences when they were together, and they were content in giving each other their space. It was Monica who broke the silence.

"You fought very well tonight,"

A quiet fell over the room again. How many times had she played the tape of the fight over in her mind. She had the ability to remember every punch and every nuance of a fight and she would play it over and over breaking it down into its various components. She would look at it from a defensive point of view before flipping it and seeing what things she liked on offense and where he needed to improve. That's where she was now. Naz smiled. He could see the wheels turning.

"So, what's the surprise?"

Monica got up and walked to the door where she'd dropped the Gucci knapsack. Handing it to him Nazar looked at her.

"What's this?"

"Open it."

Opening it Nazar's eyes couldn't help but widen. A minute later Monica returned with her gym bag only it too was filled with nothing but cash.

"I took everything I had in the bank and gave it to Trip to bet on you. Only wish I had had more to bet on you but we made a little over a quarter of a mil. Now the question is how we invest it in ourselves to keep it growing. That's the question."

"Whoa! Slow your roll sweetie. You had that much faith in me that you took everything you had and bet it on me?"

"I trained you, didn't I?" she said stone-faced.

Naz had to laugh.

"You're a trip. You really are."

"I suppose but you know they had you as an underdog. I think that anyone and everyone that really knows you picked up a little money tonight. People like daddy and Trip that know you and know what you stand for and who are as a person knew that you were a lock. It was like Ali-Frazier. People didn't even consider that Ali was a superior boxer, but Joe's left hook could easily even the score and real quick.

But it wasn't about that. People bet on Ali because Ali stood for good. He was the people's champ. He opposed the war and the killing. And because he stood

for good he could not lose. It was like you tonight.

There was no talk at the weigh in from our camp. And

you know why?"

"Why's that baby?"

"Because that's not how we're built

baby. When I look at Team Nazar I like what I see.

We are simple God-fearing folk. So, when they started

with the stupid shit at the weigh-in about who was

fucking me we all knew that One-Time had to too much

discipline to even enter into a game like that. They

tried. Boy did they try but you held your head high and

refused to allow them to bring you down to their level.

It was beautiful baby. Never was I so proud of you. But

after walking out of the weigh-in all I had to do was

look at Trip. We both knew the fight was over at that

point. We knew. We felt it. It was almost like good

going against evil and that's a no-brainer, so you see it didn't require much."

"So, you didn't even take my boxing skills into account?"

"No need to in this situation. Some fights are won or lost long before a fighter enters the ring."

"That's what I was telling you long before the fight when you told me how he'd gone away and changed his whole fighting style. It doesn't matter what style he changed to. I have his number. And he will never be able to beat me in the ring."

"But that was a great move. Wish you had told me though."

"Why? That would have only placed more undo pressure on my baby. You've got to learn to have faith and be able to trust in me. We've really

266

gotta work on the trust factor. Now what we gonna do with all that money?"

"It is a whole lotta money and you're right I do need to have more faith in you and your judgement. You are absolutely right and you too for that matter," Nazar said agreeing hardheartedly.

"And how is that Mr. Muhummad?"

"Well everyone that is apart of our camp is only interested in the success of us all. Our own best interests are all that concern us isn't that true?"

"It is but what does that have to do with you and I at this particular moment?"

"Well, let's head into the bedroom

and see what Ms. Medinda can do for the general health, well-being and morale of Team Nazar." Nazar said smiling broadly.

"Boy, if you don't stop sweating me!" Monica yelled scooting Nazar a nasty look behind a lazy grin.

"Had to take a shot," he grinned.

"You already know," she smiled.

"Well, let's see what you know about this," Nazar said grabbing Monica and slowly pulling her to the center of the room before dropping to one knee.

"I need to make this official," he said rendering Monica speechless. "Monica will you be my wife?"

"I believe I already answered that question

Mr. Muhammad.

"Then take this ring as a symbol of my love
and affection," he said opening the box.

"Oh, my God! It's huge! Oh, my God!"

"I wanted everyone to be able to see just
how much I loved you. Do you like?"

"Do I like it? I love it," she said holding
her hand out in admiration. "Oh, Nazar you are the
best," she said reaching for a kiss.

"Does that mean we can?" he said
smiling and nodding to the bedroom.

"You don't quit, do you?"

"I was always brought up to believe that
persistence overcome resistance," Nazar smiled before
falling on top of her and tickling her.

"How's that working for you so far?" she shrieked pushing him away.

"Bump you Monica," Nazar said a bit frustrated by this time.

"Patience is a virtue, sweetie," she said smiling.

"You know we have a pretty nice lil' nest egg right through here. We could and probably should shoot down to Jamaica right through here. I have a feeling things are really going to get hectic from here on out."

"They've already gotten a little more hectic than I would like to see," Nazar mumbled.

"What's wrong baby?"

"Nothing really. It's just that the

closer we get to this thing the more people seem to be

coming out of the woodwork with all kinds of schemes and

offers. I'm seeing people pop up that I haven't seen since

second grade. At least that's what they tell me. It's like

I'm attending my second-grade reunion every day now.

And they all remember when we were best friends.

If I had my choice, I'd build a little

villa on my own little beachfront property. Nothing

extravagant. No more than two hundred grand on the

place and maybe the same for the Beachfront property

and I'd spend my winters down there and any time I

wasn't in training."

"You're serious?"

"I wish you would make that happen

for me."

"I'll start on that tomorrow and thank you for another incredible day Naz," she said kissing him long and passionately.

"No. thank you baby. I didn't know where I was going to get the money to pay for that ring." They both laughed.

"Tell you what. You can come and sleep in the bed with me tonight and that's it. Sleep. Do you understand Mr. Muhammad? No humping or slow grinding, no rolling the hips. No nothing but sleep. Is that understood?"

"Can I hold you in my arms?"

"Yes sweetie, I think I'd like that. So, you seriously want me to look into finding you affordable housing in the islands?"

"Not in the islands. I want

something, comfortable and affordable on the beach in Jamaica close to Montego Bay."

"Were you even going to discuss this move with me Naz? I thought we were supposed to discuss any major moves or decisions with each other just as a matter of courtesy."

"I agree but this is something that I consider paramount for my mental stability. You know I love this city. I haven't gotten to travel much so I don't want to make statements like New York is the greatest city in the world when I haven't really had anything to compare it with but sometimes New York makes me want to scream and pull my hair out. There's no place to breathe, to let your hair down. I just need some time and space or I'm going to lose it."

"So, you figure you'll just run away and hide from the world."

"That's all a matter of perspective. I went there twice as a child and loved it. My daddy thought it important that I knew where I came from so he took me when he went to see my grandparents and I fell in love with the island and the people. Everyone seemed so relaxed and laid back. It wasn't like here. There was no rat race. And I like that. You know after racing from school to the gym and then wondering if I'm going to be mugged or hit in the head when I do go home at night isn't exactly what I call conducive to living the city life. Seriously though. I just want to take a year off and lie on the beach before returning to school and taking the bar and before I start defending my championship. That's what Id like to do. I want to be far from the maddening crowd. Do you feel me?"

"I guess I understand. Things can get mighty congested here at times. I just hope your little man cave has a place for me?"

"I'm not sure I could leave you out at this stage of my life. I'm not sure I could function without you right through here."

"Well, that's certainly good to know 'cause I didn't hear the name Monica once in this whole proposal."

Naz was forced to grin.

"You should know that when I say I nowadays it just natural refers to us."

"I didn't know."

"Well, now you know. Listen I'm going to ride uptown. I need to see Trip and wanna check on mama. You want to ride with me? Or should we wait 'til tomorrow and just head for the bed tonight?" Nazar said smiling and grabbing her hand in an attempt to pull her to the bedroom.

"I'm good. Just had a rough day is all."

"Okay. I just don't want you getting sick right through here. I need you more than ever but the way you've been running you're going to wind up right back in the hospital. If you ask me, you need to slow it down sweetie. You're trying to train, manage and market me all at the same time. And if that's not enough, you're graduating and trying to plan a wedding. I don't know if you know it or not but they have teams set up that are simply responsible for managing and marketing for a small cost," Nazar suggested sitting down and focusing on the love of his life before him.

"Trust me Naz. I went over all this with daddy and we came up with the conclusion that no one will ever invest the interest that you would invest in your own future."

"That may well be all well and good but if you don't take care of yourself there may not be a future."

"Oh Naz, stop being so dramatic. I'm fine. Now go handle your business." Monica replied tired of all the talk of her health. "Seriously though, I appreciate the concern. But trust me. I'll be fine. Now get out of here. It's getting late."

Monica's graduation was a resounding success. The crowd seemed to be made up of mostly of Monica's family. She was the first of her family to graduate from college and they all seemed like they had had a piece of her success. Even Dez showed up looking like the proud father. Mr. Medina didn't say much although it was obvious that no one could be prouder.

That Saturday, one week before the
upcoming fight Mr. Medina watched as Nazar worked
out on the heavy bag.

"I need you to put your whole body into it
son. Use your hips. Put your hips into it. When you
throw your punch, I need you to put your whole body
into it Naz. That's where your power emanates from.

You have to turn putting your hips and whole body into
it."

Nazar followed the older man's
instructions as best he could but somehow couldn't
seem to adhere to the man's wishes.

"Stop!" Mr. Medina yelled his
frustration beginning to show. "Here. Follow me," he
said getting into the ring and showing Naz exactly what
is he wanted. "Now you try it."

278

Naz did his best to follow the old man's lead.

"That's it. Now turn into the punch. That's it. Good son. Again," Mr. Medina was thrilled with how quickly Naz picked up new concepts that would only help in his growth as a boxer.

Monica sat watching, taking note but never muttering a word. It was no different when Naz entered the ring. This was her domain and she was liable to say anything to push Naz's buttons. If there was no one else who could she knew she could motivate her fighter. He would always, but always, respond to her demands for ring perfection if for no other reason than as not to disappoint her. Naz who yearned for perfection would always comply if for no other reason than to stay in her good graces. Today was somehow different though. He was sparring three rounds with a journeyman who had seen better days but who was giving Naz fits today. And still Monica never said a word. When it was all over a frustrated Naz approached Monica.

"You were awfully quiet today. You feelin' okay sweetie?"

"Feelin' a lil' under the weather but I'll be okay," she muttered.

"Let me grab a quick shower and then I'll grab a cab. Let me get you home and in bed where I can doctor you up. Do we have any Rock & Rye at the house?"

"Yes. I'm pretty sure there's a bottle on the bar."

A little worried Nazar did his best to keep the conversation light in an attempt to ward off his biggest fear. He only hoped he could somehow persuade her to relax and remain cool until the fight.

This he knew was going to be one tough battle but now that school was out of the way there was no reason for her to be overwhelmed. Normal folks worked two sometimes three jobs and never but never faulted under the pressure. And he'd personally taken control of her activities and recuperation since her last visit to the hospital. They'd spent hours at home doing nothing more than enjoying each other's company and discussing whatever was trending that day on CNN. About the most they'd done in terms of going out was going to a Knick's game. An avid Knick fan she was infatuated with the newest Knick sensation some seven-footer named Porzingas. But that had been it. The rest of the time they'd spent in the house with she ordering items for the loft. He, on the other hand, spent his time reading and preparing heart healthy meals for the two of them. After dinner the two would curl up on the couch, she in his arms and watch a movie. No. It had to be more to this exhaustion thing than they were telling him.

"My mom would always put a little Rock & Rye in my tea anytime she thought I was coming down with something. A hot toddy and a hot bath and I'd be fit as a fiddle."

Much to Naz's dismay all of his efforts at playing doctor failed and when Monica wasn't feeling any better by Tuesday it was decided by all to check the blustery, fireball back into the hospital for further tests. After doing some bloodwork Dr. Ali decided it was in Monica's best interests to have more tests done. By Thursday they had the results. The sickle cell had expanded to epic proportions.

"She's complaining of chest pains which is not unusual and is a clear indicator that little or no oxygen is getting to her lungs a common symptom where sickle cell occurs but what concerns me even more is that she has a bacterial infection."

"I concur with your prognosis," Dr. Ali said recounting his findings with the on-call doctor.

"Let's start her on some antibiotics to combat the infection and let's just hope we're in time. You realize that bacterial infection are the most dangerous to a patient having the sickle-cell trait?"

"I'm quite aware of that doctor. Let's just hope that's not the case in Ms. Medina's case. I don't know if you know it or not doctor but I was the one that brought Monica into this world."

"No. I wasn't aware of that Dr. Ali but

trust me we are doing the best we can in Ms. Medina's case. We will call you if there is any progress or change in her case."

"I appreciate that."

Naz was the last to know that Monica had admitted herself. He'd made a run to pick up some tapes Monica had suggested and returned home to find a note. He was visibly shaken by the news and rushed to the hospital only to find Monica in high spirits. That was Monday. By Thursday Naz was a bundle of nerves. No longer was the woman he had come to know so well almost incoherent, but she'd taken a turn for the worse and looked bad.

At Monica's request the doctors were not at liberty to divulge anything concerning her health to anyone other than her father but Naz knew it was something serious.

284

"Baby how are you doing," Naz said leaning over and kissing her on her forehead.

"I'm good. Just a little weak. Doctor's are calling it a virus and treating me with antibiotics," she said motioning to the intravenous which hung overhead. "They said within a day or two I should be swinging from the chandeliers," she said in her best attempt to smile.

"So, you should be out before the fight?"

"C'mon Naz. You don't honestly think that I'd let you go into the biggest fight of your life alone do you? Hell. We fought too long and hard to get here for me to be a no-show. Did you watch the tapes daddy gave you on this joker?"

All Naz could do was smile before kissing her again.

"You already know. Listen. I've got

285

some errands to run. Trying to get mama and Sin to move down to the islands. Gave mama a nice little piece of change so she wouldn't have to spend the rest of her days cleaning up behind some white folks and the funny thing is with all of her complaining about her legs and back hurting she turned me down. Can you believe that? Found her a nice lil' three bedroom in case you ever decide to put me out and she turned me down. Can you believe that?"

"Don't take it personal sweetie. But your newfound success doesn't necessarily translate to her success. As much as she may fuss and complain what else does she have besides work. She's afraid of giving up all that she knows. You may have suggested that she cut her hours down instead so so it won't be so strenuous. Don't you worry about that though she and

286

Sin are stopping by later. Leave that to me. I'll talk to her. Now come and give me a hug," Monica said now looking tired and fatigued again.

"Okay. Let me know how that works for you. I'm telling you the woman is stubborn. I don't know how my father put up with her for this long." Nazar said forcing a smile.

"The same way and reason you put up with me. I think they call it love," Monica grinned.

"Alright baby. Don't know if I'll get back by here tonight but if not, I'll see you in the morning. I love you," Naz said before making his exit.

He was to meet Trip at six. Looking at his was watch he saw that it was already a quarter of six and he still had a ways to go.

Grabbing a cab, he rode uptown. As the cab drove by a thousand sights Nazar saw nothing. His mind raced and, yet he felt mired in his own thoughts and frustrations. It was a time when he for the first time in his life was financially comfortable. It was a time when he could get away from his neighborhood and create his own world according to his specifications. But with all his new-found fortune he couldn't do anything to make Monica better or show his family a better way of life. And with the money there was a price to be paid. No longer could he walk the streets without reporters harassing him about this or that. In more instances than not the questions centered around things other than boxing and this intrusion into his very personal life bothered him immensely. Was this the price of fame and success?

Growing closer to his destination. Naz saw Trip heading for the black jeep.

"Yo, Trip," he yelled.

"What up Blackman? Another minute and you would have missed me for sure. You know time is money my brother and I ain't got time. You said meet you at six and here it is six-thirty. I thought you were serious Naz."

"I apologize. My bad. I had to stop by the hospital and see Monica."

"Oh no. Don't tell me she's back there again. What's wrong? Is she alright?"

"I really don't know. She and her daddy are trying to downplay the whole thing as exhaustion, but I think there holding back something more serious. But like I said I really don't know. I only know what they want me to know."

"What hospital is she at?"

289

"St. Lukes, up by Columbia."

"Let me see who I have up there. Give me a day or two and I'll see what I can find out for you."

"Appreciate that Trip."

"No worries baby. You know how we roll. How you feeling anyway? You ready to go in here and stomp a mudhole through this niggas ass'?"

"Yeah. I'm good."

"Okay," Trip said pulling the car over and parking it. "I usually try to stay clear and let Monica handle the motivation and training. I handle the finances. That's my forte but with her in the hospital and you looking like you lost your best friend I think it's time I spoke up. I am still in charge of the finances and from my vantage point I really don't like what I'm seeing. That attitude alone let's me know that

you are not focused on this fight which means you're

fucking with my finances. I love you Naz. I love you

like a brother, but I will not let you fuck with my

finances. Out here on the street I will maim or kill your

ass if you fuck with my money and we're talking

twenty or thirty dollars. Just imagine what I'd do if you

fucked up twenty or thirty large because you're on

some depressed shit. I'm not threatening you my

brother. I'm just telling you whether it's pop's passing

or Monica's being hospitalized you have to gain the

inner strength to know that life goes on and you still

have a responsibility to go out there and do your best in

spite of it all. Do you feel me Naz?"

"I feel you bruh."

"You know Monica and I bet the whole

shhbang on you your last fight just based on how you

came across. You were looking forward to fighting Hector. We all knew it. There was no question. That woman has the ultimate faith in you. I want to feel that way this fight, but I don't, but I'll tell you what would help."

"What's that Trip?"

"Place a sizeable bet on yourself."

Naz had to laugh.

"And what's a sizeable bet?"

"What would hurt you to lose?"

"A dollar."

"Damn bruh, you always were tight, but I'll tell you what I'm going to put twenty-five grand on you at five-to-one odds. That means you collect a hundred and twenty-five grand should you win. Is that enough incentive and motivation for your ass? With your winnings you can take mama and Sin and get them some decent housing someplace nice."

Naz laughed.

"That's funny," Trip said looking puzzled.

"No, not really it's just that I tried to get her to ride out on the island last night to look at a little place I picked out for her and she would have nothing to do with it. Said she likes her home just fine."
It was Trip who now smiled.

"I guess I can understand that. It's the only home she's really ever known. She raised her kids there and now that I've provided security she knows she's safe day and night. Why would she want to leave?"

"Basically, the same thing Monica said."

"Speaking of Monica. Will she be out for the fight? Not saying anything about her father. I know he's the one with the rep but for some reason I just like her being in your corner better."

"You and me both. She says she'll be there but if the doctors say no then who knows."

"If I know Monica ain't no doctors gonna be able to hold her down if she gets ready to go."

"You right," Naz agreed hoping that Trip was right.

The ride to Jersey was relatively quiet aside from the radio which blasted the new album by Childish Gambino. Both men seemed to be focused on other things that took them faraway.

"You called your man and told him what I was looking for T?"

"Yeah bruh," Trip said pulling into the used car parking lot.

"And he said he had one?"

"No. Actually, he has two but only one red one. I think the other one's black. Hold up," he said opening the console and taking two stacks of cash and putting them in his jacket pockets. "We about to see." In an hour they'd concluded their

transaction and a smiling Naz jumped into the front seat.

"Listen Naz, I don't care what you tell her but I'm paying for it. It can be from you but I'm paying for it. As much money as you two have put into a niggas pocket this is the least I can do. Call it a wedding gift if you like but I got this."

295

The two were back in the city in no time and Naz had fallen in love with the pep and get up of the little, red, two-seater, Audi sports car.

As planned he was at the nurse's station by eight o'clock the next morning begging and pleading until after receiving an uneasy okay from the head nurse and the doctor on duty he returned downstairs to the lobby.

A few minutes later an utterly confused Monica found a bevy of nurses and attendants around her disconnecting her I.V.'s before placing her in a wheelchair and taking her downstairs to the lobby where she was met by a jubilant Nazar who stood beaming in front of the cherry-red, two-seater Audi sportscar. Handing her the keys he smiled broadly. Monica, on the other hand, was speechless. The tears welled in her eyes and then cascaded down her soft brown cheeks like raindrops on a warm, spring day.

For the first time since he'd met the vivacious, and overly, talkative young woman did he find her speechless. The nurses and orderlies in attendance were also speechless as Monica circled the car inspecting it before getting in. Starting the car, the head nurse turned to Nazar.

"Mr. Muhammad," she pleaded. "Please tell her not to leave. I took an awfully big risk to even bring her downstairs. If she leaves we could all lose our jobs," she said as Monica pulled away from the curb.

"I'm truly sorry nurse. But if you go back upstairs I promise I'll bring her back up to the room just as soon as she gets back. I'm as surprised as you are. I never expected this," he said almost apologetically although he was hardly sorry at Monica's response. Having a seat in the lobby Naz picked up a copy of Ring magazine and flipped through the pages. He hardly read articles when it came to boxing and was surprised that there was not a single article mentioning his meteoric rise to fame. Looking at the power rankings he noticed that he was the number one contender in his division. His thoughts drifted, and he wondered what his father would say if he could see him now.

"Oh, baby I absolutely love it. I took it out on the highway for a test drive and she has some power. Everything I read about her was true. They didn't lie and neither did you when you said you love me," she said hugging and kissing him all over his face and neck her happiness spilling over.

"Glad you like it," he said laughing and pushing her away at the same time. "Stop now. You're making a spectacle of yourself," he said laughing as she ignored him content to do just that.

"Trust me. If any of these women had a man like mine they'd be making a spectacle of themselves too. My man just bought me my first car and not just any car but an Audi TT. Oh, my goodness," she said stepping away from Naz as the tears began flowing again.

"Goodness woman if I'd known this was how you were going to respond I would have gotten you a Ford Pinto," Naz laughed.

"It wouldn't have made a difference. The thing is my man loves me and was thinking about me when I wasn't around."

"Lord knows I wish I'd known. That lime green Pinto was a whole hell of a lot cheaper," he laughed. "Come on. Let me get you back up to your room. That head nurse can be a handful. I had to damn near bribe her to let her let you come downstairs and when you drove off I thought she was going to have my head," Naz said helping her into the wheelchair and onto the elevator.

"Now let me ask you. How have you been doing?"

"I'm good."

"Did you get a chance to go over the tapes with daddy?"

"Yes, love. He spent Tuesday and Thursday with me. If it weren't for his hat I would have sworn it was you."

"Did he go over Munez's tendency to drop his left after shooting the jab?"

"Yes, sweetie. Like you he left no stone unturned."

"Good and you've been eating?"

"Yes dear," he said pushing her into the room to disapproving eyes. "And by the way Trip sends his regards. He's actually the one who found me the car and when it came down to paying for it he was the one who paid for it."

"Are you serious. You know when I first met him I was quick to judge. But he's really turned out to be a pretty decent person to be a drug dealer. I think what separates him from the Dez's of the world is that he loves you."

"I don't know about that. I think he's grown to love you as well for putting some coins in his pocket. That's the only thing that Trip loves. He damn near said so on the way over to Jersey to pick up the car. "This fool said he didn't like what he saw looking at me. Said I didn't seem as focused and motivated as in my other fights and he didn't like the fact that you may not be in my corner for this the biggest fight of my career. So, he made me bet twenty g's on myself to motivate me. I'm telling you the only thing he cares about is the money. And whether you know it or not we are his avenue out of the ghetto."

"Wow. I didn't know that," Monica replied.

"It's all good though. He's always been straight up so I can deal with him."

"You know him better than I do. I still think he has your best interest at heart regardless of his motives. He seems to have love for you."

"He does but he gets a little crazy if he thinks you're messing with his money. Word on the street is he's got a few bodies on him for a whole lot less than what he's betting on me."

"So, tell me something on the real and I want you to be honest with me."

"Has there ever been a time when I wasn't honest with you?"

"In that case, tell me how you're really feeling about this fight."

"Oh, no not you too."

"Yeah me too."

"C'mon Monica. You know how I look at this fight. It's the same as any other. I'm in the best shape of my life with two of the best trainers a boxer could ever hope for in my corner there's no way I could lose. Matter-of-fact, if you're in my corner Saturday night, I'm looking for a first-round knockout."

"That's what I'm talking about. That's all I needed to hear from my baby," she said reaching out for a hug.

"Hi, Ms. Medina and how are you doing today?" the little shriveled up old white nurse said knocking before peeking her head in the door.

"Excuse me ma'am but we were having a conversation," Monica said cutting the nurse off.

"Oh, excuse me," the nurse said apologetically.

Naz could do little more than smile.

"Let me get outta here," Naz said bending over the little woman and kissing her before making his exit. "I've got to meet pops," as he now referred to Mr. Medina. "Says he wants to go over some prefight matters. I swear you two are relentless."

"We build champions," she replied. "Now go on get outta here. You know how daddy is about tardiness. I'll call and tell him you're on your way."

"Thanks. Do you want me to take the car keys? I don't need Nurse Ratchet tracking me down and putting an APB out on me."

"Get on outta here silly," she said smiling and reaching out to hug him again. "And thank you so much Naz."

"For what?"

"For keeping me happy."

"That's my job."

Naz left the hospital with a renewed pep in his step. At least the new-found fame had allowed him to make one person happy. Well, maybe two. The added income had allowed Mr. Medina to move his family to a larger more spacious apartment although Naz was puzzled to find that Mr. Medina like his mother had also chosen to stay in the ghetto. When questioned about it Mr. Medina was curt but truthful.

"I love the Bronx. I love the community. The people know me and respect me here. It's my home. I'm no different than your father. He spent all of his life in Harlem. He could have moved but he chose to stay, and he did the right thing He was a pillar of the community. He needed Harlem and whether Harlem knew it or not they needed him. That's one of the problems we have. There are not enough good, strong Black men out there dedicated to make a change." he replied matter-of-factly.

Up 'til now Naz had never thought about it. Now though with the chance to get out these men he'd held in such high esteem had never considered leaving

306

the grimy, dirty, streets of the ghetto. Was he wrong for wanting to escape?

"I know Mia doesn't believe in doing anything physical the week of a fight, but I like a fighter to familiarize himself with the ring, the ropes and everything before he steps into the ring. You okay with that?"

"You're the boss now," Naz said.

"Okay. I have a friend down at the Garden who's going to give us access. I think this will help give you a little advantage come fight night. Oh, and by the way, Mia called me. That's a beautiful thing you did for her. You're a good boy Nazar. Your father would be proud of the man you've become. And I'm not just talking about the car. I'm talking just about the way you treat my daughter. I'm talking about the way you've embraced me and just the way you treat people in general. You'll be a boon to our community just the way your father was. And believe you me that's what these young cats out here need. Nazar loved the old man but this was one conversation he would rather have not had. Little did the old man know but he was one payday from getting the hell out of this jungle. He may have been able to help but he had no inkling of doing anything other than getting out. What was it they didn't see? He remembered watching television as a kid and wondering why he didn't live in a house with a white picket fence. He loved his people and here in Harlem he had every hue and color. It's just that there were so many that at times it was hard to breathe. And now he was at a stage in his life that he felt he was suffocating. He needed space and air. The media had become almost overwhelming posting up in front of his building until Trip had enough of them interfering with his business and shooed them all away. Sometimes he wanted to tell them all where to go but it wasn't really

in his temperament to do so and anything than his absolute correctness would not only ruin his career but more importantly be an embarrassment to the standard his late father had established. No, he couldn't do that. He just needed to get away. In his mind, he knew that Monica was right. After Saturday he'd be preparing to fight for the title, getting married and Jamaica would make for the perfect getaway, but he needed to go now. And with the twenty grand Trip made him bet on himself there would be no financial burden. He'd invite
Monica but if she chose not to go he wouldn't let that stop him. It was time to get out of New York. It was closing in on him.

The workout was light, and it was more of a rehearsal for a play with pops calling out a scenario and he enacting it.

"I want you to close your eyes. You're on the ropes son. He's shooting rights and lefts to the midsection. Feel them then roll with 'em son. Now turn him. Get off the ropes. Now shoot a jab. Again. Now double it. Come on son. If you're gonna shoot the jab, then shoot it. Make it strong and crisp. The way you practice is the way you'll perform. Always do your best. Now shoot it."

This went on for another half an hour or so until pops yelled stop. An hour later Naz entered the loft downtown after putting Mr. Medina in a cab heading uptown. After fixing a protein smoothie and watching some tape of his upcoming opponent Naz lay down on the sofa where he broke a broad grin as he thought of Monica's face when she saw the car. He wished she were there now but she promised she'd be there for the fight and he'd have to be content with that.

Naz had always hated the day before fights. Everyone would be on him to do as little as possible and he'd just laze around and watch TV, nap and read a little but it was always eyes on him with his father suggesting limited or no movement. Today was no different. His sister, Sin stopped by the downtown loft, fixed breakfast for them both and shared some memories on her way to work. He then turned his phone off and took a two-mile run to try and clear his head. It was unseasonably warm for this time of the year and the soft spray of the water from off the East River was a cool relief. Returning he was surprised out how good he felt. After a quick shower he picked up his phone to find at least twenty missed calls. Monica, Trip and pops had all called as well as his mother. There were a host of other calls including one from his old friend Noah. He often wondered how Noah was doing. He'd always made it a point to search Noah out and slip him a little money, so he wouldn't get caught up out there in the streets but

Naz knew from all the reports he was given that it was only a matter of time before he'd be notified about one of his dearest and oldest friends.

"Your boy's 'bout to hit bottom, Naz. He's bad right through here. I was kinda proud of him 'til about a week ago. He was keeping it Afro-centric like I said 'til about a week ago. He was sticking up all the white bars down around mid-town and was kilin' them. I don't know what he was doing with all the money. Ain't no way he was spendin' all that he was making, and I mean he was out there every day like he it was a true nine-to-five with benefits. I don't know what ticked him off to go after it like that but then I don't know what happened but one night about two weeks ago I heard these fools screaming so I threw on some clothes, grabbed my Roscoe and headed downstairs only to find that he's stuck up my boys. I was like,

'Are you sure it was Noah? And to a man they swore up and down it was that fool. Put me in a real, bad situation. He'd punked and disrespected me in the streets which meant I had to either have him beaten to within an inch of his life or dead him. But the funny thing was that when he rolled the fellas had somewhere in the neighborhood of ten to twelve g's on 'em and all he took was a sixty dollar bag of boy. Two days later he walked right up to me and gave me the sixty said 'sorry for the inconvenience' and just walked away. Fucked me up so bad I just stood there with my mouth wide open. If you ask me the nigga's truly gone. I owe him one but hell it's Noah. He's like you to me. I mean we like fam. We came up together. But we still gotta to work this shit out. You know what I'm sayin' fam. We gotta scrap or talk or something but it can't just go unattended. You feel me? Brothas gotta work it out." Trip said breaking onto the Curtis Mayfield song.

"I didn't know. I used to check on him once a week, give him a little money but since I moved downtown I don't see him like I used to."

"Don't you have a fight tomorrow bruh?"

"Yeah. I'm good with that. It's just that I got other things in my life as well."

"No bruh. But you don't. The only thing on your mind right through here should be the fight. You need something done then you let me know and I'll take are of it for you."

"Listen Trip. Because you pea brained fools can't hold but one thing on your mind at a time does not mean an intelligent brother like myself can't multi-task."

Trip literally laughed out loud.

"I know you didn't just go there. Okay, Naz I'll round that knucklehead up and see what's up with him and where his head's at. I gotta couple empty one bedrooms I can put him in after I whoop that ass real good."

"Leave that boy alone Trip."

"I might. Good luck tomorrow bruh."

"See you in the winner's circle."

In his mind he knew Trip wouldn't hurt Noah. He loved Noah almost as much as Naz did and though he too was disappointed in what Noah had become he still loved him. There was no forgetting what the two had meant to each other. They were the family when there was no family. No. He would take care of Noah until they had a chance to sit down and work out some kind of viable solution. For now, though that would have to suffice. Laying back down on the sofa Naz fell fast asleep only to be awakened what seemed like minutes later by the steady staccato of his phone.

"Naz here," he said wiping the sleep from his eyes.

"Bay. It's close to mid-day. Why haven' I heard from you?"

"Hey sweetie. Sorry about that. I guess I fell asleep."

"Rough night? Your little girlfriend's wear you out last night?"

"Maybe that's it. How many were there?"

"I hear four."

"Yep. That's what I hear."

"Actually, there were five. You see I'm in training for my heavyweight debut a little later this year," Naz said grinning broadly.

"Heavyweight debut?"

"Yeah. You see I'm in training since the love of my life doesn't believe in pre-marital sex so in order to stay in shape I have to call in four or five of those lil' Oriental gals just to measure up to my girl."

"So, your girl's, how can I say it, a big girl?"

"Okay. I'm going to say this in the deepest of confidentiality and I hope to never hear this repeated because she would have my head if she ever came to know that when I met her she was what one might call thick."

"And now?"

"She's blossomed."

"Blossomed? Blossomed into what?"

"Why she's blossomed from thick to fat. I mean ain't too much to blossom into if you're already thick," Naz said doing his best not to laugh out loud but once Monica started it was hard for him not to. When he finished tears were running down his face.

"I'm not even gonna entertain that," Monica said still chuckling lightly. "So, how are you feeling?"

"I feel good. Better yet, how do you feel? They gonna let you out today?"

"I don't know Nazar. I haven't seen the doctor yet. I feel weak as hell and tired too. I feel like I could sleep for three or four days straight. That's

how tired I feel if you can imagine that."

"Funny thing is in a way I can and

that's why I'm getting out of the city after this fight. I

thought about it and it does make a lot more sense to go

after the championship fight for our honeymoon but I

gotta get out of here before I explode,"

"Doesn't sound so bad and my

doctors would probably applaud that. Let's try and get

a flight out the morning after."

"I'll put Sin on it as soon as I get

off with you."

"What do you have? ESP?

Twenty-three people just walked in the room in white

coats."

"You get some sleep. I'll talk

319

to you later."

"In person I hope."

"Love you sweetie."

"Love you more."

Naz turned the ringer off on his phone and slept for most of the day. It wasn't until later that evening when he heard the sound of pots and pans clanging together that he remembered giving Sin the key so she and mam could come fix a pre-fight dinner. This had been a family tradition since he first entered the ring at twelve and little had changed.

"Ma. Is that you?" Nazar yelled.

"Yes dear. It's just me and your sister."

"Hey little brother. How's my girl doing,"

"She's in good spirits. Says she still feels a little weak though. Now they're saying she has a bacterial infection and are treating her with antibiotics. But for some reason I get the feeling that they're not telling me everything."

"Mia probably told them not to tell you anything. She would never want you to worry about her."

"And especially at such a crucial junction in your career," Sin chimed in. "All she wants is for you to succeed. She not only loves you she's devoted to your success. And when I say your success I mean she's devoted to her success as well as yours. She sees you two as one now. You're a unit now and she is driven and is going to make sure you're a success. She's not going to let herself get in the way. She loves you too much to do that. So don't blame her for not giving you license to worry unnecessarily."

"Thanks for that Sin. That doesn't exactly

make me feel any better." Naz said knowing his sister had just put everything in its own proper container and properly organized his thoughts, so he could think logically. And she was right. They were keeping something from him in lieu of the fight.

Well, all that would end as soon as this fight was in the books. There would be no more secrets. Nothing was more important to him than she was right now. And if something was wrong Monica certainly held the higher priority. The fight could wait. It was time he had a long sit down with her. It was time she knew that this was an equal partnership and her well-being was just as important as his. But first he had to get the fight out of the way.

Dinner was delicious with mommy boiling a couple of lobsters in beer the way daddy used to. She followed this with a large plate of manicotti she'd learned to fix from the Italian cook she worked with at the Lansing home. On the side she fixed a tossed salad with fetta, black olives, banana peppers, chick peas and so much more. For dessert there was strawberry cheesecake and coffee.

"That dinner was fit for a king. I can't remember having a dinner that good. Thank you two. That was absolutely delicious."

"That's the least we could do." Mrs. Muhammad said leaning over the sofa and hugging her son.

"You know I was beginning to have my doubts that you'd snap back after your father died and then God put Monica into our lives and my son picked himself up and I could never be more proud of the man he has become. C'mon Cynthia. It's starting to get late."

"You know you can stay here tonight.

Tomorrow's Saturday. Neither of you has to work tomorrow so why don't you spend the night. I could really go for another of those breakfasts like I had this morning."

"I wouldn't be opposed but you know mama can't sleep anywhere but her own bed."

"Sin you need to get your license."

"For what? I don't have a car."

"Let me worry about that. You just text me what you like."

"Don't waste your money on me lil' brother. You save your money for that lil' white house with the picket fence and my nine or ten nieces and nephews you gonna give me."

"I'll do that. Well, at least let me call you a Lyft."

"Not necessary. We'll take the subway.

You ready ma?"

His family was an odd lot. Most people

worked their lives to afford better but not his. As hard

as mama and Sin worked they seemed satisfied with life

as it was. It was the little things that made them happy

like coming over and fixing their favorite son dinner

and watching me smile with each forkful. That's what

got it done for them.

He slept fitfully waking up several times to

Monica's voice calling him to rescue her from her pain

but there was nothing he could do. He thought about

calling her but he was sure she was sleep. In the

morning he did just that though.

"Hey baby. It's your big day. How are you

feeling? How did you sleep?"

"I didn't. I thought of you the whole night and when I did fall off I had nightmares of you screaming out in pain for me."

"Oh baby, why didn't you call me, so I could have put your mind at ease."

"Didn't see any reason both of us should be awake."

"How are you feeling otherwise. You still have a chance to take a nap. Fight's not 'til tonight."

"True. What time are you coming home?"

"Still waiting for the doctors. They tell me if I walk out again against medical advice then they won't admit me again so I'm trying to do this correctly and by the book. But I think once they see me they'll discharge me. If not we'll just have to find another hospital."

"You know you're crazy, don't you?"

"Crazy in love with you 'One Time'. Get some sleep. I'll see you tonight."

"Love you mommy."

"Love you more papi," Monica said sending warm shivers through Naz. Damn how he loved that woman. She was an angel that God had sent him to replace his father. That was it. That had to be it.

Setting the alarm for five-thirty Naz hit the snooze. At six-thirty he found himself rushing to hail a cab. He was the second fight on an undercard that featured up-and-coming heavyweight contender Jarell 'Big Baby' Miller. The first fight was slated to go off at eight. He should have been dressed and already broken a sweat.

Minutes later Naz entered the rear entrance to
the Garden and soon found himself standing before
Mr. Medina in the dressing room.

"Sorry, I'm late sir. Traffic and all.
Where's Mia?"

"She was too weak to come."

"Sir, there's something you and your
daughter aren't telling me, and I think I have the right
to know."

Mr. Medina dropped his head. It was
obvious this wasn't the first time he'd given the subject
some thought.

"I asked Mia if she were going to tell
you and she said she would when you didn't have so
much on your plate. I guess she just didn't get around
to it but it's not for me to say. I don't get involved in

my children's affairs. I'm sure she'll tell you after the fight. But for now, let's focus on why we're here. This kid ain't to be taken lightly so I want you to let the thought of Mia go for the next hour or so and concentrate on getting this guy outta there. Jab him until he drops his guard then I want you to drop him."

Naz did as instructed often going toe-to-toe with the smaller man once he found out the smaller Nunez had no real power. But neither could Naz get him out of there either. It wasn't until the seventh when Naz caught him flush on the temple with a lethal left hook that Naz could feel the tone of the fight turn in his favor. Early in the eighth he followed the jab with a double left hook that sent Nunez to the canvas for the final time.

Naz returned to his corner smiling in relief. He was free. It was over, and he was out. He'd grab Monica in the morning and grab the first flight to

Jamaica. And then he noticed a pale, almost eerie gloom hanging over his corner. This was not the corner of a winning fighter who had just pushed himself into a title fight. Where were the cheers, smiles and congratulations? Where were the pats on the back and the cries of 'Good fight or Good job son?' Why did everyone look so gloomy, sad and down.

"What's wrong pops? I did get him outta there didn't I?"

"Yes. You certainly did that son. Sit down on your stool. I have something to tell you. Listen. Mia passed away about a half an hour ago," the man said his eyes welling up with tears.

"What are you saying pops?" I couldn't believe what I was hearing. Was this some type of bad joke they were playing on me? But then why would pops do that to me? No. He had never lied to me. I needed further clarification of this horrible tragedy now bestowed upon me.

"What happened sir?" I said staring at the now fallen man sitting on the floor of the canvas next to me letting his grief spill out in buckets and still having a hard time grasping what he'd just told me.

"She had sickle-cell. She was warned countless times to slow down but that just wasn't who she was. That's not how she was built. So, she just kept pushing until she contracted this bacterial infection that attacked her lungs. And from what they tell me she'd disconnected the I.V. They found her dressed and on her way to the car. She was headed here and didn't or couldn't make it. They say she was still breathing when they found her but their attempts at resuscitation were unsuccessful."

The recounting of his daughter's final

minutes must have been too much, and I watched as Mr. Medina went into shock which was followed by a seizure or a stroke I'm not sure which.

Me. Well, I don't know how long I sat there on that stool alone in the corner of that ring and I'm not sure who instructed that team of first responders to stand by but all that I know is that Nunez had gotten nothing compared to what they'd get if they tried to approach me. Then just like that I was face down with my arms firmly pinned behind me. I could feel the prick of the needle and then all was Black.

I was awakened to the sound of my mother's voice and from what I could make out as I did not want to open my eyes, and this be a dream or nightmare of epic proportions. That's what it was. It was a nightmare of epic proportions just like the other night when I felt her screaming, calling me to save her from the pain. But then it had all seemed so real. The fight. Them carrying Mr. Medina away on a stretcher. He could make out the voices. There was Sin. Trip was teasing her. They were having fun. Trip was always teasing Sin about something or another. He needed to open his eyes to know the truth. Opening his eyes he saw that they were all there. And they all sat there with smiles etched very carefully on their faces almost as if someone had carefully drawn them on. "Congratulations son," my mother said kissing me on the forehead followed by Sin before Trip bent down hugging me and whispering in my ear.

"You know you won a hundred grand. You had me scared though. You was really hitting Nunez, but he just refused to go down. Well, that was until you caught him with that double left. It was a thing of beauty. Anyway man, I am deeply sorry for your loss. Mia was truly a beautiful person."

So, it was true then.

At first, I was beside myself with grief. The fact that I had money mattered little now. I put Sin in charge of all my financial affairs and took a little over ten grand with me and rented that little, cozy, warm villa I'd been dreaming of on the edge of Montego Bay in Jamaica. And though I had never been what you might call a drinker I started my new career in earnest now. The liquor store was only a five-minute walk from the villa and I spent most of my days either going or coming from that well honored institution. Often,

I'd just sit alone on the beach. I'd never been what you might call a deeply religious sort of person, but I never doubted the existence of my God. I just never thought that I needed an intermediary or spokesperson to translate what my God had in store for me. Mama used to say that I wasn't religious in the manner of going to church but said I was spiritual and she'd take a hundred-spiritual people over one of her holy-roller, born again, church going, hypocrites. I never exactly knew what this meant but I knew it was no condemnation of where I stood concerning God. To me God stood for good just remove an 'o'. The devil stood for evil just remove the 'd'. It was just that plain and simple.

Well, it had been that plain and simple up until now. Now I was confused. I wanted to know how God the Father, my father, could take this woman who had caused no one any harm but worked always with his

'word' in mind. How could he just take her? She who had pulled me through the fire when my own father had passed, and I was on threshold of throwing my life away. How could He who professed to love me just snatch the most important person in my life away from me? Does he not know the pain He has caused me? Does He not care? Does He not love me? I asked myself these same question a hundred times a day between the tears and the bottles and then when this did not suffice in ending my grief I drank some more. I

thought of Job and how his faith would not allow him

to question the Lord and chose to take this approach in

dealing with my grief.

There were days that I woke up with my head

throbbing and would go to bed with it still throbbing and

with all that I consumed it did little to ease the pain. I

just couldn't understand how she could be standing in

my corner one minute and gone the next.

I could feel the tears coming on again. By now I didn't

care. There was no holding them back these days.

Sometimes I could be out at the little bar on the beach.

Might be twenty, twenty-five people there and I'd see

or hear something that would remind me of Monica and

be a mess again.

There were times when I thought I was

having a nervous breakdown. Daddy's passing hurt.

When I finally came to realize. and it really hit me that he was gone for good I knew at that point that I'd never felt a worse pain in my life. And no matter what I did I could not get it to go away. The truth which I had yet to come to accept was that my Mia was now gone never to return. And no matter how hard I tried to come to grips with the fact that she was no longer in my life I was unable to do so.

Mama and Mr. Medina called me regularly to check on me but aside from that I spoke to no one. Trip would call occasionally, maybe once or twice a week and tell me how crazy things had gotten in the city and then laugh and joke that if he wasn't so goddamn greedy he'd probably be right alongside of me sippin' Mai Tais on the beach. I invited him down and he promised he'd come just as soon as he could get a break, but I doubted that Trip could ever leave the streets. I invited mama who insisted that she had to work but promised she'd come as well. To be honest I didn't expect either of them but was shocked when that very weekend mama showed up at my doorstep.

"Hey sweetie. How's my favorite son?"

Much to my surprise I was elated to see her. When I looked out over her head there stood no other than Cynthia having a good ol' time playing with the cab driver who seemed enamored by her.

"Think I'm coming to stay with you baby brother. The men are so flirtatious here," she giggled before hugging me.

"You're quite welcome to. I've got plenty of room. Come on in and check it out."

They stayed a week and had a ball spending almost everyday shopping at one of the thousands of outdoor markets around Negril and laying

on the Beach at night sipping one Pina Colada all night

long. It was the first time in a long time where mama

looked happy and at peace with the world. It made me

feel good that I could for the first time elicit the same

spark of life and happiness that I used to see when

daddy was alive. It was almost as if she didn't have a

care in the world.

Mama kept me by her side. I guess she

was a little worried about me and I did my best to keep

my chin up when I was around her, but it was tearing

me up on the inside. Cynthia knew and when mama

went to sleep we talked.

"God put that woman in your life for a reason.

She took you to another chapter in your life.

She did her job. If you could only see how far she's

taken you in only a couple of years. If you could only

see yourself baby brother. If you could see how far

you've come. When you met her, you were just a boy.
She helped create this beautiful Black man that stands
before me. I'm proud to call you my brother because
you're a good man Nazar. You've risen to the top of
your profession .and remained humble. You try to do
right by people almost as if you're a saint Nazar. So,
hard as it may seem put this lesson behind you. You've
got to take the goodness and positives from her memory
and move on my brother."

"I wish it were that easy," I replied.

"Didn't say it was going to be easy. Just
said that's what you have to do. You've got to keep
spreading her love and goodness in your own way."

I hung my head knowing she was right
but not knowing if I was capable. I wanted to and not
only because I never wanted to let Sin down but for my
own sanity. I couldn't keep trying to drown Monica's

death in a bottle. I knew this wasn't me and I was killing myself. Monica wouldn't want this. And so. I made a conscious effort to try and put her death behind me and turn my life around.

The next morning, I waved as the cab pulled away from the villa. My thoughts were still full of morbid thoughts and I wondered if I was seeing my mother for the last time. Monica's death had taken it's toll on mama who had taken Monica under her wing like another of her children and loved her as much if not more than I did. Her death had taken its toll and mama had physically aged since I'd last seen her at the funeral. It was frightening and let me know that she too had more days behind her than in front of her.

I vowed not to drink today and stay active, so I threw on a sweat suit and decided to run a few miles on the Beach before it got too warm. I ran maybe a mile or so before I began throwing up at regular intervals. I kept running and when I returned I showered and decided to take a nap. When I awoke it was somewhere around eight that night. I showered quickly and donned the new white and gold sweat suit designed and given to me by the Nike representative after my last fight in hopes that I would sign with Nike once I won the championship. I knew

Monica had been behind the whole the whole affair, but I didn't care. Nike was a reputable company and I loved the sweat suit. The music was blaring some Gregory Isaac, I didn't know but I fell into the groove when the bartender asked me what I wanted.

"Hello my friend. What's it going to be tonight? The usual?"

I got ready to say yes when I remembered my vow.

"No. Give me a ginger beer."

"A ginger beer it is," he said wiping off the bar in front of me without flinching. A cute little dark-skinned girl slid onto the stool next to me. Her close-cropped haircut and simple black dress made her stand out in the crowd.

"I love the sweat suit but a ginger beer? No. Give him a Long Island Tea, Boston," she said never taking her eyes off of me.

"You're a cutie. What's your name?"

"Nazar," I said extending my hand. "You're not too bad yourself. You want to grab a table?"

"That accent. You're not from here that's for sure. Oh, I know that accent. You're either from Boston or New York. Don't tell me. Just keep talking I'll get it. So, what brings you to Negril, Nazar?"

"Vacation."

"Oh, you've got to give me more than that if I'm supposed to figure out where you're from," she smiled displaying a most beautiful smile. She had his attention now. Along with everything else he loved her Jamaican accent.

"Why did you choose to come to Negril?"

"Actually, my father brought me when I was younger to visit relatives."

"New York. That's it. New York. Am I right?"

Nazar smiled broadly before sipping his drink.

"Thanks Boston."

"No worries. Shall I run a tab Ms. Bea?" the bartender said clearing the now empty glasses.

"Sounds good," she said handing him her card and crossing her legs exposing her dark, shapely thighs.

"You don't have to do that," Nazar said reaching in his pocket.

"So, was I right. Are you from New York?"

"Yes, I am?"

"Uptown? Harlem?"

"How'd you know?"

"Brothers and sisters from uptown have a unique swagger about them that separates them from everyone else. But once you live there you can pretty much tell who's from what borough. They all have their own kind of swag."

" You know a lot about the city."

"My mother lives there so I spend a lot of time between here and there. I actually have an apartment in Manhattan on the lower eastside."

"Get out of here! So, do I. And you live here as well?"

"I do. My daddy had the good foresight to try and buy up all the beach front property and so now I do all the rentals."

"Wow! That's great. You might be just the person I'm looking for."

"You do move fast Nazar," she said teasing.

"No. Seriously. I'm renting a villa on

the beach not far from here. My intentions were and still are to buy but something came up."

. "Don't they always. What's the address?"

Naz repeated the address.

"Yellow Spanish villa with a fountain and garden in the middle. Yes, that's one of our properties," she smiled.

"And it's for sale?"

"Everything has a price," she said smiling.

"But let's set another time to talk about business. I do that all day. Let's talk about you Mr. Nazar. What is it that you do in the big city that made you come join us common folks in the islands. It must be intense."

Nazar hated this part of meeting someone. He'd never liked talking about himself. It made him feel uncomfortable almost egotistical and that wasn't him.

"I'm a boxer."

"A boxer?" She said almost choking on her drink. "I would've never guessed that in a million years. Are you good?"

"I don't know. I've been boxing for close to twelve years and I've never lost. Better yet google Nazar Muhhamad." There that would end all this talk about who he is.

"My God. You're famous. Guess I don't know as much as I thought I did about what's going on in New York."

Naz smiled.

"So, from what it says here you're the overwhelming the favorite going into a championship fight. Says it's the biggest fight of the year. Oh, my goodness! You're the headliner at the Garden. Oh, my God! I'm here with a celebrity," she yelled.

"Stop! You're embarrassing me," Naz grinned uncomfortably.

"You're going to be on Pay-Per-View and HBO. They're saying you're the most complete fighter in the last twenty-five years. Okay and who's representing you as your publicist and agent? We need to put together a whole marketing team. We'll make you a brand and take you national.

No international.

We've got to get you to book more fights overseas. We

need to make your name a household name overseas as

well. We've got to nail down China. I know you've

considered all these options already."

"I thought we weren't talking

business."

"I'm sorry," she said before fishing in

her purse for a cigarette and lighting it. "I can't believe I'm

sitting here with the next welterweight champion of the

world."

"Let's pray."

"You don't feel confident?"

"I always feel confident because

I know what skills I'm bringing to the table but for some reason I always feel better climbing out of the ring than climbing into it."

"That's interesting. Are you going to win?"

"I expect I'll rough him up a little bit before the ref steps in and stops it."

"Wow! You know you could be the biggest thing to hit New York since… Seriously, what firm is managing your marketing?"

"My fiancé handled the marketing and all financial aspects."

"I knew it was too good to be true."

"She passed away a month ago."

"Oh, I'm sorry to hear that." The young

woman said the concern in her voice showing. "You must be devastated. How are you handling that?"

"I think I'm going to make it. My mother and sister just left. They came down to check on me. Kept me busy and my mind off of it."

"Well let me see if I can help any. How 'bout I pick u up at say eight tomorrow morning and we'll take a tour of Negril. Maybe end with lunch and I can show you some of the other beachfront properties I have available."

"Sounds good. I guess you're leaving," Naz said watching the woman gather her belongings before holding out her hand to Naz.

"Nice to have met you Mr. Nazar."

"Why are you leaving so early? I was enjoying the conversation."

"I always put business before pleasure and I was just informed that I had a showing in the morning. Seems the gentleman is looking for a beach house. Cute little devil. I need to be on my toes. You never know what else may transpire" she said winking at Nazar. "See you at eight." Nazar stood as the fine, young, dark-skinned woman walked away.

Nazar immediately felt guilt. Was he being unfaithful to Monica? What would she tell him to do? She would want him to go on with his life he was sure. Still, he felt like he was betraying their love.

The next day arrived quicker than Naz expected and when he looked at the clock in the morning he couldn't believe the time. Throwing on a white shirt, some jeans and penny loafers he rushed out the door to a waiting car.

"Morning Mr. Muhammad," the stately

looking woman wore a navy-blue suit that exuded money.

"I'm sorry I didn't get your full name last night,"

"Kree. Kree Edmunds," she said holding out her hand again. The windows were tinted black and the driver was white. A bowl of fresh strawberries sat on a bed of ice.

"Nice touch," Nazar said dipping a strawberry in the cream.

"Is there any other way?" The woman said before handing Naz a folder.

Here's a listing of houses that we'll be visiting with all the amenities listed and the prices they're going for on the current market. Feel free to negotiate.

Two hours later Naz was virtually speechless. His villa that he was paying close to five thousand a month for paled in comparison to most of the other properties he saw. And Ms. Edmunds was the consummate professional not needing to refer to any notes or paperwork as she pointed out all the unique and positive amenities of each dwelling. By the time they reached Negril for lunch Nazar was exhausted. Kree, on te other hand, looked like she had hardly broken a sweat when they sat down at the little outdoor café in the heart of Negril.

Naz was amazed at all the people in the small square at mid-day and wondered what they did to sustain themselves since he saw no signs of industry though there was plenty of commerce. He was just about to ask when she smiled at him making him lose all thought.

"Anything impress you?"

355

They all did but what really stood out was the proficiency of the realtor.

"You really know your stuff," Naz said humorously.

Kree was surprised by this but answered rather matter-of-factly.

"A good realtor is supposed to know her properties better than she knows herself," She responded. "That's just something daddy used to stress."

"Well, he did a good job getting that point across."

"I'm not sure if you're merely being sincere or just being flirtatious."

"Is there any harm in being both?"

"No. I suppose there isn't, but it does make it a bit difficult to concentrate on work."

"I sincerely doubt that from what I've seen from you so far."

Kree seemed visibly shaken by Naz's forwardness although she hadn't had a problem last night when she was on the offensive. She laughed before doing her best to compose herself.

"Seriously though was there any one that stood apart from the rest?"

"Aesthetically yes but financially I'm not sure if I could stand it. I'm a boxer. My job security is if nothing else very precarious. A lucky punch and my career can be short-circuited and I'm unemployed, so I don't want to get in over my head."

"Makes perfectly good sense

which is why you don't want to depend on boxing as an income. You want to build a brand so that you become a household name, with hundreds of endorsements. That's where the real money is Nazar. Tell me honestly and I know we just met but do you have a marketing team out there right now working on your behalf?"

"No, to be honest all that died with Monica,"

"Well it's time to resurrect it. Excuse me for being so forward but I'll make a deal with you. Tell you what. I notice you have a six-month lease on the villa with three months to go. That comes to fifteen thousand dollars owed me in rent. I will waive the rent if you let me act as your marketing team for the next six months. All I ask is that you watch the endorsements grow as well as your assets and at the end of the six-month probationary period you decide whether or not you want to keep me on. Fair enough?"

"Let me give it some thought. In the meantime, tell me about the beach front property with the stone wall around it and the tall, black, wrought iron fence. It says it sell here for seven hundred and fifty thousand. I like that one, but the problem is that one's clearly out of my price range and my mother and sister love the villa I'm in. Thank God, they didn't see the other ones. So, you see my problem."

"So, let me see if I'm understanding you correctly. You're interested in a property that I have listed at three quarters of a million and another that I have listed at a quarter of a million bringing you to a cool mil for both properties. Is that what I'm hearing?"

"Yes ma'am. Can't hurt to dream," Naz muttered when the numbers came up.

"Let's see if I can't make that dream a reality. But first I want to be frank about some things. I can get maybe eight or nine humdred thousand from that walled in beach front property so seven fifty is a bargain but what are you going to do with all that house. That's meant for a family Nazar. The share cost of it would be substantial in itself."

"But with all the money you're going to make me in endorsements should take care of the overhead I'm sure."

Was he baiting her? Not one to back down from a challenge.

"I'll tell you what Nazar. If you allow me to represent you for one year I will sell you both homes for half-a-million and I will guarantee in writing that both houses will be paid for within the upcoming year."

"And you will put that in writing? We can sign off on it after our lawyers look over the terms and okay it."

"Absolutely," she said grinning. "Come on. Let's go somewhere a little quieter and celebrate our first of many business deals."

"I know just the place," Naza said smiling at the stunning Black woman who sat across from him. Picking up her phone she called her driver who appeared within minutes.

"Just tell James where you want to go."

"Same place you picked me up this morning." "Oh, this day may turn into something after all," Kree snickered.

"You sold two houses for half a million and made a deal for a contract with potential to be in the millions and your discounting your day."

"You've got misplaced priorities Mr. Muhammad. "Money is wonderful, but it pales greatly in lieu of happiness. I am sure if you had he opportunity you would give your last dime and all that you will make in your career to bring Monica back. You see money cannot in any terms replace the real joy of being in love and having someone love you."

"You're right. Have you ever been in love?"

"No. But I'm starting to see the possibilities."

They were at the villa and Naz routinely went to the Wave Sound System and threw on some

Sade before pouring a couple of glasses of Merlot before pulling her forward and kissing her. Kree Edmunds did not resist.

"Wow! And what was that for?"

"No reason. Just because."

"Then just because again," she said grabbing and pulling her head to his.

He couldn't remember how many times they made love that day but he couldn't help smile when he thought of her non-stop chatter and instructing him to concentrate on her feel good spots. Kree Edmonds, young millionaire real estate broker was a mess. Naz had assumed this young ebony princess was rather well-to-do just in how she carried herself. She exuded confidence and culture. She embodied class and mystique, but it was not until she took Naz home to the castle on her estate that Naz had no-doubt. This was old money and this woman had been born into an empire and was just the latest gatekeeper.

Days were simple and easy. The weather was warm but not unbearable. And Kree for all intents and purposes had moved in. Everything seemed perfect. They would stay in bed and make love until the early afternoon when Kree would suggest a restaurant and off they'd go. At night they'd take long walks on the beach and talk about whatever came to mind before stopping to see Boston at the beachfront bar. In all life was good. He liked this woman. She was good company in a time he didn't need to be alone. Like mama and Sin, she kept his mind off of Monica although she could never hold a candle to Monica Medina. There were still those nights he woke up soaked in sweat after reliving Monica's death.

"So, what would you consider what we have?" Kree said turning to him one night right after they'd made love.

"On what level?" Naz asked knowing exactly what level she was asking.

"C'mon Naz let's not play games. I'm aware that we exist on a business level and I would call you a rather good as well as intimate friend but do you think it's anymore than that or has the possibility to be any more than that?"

"That's something that I give a lot of thought and everything's in place for us to move forward but I'm not sure I'm emotionally ready to take that step."

"I guess I understand. It hasn't been that

long but I want something more from you. I want you to be mine, to be devoted to me. I don't want your physical presence with your heart and soul with someone else. I want all of you so I guess I'm going to step aside until it's all of me you want."

That was Thursday. By Saturday there wasn't of Kree Edmunds to be found in the chateau. Naz returned to his dinking and grieving and was in the middle of another binge when he received the phone call.

"Will you please tell this nitwit your address. My God. No wonder you're a goddamn cab driver. You're dumb as soap. C'mon man how many yellow beach front houses can there be?"

"Trip! Trip! Is that you?"

"Yeah!"

"Where you at man?"

"The airport."

"Stay there. I'll be there in five."
Ten minutes later Trip sat across from Naz in the chauffeured limousine Kree left at Naz's disposal during his stay on the island.

"I see you. You doing big things. Riding in the limo and all. So, what's up my brother? I know you didn't expect to see your man Trip anywhere but on the block. I surprised yo' ass thougth didn't I?"

"Things must be really getting' twisted if you left town," Naz said grinning glad to see his friend. This past week and since Kree had stopped coming by had been particularly depressing and when he wasn't drenching himself in the liquor he was crying buckets fool of tears. He wasn't getting any better and this time alone he had so wanted when she was alive

was becoming his undoing. All he thought about was

what could have been. And no matter how much he

thought about it he couldn't find the answer as to why.

"Every time I see your moms or Syn all they did was

talk about how you was living down there in the islands

so I said 'let me go down here and see what this

Blackman has done.'

Trip was outdone when he saw

the chateau and after he showered and changed the two

men walked up the each to the bar.

"I want to meet this lady realtor

in the morning,"

"I'll see what I can do but what

are you going to do about New York?"

"I gave it to Murph. You know he almost killed Dez. I guess Dez really didn't know Murph. You and I know he's the nicest guy on earth but if he snaps someone's gonna get hurt. Guess Dez found out the hard way. But yeah, I'm out. Took my investments from managing you and invested them along with some loose change I had lying around and now just living off the residuals and now I've found my home. Damn this is nice."

"Yes, it is. Makes me want to retire now."

"Don't even play like that. That's the other thing I wanted to talk to you about. There offering you a million five plus a percentage of the gate and Pay-Per-View."

"And? Come on. I know there's more."

369

"Well that's the good news."

"And the bad?"

"They want you to take the bout on only four months' notice."

"Okay and?"

"Well usually in a title fight you get at east six months to prepare."

"Take the fight Trip."

"And you'll be ready?"

"I'll be ready."

"The two men stayed up 'til the wee hours of the morning talking about old times when things were better and what the future would bring. At nine there was a ring at the door. Naz opened it to find

Kree looking just as radiant and beautiful as ever.

Bending over he kissed her on the cheek and whispered.

"I missed you."

"Fix it so you don't have to. I think I'd

like that too."

The two left and returned at around six

that evening. Nazar found himself thinking about Trip

and Kree. He didn't know why thoughts of them

together kept reoccurring. He had no room for her in

his life right now but for some reason he felt a tinge of

jealousy.

Trip came in carrying shopping bags.

"Did a little shoppin' bruh," he said

smiling. "I love it bruh. Absolutely love it. I'll be

moving in within the next two or three weeks. Just

think about it Naz. You're going to have a new

neighbor. And we can set up training camp right here.

I mean we'll have to go back for you to get quality

sparring partners, but this is it. Ya' feel me?"

Kre followed him in and had a seat in the

living room.

"Naz, be a prince and bring me a

Hennessey over ice," Kree smiled.

"That woman is a charmer Naz. Such

elegance and style. I really enjoyed your company Ms.

Edmunds."

"It was my pleasure Trip. And please

stop calling me Ms. Edmunds. It's Kree. Just plain

Kree" she said smiling her eyes never leaving Naz.

"Okay, Kree. Listen. I'm going to run

these bags upstairs and grab a quick shower. If you two decide to do anything tonight don't forget about me. And thanks again for making it quite the day Ms. Kree." Trip said before heading up the stairs.

"Oh, that man," Kree said easing back into the plush leather sofa. "So, what's the relationship between you two. You seem to be complete opposites. You appear to be so serious and he seems so carefree."

Naz laughed.

"I think it's the environment. You caught us both out of our natural environment. He's the businessman at home, always on the grind. Me. Well, my life isn't or at least it wasn't filled with that much stress until recently which is why I'm here."

"Okay. I buy that. By the way I received your first inquiry about you doing a photo shoot and an endorsement for General Mills on Monday in New

York. You do what General Mills means don't you?"

I didn't but the expression on her face told me it was huge.

"Win the championship and you'll be on the cover of the Wheaties box. And that will in itself make you a household name."

"Oh really?"

"I told you I would bring you to national prominence. Excuse me. International prominence. And this is a helluva first step. I may just win you over yet."

"Who says you haven't? I'm just dealing with the skeletons in my closet right now. I'm hoping I can put them behind me sooner than later but I'm still dealing with them and I don't think there's a lot I can do about it. They tell me only time will heal this."

"I'm aware of all of that Nazar. I wasn't born yesterday but that isn't my objective. I know we've only known each other for a month or so and I don't know if you've noticed it or not but I'm goal oriented and my objective is to have you. All of you. And with our business contract we will be in contact at regular intervals so I'll be able to see you." Nazar smiled.

"Is there anything you may be holding back?" Naz grinned.

"Just wanted you to know where I stood. You think we could get away for an hour or so?"

"I wish I could but that would be rude with Trip just arriving."

"Okay, well let me get out of here. I'll

send the car back in case you two want to go out tonight. And if I don't see you remember we're in New York Monday morning to sign with General Mills so don't turn up too much," Kree said kissing Naz on the cheek before making her leave.

The weekend sped by and it was all a blur of taxi cabs, flashing lights, always one too many drinks and half naked women. And then just like that he was arriving at LaGuardia. In another forty-five minutes he was sitting in the boardroom of GM with the lovely Kree Edmunds by his side. She was as comfortable and knowledgeable in the boardroom as she had been walking barefoot on the beach showing

her properties back in Negril. An hour later Nazar Muhammad was the newest face for GM and was responsible for signing the most lucrative deal in company history at more than sixty million dollars.

"This I think calls for a small celebration in your honor Ms. Edmunds."

"I must say that I do agree Mr. Muhammad. And then we need to start working on your investment portfolio. You're going to need some tax shelters and a pretty good accounting team to prevent the government from taxing every dollar you earn."

"Slow down Kree," he said grabbing her and hugging her tightly. "Thank you, Kree," Naz said. She couldn't see the tear that rolled down his face.

"Come on. Let me show you how you can thank me," she said hailing a cab.

Moments later they got out somewhere down in Soho and entered what appeared to be a grimy old warehouse. Inside Nazar found a rather large, tastefully renovated loft.

"Something to drink?"

"Whatever you're having is fine. Kree darling, I have a confession to make. There were times when you said that you wanted to market me when I had my druthers. You know what I'm saying? The fact that you sold real estate locally doesn't really equivocate to marketing me internationally."

"I feel you. And I'm sure you did your research on me and then you had enough faith to take a chance and I guess today we saw the fruition of our efforts. And that means what?"

"That means we're rich. Come here baby!"

Kree let the black suit jacket fall from her shoulders before the little black dress joined it on the floor. They made love countless times until both passed out, spent, in each other's arms.

Kree had to be at work on Wednesday and Naz had all intentions of returning with her but he had too many loose ends to tie up to leave then. The first ting he had to do was check on mama and Sin and make sure that they had everything they needed to make life a little more comfortable and then do the same for my other family, the Medinas.

I was going to take mama and Sin back down with me now that the villa was more conducive to women. Kree had seen to that, having an interior decorator come in and do the whole thing over for the two women. Both bedrooms had the bed with all the mesh and web curtains going around like they're in a hut out in the backwoods of Africa. I think they call it a canopied bed with the seventy-inch television

and all the other frilly furniture that women tend to like.

Had a fruit basket put on each of their beds with all the

local fruits and a thousand dollars' worth of gift cards

to all the most prominent stores.

I had a difficult time convincing mama that it

was okay for her to take off from work for a couple of

weeks but after Sin gave her a firm lecture on 'slavin'

for white folks' we made reservations.

"Just the fact hat your baby boy says he has

something to show you should be reason enough for

you to go see. Your son is a success and says you don't

have to go cleanin' up behind no white folks and the

fact that you're still thinkin' about it is a disgrace in

itself. I can't believe that they have you that

brainwashed mommy."

Naz didn't have the heart to go uptown and

meet with the whole Medina clan but did however manage to meet Mr. Medina down at the loft. Three times the size of his current apartment in the Bronx Naz convinced him to take it and handed him an envelope with fifty thousand to hold him over until they began training again. He then apologized for not staying in touch more. The two men hugged for a considerable time. And the tears flowed freely. They had a bond, a commonality that bound them and yet allowed them to be men in each other's company. And so, they sat in each other's company and cried some more."

By the time Naz arrived back on the island Trip had already had a gym installed at his new home and was in the process of moving in.

"I want you back in the gym no later than next Monday bruh. Mr. Medina will be flying down Sunday night. With k Kree promoting you and you flying back and-forth you're going to miss a lot of training, so we've got to got to get you in the gym every chance we have.

Right now, you're the odds-on favorite in Vegas but once we publicize your flying back-and-forth to New York and hanging out at the popular night spots they'll get to talking about how you're not taking training seriously. Together with the reported wrist injury we're going to lower the odds where we can make a bundle off of the side bets."

There was nothing to say. Both he and Monica could switch from friend to manager in a hcartbeatbeat. He was into his manager's mode and I had little to say.

"You know I think the world of Kree and what she's trying to do as far as promoting you. But I'm going to need to meet with her and make it plain to her that she's going to have work around your training schedule. She's got to realize that all the work she's doing is contingent on what you do in this championship fight. Lose and see who wants you to sponsor their product. You feel me bruh?"

"I feel ya. Go easy on her though Trip."

"Oh. No doubt. But Monday is the beginning of camp and the rules need to be laid down. First of all, the partying is over. After this weekend there ain't no more bar and drinking and we need to get you a dietician, cook and nutritionist to move in pronto. This is the biggest fight of our young lives and Team Muhammad needs to come together and show what a winning camp looks like."

I knew Trip and if there was one thing I knew about him was that the way he was acting now babbling and running off about the obvious meant one thing. There was something that was troubling him deeply.

"What's wrong bruh? What's troubling you

Trip?"

He looked at me and I watched as his eyes
as they filled with tears.

"I just got the call. Someone shot Murph.
He ain't been running things a week and someone shot
him."

"Nah, not Murph. Don't say that. How is he?
Is he breathing?"

"They have him in intensive care. Boys
don't know. They're standing by. They're going to
call me as soon as they get an update. Damn man! I've
been in the game ever since I can remember.   Always
said I was gonna make enough money and get out. And
I did. I was trying to give Murph the same opportunity
and look what it gets him."

"Can't blame yourself for tryna' help a brother out. He just ain't built like you. You have any idea who might have done it?"

"If I had to bet I would bet on Dez. He was the one always talking about consolidating the heroin trade under one council with him at the top like the Italians. He always wanted to be kingpin. I've got some of the boys checking it out. If he's behind it, we'll hear about it. You know how he likes to run his mouth."

"And then what?"

"Best case scenario is that we body him. Worst case scenario is that we have to go to war. And if we go to war a lot of innocent bodies are going to be involved but Dez we'll get his wish in the end when the winner takes all and one of us ends up with all of Harlem and the Bronx. How's Pacino say it? 'Every time I try to get out they pull me right back in...' It

385

was more than obvious that this latest turn of events was more than Trip had bargained for.

"Let me see if I can get a flight out of here tonight," he said aloud to everyone and no one in particular.

Trip arrived two hours later. There was yellow tape everywhere. Trip tore it down and moved to the back of the cut as though he hadn't left. Murph was still in intensive care but had been moved to stable condition. He would fully recuperate, and this eased Trip's mind and allowed him to concentrate on retaliation. Almost to a man his soldiers came to the conclusion that it had been no one but Dez's grimy ass in response to the ass whoopin' Murph bestowed on Dez for disrespecting him once too often. It was maddening. The senseless violence made Naz only too glad to be back in the islands.

"So, you're heading back up top tonight? Do you need me to ride along?"

"Hell no. I don't want you anywhere that craziness. I don't want to be there. Nah bruh all I want you to do is put in the roadwork and get back into shape. That's what I need for you to do for me. Can you do that bruh?"

"I gotcha. You just be safe Trip. Lotta uncovered treasures just waitin' for you to uncover."

"Speakin' of which. You're aware that Ms. Edmunds has eyes for you, aren't you?"

"Yeah."

"And?"

"I'm not ready yet."

"Look bro' you've got to shake it. The way you are right now you're not good for yourself or anybody else. You've got to snap out of the funk man. If living here and waking up to the sun over the water and a beautiful, bright young woman that carries herself like a queen is not enugh to make you give thanks and praise I don't know what is. Take Ms. Edmunds and embrace her. She's not Monica. There will never be another Monica but there will never be another Ms. Edmunds either. Don't sleep bruh."

I gave some thought to Trip's words. I was still trying to shake Monica's memory and in two days I would have to get back to work with Mr. Medina who was the very embodiment of Monica. This might be the the toughest thing I'd done with since her passing.

Mommy and Sin were in love with the villa even more so than when they'd first visited. And when I put the deed in both their names and handed them it I thought they'd died and gone to heaven. They loved

what Kree and the decorators had done with the place

but mama was insistent on putting her own touches to

it. Cynthia was the same rearranging almost everything

to her own specs. They were comfortable and for the

most part happy although mama protested vehemently

about the maid and cook coming in once a week.

"Been doing these things all my life. Don't

know what makes you think because you got a few

dollars that I can't do them now. Next thing you know

you'll be tryna' ship me off because you got a nice little

pamphlet in the mail sayin' how they have more

amenities than you have at home and caring adults to

assure quality assurance for your loved ones."

Both Nazar and Cynthia fell out.

"Got you two heathens pegged, don't I?"

Mrs. Muhammad said grinning broadly at her two

children. "Probably ship me off the first time I close

my eyes to take a nap. Your daddy always warned me that this day was coming. Probably turn this place into a den of inequity with liquor and drugs just a flowing, with half naked women and the music at fever pitch."

"Your mother has quite the imagination, baby brother," Cynthia said wiping the tears from her eyes.

"Funny thing is I like it so make sure she gets the extra tablet in her tea at lunchtime."

"Gotcha."

"I wouldn't put it passed either of you. Lord! Now I've gotta watch my food."

Both of Mrs. Muhammad's children laughed but not before Naz interrupted.

"Listen ma. I've got a meeting with Ms. Edmund in a few minutes. I'll swing back by and take you two out to lunch if you're of a mind to."

390

"Don't let that money burn a whole in your pocket son."

"I don't think mommy can even conceive of the contract you just signed, baby brother."

"Mommy may be more cognizant than you or I of how easy

money comes and goes," Naz said winking at his mom and kissing his sister on her forehead. "Listen do you want to do lunch after my meeting?"

"Your sister may. I'm going to spend my first couple of days relaxing and catching up on my soaps and watching my food. But you two have fun."

An hour later, Naz pulled up in Old Negril in front of the tallest and only high-rise office building in the downtown square. The elevator ascended with all haste and he soon found himself at the penthouse suite on the sixteenth floor.

The receptionist was a thick, buxom woman of about forty who was attentive to all of the nine or ten clients in the lobby. The men couldn't take their eyes off of her and were stuck on her like metal to a magnet as she moved around the room. Nazar found the whole affair quite comical.

"Mr. Muhammad. Ms. Edmunds will see you now."

Folks who'd been sitting there a lot longer than Naz turned to each other in silent protest.

"Hey baby," Kree said pushing her way into Naz's arms. Naz kissed her before leading her to her chair and having a seat himself.

"What's up my beautiful Black brother?"

"Have an idea that I want you to

run with."

"Go ahead. Shoot," she said

shuffling through the pile of papers on her desk 'til she

finally found what she was looking for.

"I was thinking of setting up a

non-profit around the children on the island with a couple

of gyms where they have all the recreational activities

including boxing available to them, but I want it coupled

with an educational contingent."

This had not been at all what

Kree expected when Naz called to schedule a meeting.

Pushing the plush, leather chair back away from her

desk she suddenly found herself in deep thought.

Finally, and after a few minutes Kree pulled herself

back to the desk resting her elbows on it and holding

393

her head in her hands she stared directly into Naz's eyes.

"I think we've got the Pepsi contract on the table. And I was just thinking how we may need a foundation as an umbrella foundation to defer some of these taxes. At the same time, we could be doing some reputable charity work with the proceeds and you walk in with this. I think it's a marvelous idea and this addresses one of our most pressing needs and that's our children."

"So, you'll get started on that?"

"I will and will get a rough draft over to you by mid-week. Will that be all?"

"What's Pepsi talking?"

"Tenty-five to thirty million but if I could get Coke involved we would could start the bidding at fifty. There's no telling where we would have topped off at. I'm still extending invitations to Coke but this is a tricky situation. We wait too long, and Pepsi may withdraw its offer."

"Okay, well I'm sure you'll work it out and listen this is my last weekend before I go into training. Trip also informed me that I may be overlooking a gem in my midst so if you're not busy I'd like to share your company and perhaps consider reassessing this jewel in my midst."

"Sounds enticing. Give me some time to think it over. I'll give you a call later."

"Or you may consider surprising me. I'll be at Boston's place at around eight."

"I'll consider your offer Mr. Muhammad," Kree smiled before standing and extending her hand.

Things were moving now spinning almost out of control but Naz kept things simple having a cup of black coffee and a grapefruit before running two or three miles along the beach. The rest of the day met with the same routine except for dinner where his cook, Jo, a pudgy, cute little Jamaican girl who loved Gregory Isaacs would sing as she created the most nutritious and delicious Jamaican delicacies. His favorite was the codfish fried in it's own oil with onions and red and green peppers as a side and the fungi a yellow cornbread mix waiting to be used as a base. Talk about something good. That and a bottle of Red Stripe and it was naptime.

Mama had volunteered me for her little book group she'd gotten started with some local women she'd met at church. So, everyday after Joe and I'd finished my lunch I'd sit back with my book and look out over

the ocean until I was ast asleep. Every day I'd take that

book. I don't believe I've read a page yet. I really

don't think this book club of hers is a good idea. All-in-

all I guess life is going pretty well right through here.

Everyday that goes by I think of Monica less and then I

feel guilty as if I'm not giving her her time and paying

homage to her. But then how long am I supposed to

grieve. The Indians would let you grieve and then one

day say you were done. I keep waiting for someone to

tell me I'm done. I feel like I've done my time and I

know this for sure. Not one day that I was grieving on

Monica's behalf would she have wanted me to. She

would have wanted me to get on with my life and to

continue living. She wouldn't want me to waste my

time grieving. She'd want me to stand up strong and be

a man,

I felt like I was mired in quicksand. I wanted to move ahead but when I wanted to give of myself I was afraid that that person too would be snatched away so I was hardly ready for any type of relationship. I had to be the the only brother in the world who had the complete good fortune to meet two of the brightest most beautiful Black women on God's green earth and having second thoughts.

Truth was I like everything about Kree Edmunds. Bright and beautiful she was not only well-schooled with an air of class and sophistication that separated her from other women. She was the kind of sister that would draw attention just by entering the room. That's the kind of woman Kree Edmunds was and I wasn't sure if I wanted to be committed to her. This same woman who was following through on her commitment to expanding my portfolio. And though I wasn't a household name, yet my bank account had grown exponentially. We'd grown to be extraordinary friends in only a short amount of time, but I knew that the way we were living bothered her.

And like that I ran into the house and up to the safe in my room and grabbed a fistful of dollars and threw them into a small duffel bag.

"Take me to Jade's, Sam."

An hour later, I was back. The ring was small but classy. Knowing her she wouldn't want anything to draw attention. Glancing at it he could see her smiling face.

"I tried to wake you earlier, but you were out. Where did you go? By the way your dinner's in the oven. Goat rolti with peas and rice. You're gonna love it. Plenty of proteins a few carbs. You going out tonight?"

"Probably."

"You taking Ms. Kree?'

"Probably."

"That's good. I like her. She really cool. She got money. She like you though. She down to earth. You would never know she paid. She good people."

"I'm glad you approve. You know when I initially met her I said I sure hope Jo approves of this woman," Nazar smiled.

"Oh, you're teasing me again," Jo laughed. "Good night Mr. Muhammad."

"Night Jo," he said watching as she got in her car and sped away.

Glancing at his watch he noticed that it was already eight fifteen. Grabbing his phone, he called Kree. "I'm still contemplating whether I want to meet this man who's still not sure if Kree's his cup of tea or not.

I'm better than that. In all honesty, I don't know of many women that can hold a candle to me and you're not sure. Nigga bye."

Naz had to laugh. He hadn't seen the homegirl side before. Picking up his phone he called her back.

"Kree, sweetheart."

"Listen Nazar. I'm on a fast track. My business. My life. I know what I want and don't ever have to wait or be put on hold. I have entirely too much going for me to have to wait on anything. If it's not to be then I have to move on."

"Take a breath baby. I need fifteen minutes of your time is all. Can you meet me here at the house?"

"I'll be there in fifteen. This had better be worth it." Naz showered quickly and threw on his favorite blue suit and a pair of black loafers. Should he tuck the shirt in or just let it hang. Yeah. He'd just let it hang out.

The glasses were chilled, and he champagne was on ice.

Hearing the car pull up he was surprised to find a car full of women.

"Wait here. No, you can't meet him. Stay in the car. I'll be right back."

"Hey Naz. What's up? You said you wanted to see me?"

"Yes. I kinda wanted to spend some time. I had something I wanted to ask you."

"Oh well, go ahead. Ask away."

"No sweetheart. I think I'll wait for a more opportune time. You go ahead and have fun. Call me when you get some free time."

"You sure? The girls can go without me if you had something special planned."

I did but at that moment I just had an uneasy feeling. If she could be in love and yet switch it off and on like this is this really the person I wanted to spend the rest of my days with. I needed to give the idea of marrying Kree some more thought despite the objections made by Trip and Sin. After all this was my life.

That night I lay alone in the bed wondering if it were me. How could I have everything I'd always wished for and still be unhappy and dissatisfied? Perhaps it was because the one thing I wanted in life wasn't possible. I wanted my baby right here with me just as we had planned. We knew each other, felt each other, could finish each other's sentences. We were just meant to be with each other. If there were ever two people meant for each other. She was my idea of a soulmate. Now I could adapt and maybe even fall in

love with Kree but it was something that needed to be
planned and consciously worked at and that's not what I
believed love to be. Love was that old spontaneous
thing that jumped up on you without you seeing and
clinging like a flea on fat puppy. Love hangs there
unwilling to let go until you succumb into a sea of
irrationalities. That's just what it is. It can take you by
storm like a sudden spring rain that catches you only a
half a block from the crib. You don't even run. You
allow yourself to be immersed in its warmth. That's
just what it does to you. It makes you act irrationally.

This thing I feel for Kree is not love. I would be
making a mistake of monumental proportions if I were
to consider her even for a minute. She is but a friend. I
do neither yearn or crave for her when we apart. Love
will make you do both. That is why I know it s not
love.

I did not hear from Kree that weekend and it soon became apparent that she was really making a conscious effort moving forward. Monday was the beginning of training camp and if it was anything like previous training camps there was only one thing I was interested in seeing my first few weeks and that was my bed.

I met Mr. Medina at eight a.m. at the airport after doing my roadwork. He was glad to see I was still in shape and just glad to see me in general I do believe. He hadn't changed much in the weeks since I'd see him. He was still sharp-witted and focused at the task at hand.

"Brought you some tapes of Garcia. He's a crafty fighter. Real good boxing skills and has power in both hands. This is going to be your toughest fight in a lot of ways. This is going to be a chess match and if you fight the kind of fight I know you're capable of I see it going the distance with you winning a unanimous decision on points. You're going to have to put a ton of work in in the gym though. I want you to watch him, study him, know his every move before he does. Do that and you can beat him but if you're focus is anywhere but there in the next three months let me know now. I don't have time to waste. You still think about Mia?"

"Every day sir."

"I do as well but when we do remember that this fight is the one that she fought so hard to get you ready for. Let's continue to think of her every day in keeping her memory alive. And let's dedicate this fight to her memory."

Nazar smiled before embracing the older man.

"I think she'd like that."

Mr. Medina had little time to waste and soon had me in the gym sparring with some of the local talent but he like his daughter was more concerned with my defensive prowess and went even further than the one-armed defense. Mr. Medina had both his arms bound and all he had left was his feet to help him avoid trouble. It was a good strategy at this point in his career. By this time, he'd come to the realization that he could outbox his competition but Mr. Medina was challenging him to be a better defensive fighter. Showing him the intricacies of the fight game, he was taking him to the Pernell 'Sweetpea' Whitaker fight school where pure and true boxing aficionados knew that this was the purest form of boxing where the art of the game was to hit and not get hit and who to better attest to that than Pernell "Sweetpea' Whitaker.

For weeks and weeks Naz switched between the defensive strategies of Sweetpea and the offensive explosions of Garcia caught on tape. At the end of a month and a half Naz knew he was ready. Mr. Medina was sure too. No longer did he insist on Naz's jab. No. Now he just watched as it shot out in piston like precision with the snap and pop on it to snap many a sparring partners head back.

Trip would show up frequently to share the odds on the fight or just to watch me work out but now that he was retired he just seemed to have a whole lot more idle time to do some of the things he'd always wanted to do which in all appearances seemed to be little more than nothing.

"So, how did that thing go with Murph and Dez?" Murph's back out and running things again. Things are a whole lot tighter now. But he's accepted what's happened to him. He calls it an occupational hazard. He's good though. Punk ass Dez is on the lamb. Got reports he's staying over in Jersey. He's been spotted in Jersey City but the boy's seen once and then he's gone. I'm gonna get him though. It looks bad him being gone so long. Looks bad to his soldiers. Just looks bad in general so he's gonna have to show his ugly head before long."

"I feel ya."

"How are you and that pretty lady getting along?"

"Dissolved that whole issue over a month ago?"

"*Stop playing. What happened?*"

"It's not what happened. It's what didn't happen. Outside of my initial attraction I never felt that spontaneity or warmth that makes you a couple. If there was heart, there then there was no soul."

"I feel you. That's why I'm still single. Nobody ever really turned on that switch for me. Ain't no rush where you're concerned either. You're at the top of the world ma." Trip said smiling.

And he was right too.

The days leading up to the fight I spent in New York at home with mom and Cynthia. Bea offered me her place but I was intent on keeping our relationship as professional as possible and, so I politely declined.

Mr. Medina who insisted on spending the day before and eve of the fight with me watching tapes ate everything mama put in front of him hemming and hawing over each dish making he and mama fast friends.

The day of the fight was like any other day to me, but it seemed to mean the world to everyone but me if that makes any sense. You see to me it meant another day in the gym with some kid that was intent on bustin' me up and making a name for himself and that just wasn't

410

happening. It was the same every day. You see I was blessed with a God given skill to make light work out of whoever decided they had enough heart to get into the ring with me. The reputation already precedes me. They're already calling me the best pound-for-pound boxer in the world today. And I don't even have a belt yet. So, know that when you step into the ring with me I have bad intentions. My intentions are to beat you up, and get you out of there with the quickness, holmes.

And then I heard my name called and Team Naz headed for center ring at Madison Square Garden.

At the end of the first I heard pops talking to me softly, cooly.

"Beautiful son. You boxed beautifully. Reminded me of Ali the way you were dancing," the old man chuckled. "That's it son. Keep working the jab. It's frustrating him and pretty soon it's gonna allow you to get your combos in. Just keep touching him with the jab. Just keep touchin' him. And keep your hands up."

This pattern continued for the next five or six rounds and everything was playing out just as pops had said it would. Garcia was growing frustrated that he was not able to touch me and was becoming more and more wilder in his attempts to land a solid blow.

I was catching him now with good, solid, upper-cuts and hooks. I could hear my father now begging me to think for myself in the ring. And that I would never be ready for the pros until it became instinctual. And like so many times in the gym I dug two hard lefts to the body. I guess that was round eight or nine and I watched him crumple to the canvas and I knew it was over. I don't remember much after that. I went to my knees and thanked Him for blessing me. I then thanked Him for allowing Monica and Mr. Medina to come into my life. I thanked Kree for providing the security I needed for me and my family. And I thanked mommy and Cynthia for holding me down and keeping me humble. But if there was one thing I knew after that championship fight which elevated me to the elite division of champion was that I was done, finished with the fight game.

It was time to sit down and see exactly where I was financially. I wanted to go out with my wits intact and financially well off. I wanted to make sure all those that I cared about were taken care of and that such things as the gyms I had built would be self-sustaining through grants and local charities. Kree could update me and tell me what I needed to make this dream come true, so I called her and left a message that I wanted to meet.

The following day I received a call.

"It's Kree baby. I got your message and I'm not sure you got mine message but 'Cngratulations' again if you didn't."

"You are at the top of your game now man. Listen. Why don't you meet me on the square? We can decide where to go after that."

"I'm on my way."

Minutes later I pulled up in he new black Mercedes coupe Trip had given to me on winning my belt. It was sweet but a bit too much for me. Still, I drove through the streets of Negril as proud as a peacock as all the little boys and girls turned to stare at this famous person with the nice car. Pulling up outside of the café I noticed Kree but not before she noticed me.

"I like your whip. It suits you fine. Did you just purchase it?"

"Come on Kree. You know that's not me. I'm more of a Volkswagen Bug type of guy. No. That was a gift from Trip on winning the championship."

"So, how does it feel to be champion of the world?"

"Same way as it did before I won the belt."

"No different?"

"No different."

"I should have known it wouldn't change you. So, what is it that I can do for you Mr. Muhammad?"

"I'm considering retiring."

"Retiring? You can' be serious!"

"I am though. That last fight was the hardest fight I've ever had to get ready for?"

"Why was that?"

"Because I've lost interest. My focus wasn't there. I had to work just to stay locked in. I won because my skills were more proficient. I was more exact and precise. In short, I was a better boxer than he was or could ever hope to be. But what happens when I get into the ring with someone of equal ability and it comes down to heart and soul. Well, that's the end of my reign. You see the heart and soul is gone from me when it comes to where boxing is concerned."

"And this too goes back to losing Monica as well?"

"She was my trainer and my cornerman."

"And it doesn't feel the same without her in your corner? Is that where we're going with this?"

"Not exactly."

"So, what is it? Tell me what's changed since you last fought?"

"There's been no change. My father was my manager and trainer up 'til his passing."

"Oh, I didn't know. I'm sorry."

"In any case, he gave me my start and I've been living his dream ever since. When he passed I had some tough decisions to make. Did I even want to box? I didn't want to, but everyone told me it would be a disgrace if I didn't follow through on his dream. Winning the belt culminated his dreams and mine but you have to realize that I've been boxing since I was twelve. That's ten years of men trying to decapitate me every time I climb in the ring. Can you even imagine that every time you go to work there's a man waiting to beat on you with the intent of doing you seriously bodily harm? Just think about that for a minute."

"I can't even fathom such thoughts. It's both brutal and barbaric if you ask me. I watch but also recognize that it's an art form as well. A beautiful art form with so many nuances with the feinting and all. And they say you're the best at it, maybe the best to ever do it so no I can't understand your wanting to leave when you've just been christened king. See it through. And I'm not saying see it through for the sake of being the greatest boxer of all time or anything like that. I'm just saying that with each win think of how much more power you will garner and with this power and given the podium or bully pulpit you can make some real changes."

"At what price? What you're not understanding is that each time I step into that ring the closer I get to God. And much as I love Him I'm not sure I'm ready to meet him quite yet."

"I still think you're missing the point Blackman. When you are in such a commanding post as you are it is no longer about you. It used to be Naz is a contender and a good guy. Now it's Naz the champ is rich. Now the question is how does Naz change the world to make it a better world. You feel me? You have a higher calling and if boxing was your means of getting you where you are today then you ride it out for the sake of others. Make life better for others while you have the opportunity."

"That's easy to say when it's not your neck on the line."

"What it's called is *sacrifice*. I don't think either Malcolm or King looked favorably on their own violent deaths. And yes, they knew their deaths were imminent and would be violent, but each accepted it as a sacrifice they made for the greater good. Neither was forced to take on the issues of an entire race. But they readily accepted the challenge. Accept the challenge Nazar. Don't abandon your potential. Start using it."

"What are you doing tonight?"

"Don't have anything planned. Why are you asking?"

"Thought I'd come over and cook dinner for you.
Maybe smoke a blunt or two while I crawl up in your
arms and listen to some music. And talk more about
how you are going to impact the world"

"That shit you be smoking will make you stupid."

"Was already stupid so I don't have to worry too much
about that." Kree smiled. "So whatcha think
handsome?"

"Sounds like a plan to me. Shall we say eight?"

"Eight it is."

Winning the belt now had him over a hundred million in
long term endorsement deals. Kree had everything
packaged very nicely so that he would receive financial
explosions at regular intervals of his life to account for
any errors, or botched financial dealings or changes in

the stock market. On an uneventful year where none of these things occurred Nazar might have an easy ten million at his disposal.

Kree started looking past his financial earnings when he hit the hundred-mil milestone. At this rate his grandchildren's grandchildren would still be sitting pretty. The overly socially conscious Kree with all of new found wealth had never wanted for anything but with this new-found wealth she could finally follow through with her own dream of impacting the world for the better. Now all she needed was a partner. And with Trip joining she and Naz as the face they could really make some things happen. They could shake up things a little bit. They could do big things.

Still, it seemed like Naz wasn't comprehending or maybe he just wasn't understanding. He just wasn't processing. He may not have even considered his worth to the rest of us just because he was a success.

He was so goddamn humble and introverted that he

doesn't even recognize who he is, or what he is. But

Kree Edmonds was going to lay it on the line tonight.

'You ain't just on your block with the fellas now.

You're famous nigga. Wake up and smell the coffee. We

almost in the Jay and Beyonce ballpark. You know what

I'm sayin'? That money gives you one of two choices.

You can spread the money and love the way Prince did it.

You know, incogNegro and nobody now.

That's when you have true goodness in your heart.

That's some beautiful shit right there Negro. That's

some beautiful shit he did, and no one even knew 'til

after his death. Anyway, it's that or you can let that

money be used as a platform to do the same thing as

well as letting the rest of the world be exposed for not

doing enough. Embarrass them into helping you make

a better world. And you've got to keep fighting to keep

you a household name, so you can keep affecting the world.

Look at Ghandi. Look at John Lennon. One man is all it takes to change the world. You can be that man Nazar. And if you need me I'll be there however you want me to support you.

In his arms that night they listened to Masego while she recounted her thoughts from earlier in the day.

"Wow. You must hold me in really high esteem. When you mention names like Lennon and Ghandi."

"Don't forget Malcolm and Martin."

"Whoa mommy. I'm still trying to handle Lennon and Ghandi."

"But don't you see those are just men who decided one day that they were meant for something bigger than what they were doing and let their voice be heard."

"And what voice is it that you think I have Kree?" "The

same one that brought you to my office with the

proposal for me to build two gyms on each end of the

island for the children. The thoughts behind those ideas

are all good. All I need now for you to do now is

express the reasons behind you doing so. Not a lot but

just enough to say you know that guy Naz is a pretty

good guy. You just keep feeding them kibbles and bits

'til you have them eating out of your hand where you can

run for governor. Okay, that may be down the road a

piece but nothing's out of scope, out of the realm of

possibility."

"And you're going to tutor me. I am a boxer, but I have no

public persona and don't really mesh well with the so-

called upper class."

"A few months under my tutelage and you'll be as comfortable as a duck in water."

They did not make love but walked up the beach to Boston's Place where they had one drink which they babysat for much of the night as they talked and giggled under the moonlit sky.

The next morning both awoke to the smell of bacon.

"Morning. Hey girl. I saw your car out front, so I took the liberties. Nothing fancy just a little fresh, fruit, a little protein with the scrambled eggs and bacon although we all are aware of the fact that the pig is a nasty, filthy animal. And for those that can't believe that there's life without carbs you'll find half a toasted bagel with cream cheese and jelly Mr. Muhammad,"

"Oh, my goodness. Kree please tell me that I'm dreaming and that's not Jo up in here on a Saturday morning looking like she just kissed Jesus. Don't they

425

serve out hangovers in your neighborhood. Or were you just sent here to torture me?"

"Oh, stop being mean Naz. Look at this delicious breakfast. You ought to be on your knees kissing the ground she walks on."

"Kissing the ground, she walks on. I purposely gave her Saturday's off, so I could recuperate. She's a nut. She knows it. I know it. You're the only one that's not getting it. Tell her Jo. Tell her there's nothing you like more in life than seeing if you can drive me looney with lectures on the different types of foods and their nutritional value or it's some long-winded conversation on she who has a friend that is going through some male-female relationship issues. And what do I always tell you? I don't know because I very rarely get into relationships. If a relationship turns into drama then chances are I shouldn't be in that relationship. Isn't

that what I tell you. And then she has another friend

with another problem. And now she's here on a

Saturday on her day off. Who sent you? Someone

really has it in for me. Listen Jo. I'll pay you if you

you just go home and stay home until Monday. How's

that?"

"That sounds good Mr. Muhammad, but I've already

started the salmon croquettes for lunch. So, what did

you two do last night?" Josephine said grinning from

ear-to-ear. "Do you mind turning to the cooking

channel," she said pulling up a chair in front of the

television.

"Oh, hell I might as well get up," Naz said feigning

anger. By this time Kree was doubled up in laughter.

"So much for a quiet Saturday morning in bed with a

loved one. You just can't get good help nowadays."

"Oh, I'm leaving you you big baby. But seriously Mr. Naz I was thinking."

"Well, that's a first,"

"What's that?"

"You thinking," Naz laughed.

"Do you two go on like this all the time?"

"All of the time," they both said in unison.

"But seriously Mr. Muhammad why don't you have a party. This house could hold a hundred easy and me and my girls can handle the food and refreshments and my cousin can Dj. He's one of the hottest dj's on the island and he's flexible. You know what I'm sayin'. He can mix hip hop with a little reggae flavor to keep everyone happy. So, what do you think? It would give the island a chance to meet Nazar 'One Time'

Muhammad. It would be like you opening yourself up and welcoming the island."

"You may just have something there Jo," Kree said warming to the idea quickly. And I know just the young, wanna be, blue bloods to invite. They'll want to donate and pledge just to be on the ground floor with the hottest new commodity on the market. Nazar 'One Time' Muhammad. Let's make it for a month form this Saturday. Jo, you and I will need to sit down and do a budget for the whole affair."

"Sounds good girl. What do you think Mr. Naz?"

"I don't know that what I thinks makes that much of a difference."

"Oh, it does but your promotional team sees it from a completely different perspective. This is exposure and if we're to be a household name, a brand we need exposure."

"You're not getting it at all Kree. I came down here to relax and get rid of all the camera flashes in my face. I don't cherish the limelight. I enjoy my space baby, me peace and quiet. That's what I'm most looking for right through here. Not the parade and the circus. You feel me sweetheart?"

"So old to be so young but yeah I can understand. So, we won't go all out. We'll keep it an island house party. I'll invite some of my friends and some notables it might be worth you getting to know on the island and I guess Jo will invite some of her friends. You might want to invite a few of yours from up top and we can just chill on the beach for a couple of days."

"Sounds good. Especially for some of my people coming from New York. Gives them a lil' time to chill and relax before heading back home."

"We can take them up the river the first night for the festivities and take everyone shopping at the open market in Montego Bay the next morning."

"Handle your business my beautiful African sista."

"And if you get back in this bed you can handle your business," Kree said smiling coyly.

"You gonna run with me this morning?"

"If you'd like me to my king."

The two made love, then ran along the beach before making love again. Jo led the crew in party preparations and before you know it the house was filled with speakers and turntables. A nice sized dance floor was carved out of the adjoining living rooms. A

live band specializing in the cool, melodic sounds of

Lover's Rock was put to entertain the older crowd

looking to just chill on the beach. Jo and her crew were

busy designing a menu for both the health conscience

and others.

The night of the party, it seemed like half of New York

had already arrived. Trip actually had to charter a large

jet to fly some of his peeps in. Of course he charged

them all an astronomical rate to come to Naz's new

home. Each time the car returned from the airport

there was another call.

Negroes Naz hadn't seen in ages were flying in and Naz

wondered if Trip hadn't somehow constructed some

kind of early release program at Rikers. I mean there

were real live gangstas that had made the Trip on Trip's

account. I knew them all, had grown up up with most

of them. To them this was the ultimate celebration of

local hero makes good. They all seemed happy for me and all came bestowing gifts. Most were monetary but every now and then one would bestow a car on me. This was the typical conversation.

"My man. What's up my nigga? When they told me you was still undefeated and was fighting for the belt the night after I got out my niggas asked me what I wanted to do. You know the typical shit. Did I want a party? Did I want some hoes? I was like no what I really want is tickets to see my man Naz win this belt. They was like 'Ahh man you don't know no Naz.' I was like me and Naz grew up together. He used to make me run everyday in gym class cause he hated to run. But any way I went to see you win the belt and I

noticed one thing."

"What's that?"

"You sure learned to run good," Nicky B. laughed.

Naz had to laugh.

"I knew we were going to get out Naz. I'm proud of you man."

"Already."

Naz smiled at the thought of Trip chartering a plane. It was easier for his element to travel this way Naz knew. He also knew that most of them weren't leaving New York without a piece. They were a paranoid bunch always thinking there was someone trying to put them out. And in many instances, this was true.

"What's up Murph? I was hoping you'd make it bruh. By the way this is Kree."

"Nice to meet you. Damn Naz I thought you was my man. We always been boys. I really thought you was my man though Naz. I know Trip told you I got shot."

"Oh, that. Yeah Murph. Go ahead and cuss me out. You're right I should have flown up and checked on you in the hospital, but you know how I am. If it's drama and hurt I run the other way. The shit that happens to us is because of the choices we make. I'm sorry you got shot and I'm sorry that two Black men gotta resort to pulling out guns to resolve an issue. But the choice you made to take over Trip's spot put you in a position to get shot. That was your decision not mine. Choices baby. I still love you Murph and I am glad you came. You can stay here in the house with us or you can stay with Trip at the big house. Just want you to know that you're home here."

"I love you too bruh. Now let me go mingle. I think I smelled something good coming from the beach," Murph said hugging Naz tightly.

"Now I know he's a gangsta," ree said letting out a slow deep breath.

Naz chuckled lightly.

"One of my best friends. Grew up with four guys. Trip who you already know and who acted as my big brother and protector. Then there was Murph who acted as my personal bodyguard when I was a punk and couldn't fight. Murph used to beat up all the kids who would try to bully me. He was working in the same capacity for this kid who was vying with Trip for the top man in Harlem and decided to shoot Murph when he took over for Trip in his efforts to consolidate all of Harlem. That was a bad move. Brought Trip out of retirement.

You see Trip is about loyalty so when you mess with one of his family members you can pretty much expect some push back. Then there's my boy Noah who was all world at anything he touched. We're the same age and came up together. We started boxing together and he was the only person I ever stepped into the ring with that would get the better of me every time. I'm certainly glad he decided to switch sports. Went on to become the best point guard New York has ever seen."

"And what happened?"

"Wish I could call it. One day he just disappeared from the whole scene. I guess everything just became too much. Now he's sporting a two hundred dollar a day habit."

"Oh no. How's he support it?"

"By any means necessary. Robbing, stealing, sticking up people, stores whatever it takes to feed his habit. We grew up in the same building. He's like a brother to me. I don't know what happened to make him give up on life. We've never talked about it. But we know that if the drugs don't kill him someone will so Trip and I set him up in this flat, so he has somewhere to rest his head and Trip keeps him supplied so none's out there trying to shoot him over some dumb shit. Butchie would have completed the four but he was wild and got himself shot about four years ago. His crazy ass decided at sixteen to go on a grown man job and try to rob an armored car. He was shot and killed. That was Butchie always reaching for the moon and the sky."

"Wow! I only see shit like this on television. Won't be any shooting will there?"

"No. I think that as long as everyone is mellow we'll be fine."

"Let's hope so."

"From what Trip tells me there more interested in doing business and making a connect between Jamaica and New York. There will be no violence while they're conducting business and trying to establish a connection."

"So, the governor may very well be in the midst of a major drug deal going down?"

"Very good possibility."

"So, help me understand. Your friends are gangstas but you're not. How did that happen?"

"I wouldn't say they were necessarily gangstas. I'd say they were entrepreneurs and businessmen. Not a whoe ot of difference between them and the Kennedy's except the Kennedy's did it on a grander skill. Where we grew up there weren't a whole lot of opportunities and the few opportunities given they seized and have been quite successful with it. And they have the respect to push me and keep me away from the dirty side of it. I know little or nothing about their business and that serves well for both sides. But if I were to look to them for anything they would be there. They're like brothers to me."

"So, you can assure every one's safety with them all being here?"

"I'd like to think that I could and again relax. These folks were invited to a party. That's all there here to do is have a good time so stop your worrying. Remember this was your idea."

I knew the contingent from New York and was glad they were there. I knew how they must have appeared to Kree though. These brothas came hard. A pair of Levis, a fresh white tee and a pair of Air Force Ones and they were ready for the world. They had all to a man established their reps in the toughest neighborhoods in New York which somehow equated to all having belts. The biggest thing among them was respect. They'd earned it and now demanded it. Any infraction and you could very be bodied up. Overhearing a conversation from guests at the party responding to the invasion by the New York bad boys she asked.

"So, who is this Naz character I hear he's a boxer hat grew up in New York but why do all his friends seem so hard. They scare me. If he's such a cool guy why does he hang out with all of these thugs?"

"Excuse me miss but I heard what you were asking about my boy. You're right in calling us bad boys.

New York is a tough city. You do what you have to do to survive. A few of us just came together and agreed that there's strength in numbers and being that we all grew up in basically the same area we have a style of our own. As Naz goes he's like family. We all grew up together. Naz was always cool with us because he made it a point not to invade such places as business.

He had little or no interest in what we did, and I don't think he wanted to know. But you know how the streets talk and I'm sure he's now fully aware, but he wasn't judgmental. You know what I'm sayin'. If he liked, you then he liked you. And would come looking

441

for you to go run some ball at the gym. Naz was a gym

rat and he always found time to hang with his peoples

at the gym or around the way. He'd run a full court and

talk shit the whole time. When it was over he'd hug

you and then you'd sit down and catch up on how the

kids and wife were doing. You know real talk from real

people. Naz good people. He always been good people

and he always come through when a nigga needs him.

That's my nigga! that answered your questions

sweetie," Tony Rich said before lighting his Black and

finding his way up the beach.

"Some mighty fine women here and with some class

too. These are ladies not like them trifling hoes back

home, "Trip laughed.

"No doubt. Can't just grab her arm and head for the

bedroom. You got to go through the steps and put

some work in."

"It's gonna cost you a nice little tidy sum too."

"I'm gonna leave you to put that work in my brother. You know that's not how I roll."

"You might wanna walk up to Naz's crib. His cook invited some of her friends, some locals. They might be a little more to your liking. They down to earth. Same party but different clientele. These here are the movers and shakers from New York and the islands.

Naz is where the real party is. They eatin' and drinkin' and having a ball just chilling on the beach getting blunted up. And I hear his cook is off the hook. Her name's Jo. You might wanna link up you fat motherfucker," Trip said laughing at his man Murph.

"I ain't fat nigga."

"No, you're really not Murph. You just big. Murph you know that you're the biggest man I've ever seen.

443

You're like a small mountain."

"Okay. What is it? Crack on Murph night?"

"Nah, man. C'mon bruh. You know you're my heart and soul but seriously what's up with you?"

"You've been the same size ever since I've known you and I think we started hanging out when we were seven or eight and you were the same size then."

"Stop lyin' Trip."

"I'm not lying. You had th whole school terrorized because you were so damn big. Naz didn't even know you and used to walk and hide behind your left leg. You wre so big you didn't even know he was there. That way the other kids thought he knew you and wouldn't pick on him. You remember that?"

"No. And you don't either you lying motherfucker," Murph said laughing out loud. "Now what you say that girl's name that prepared the food?"

"Jo. Josephine. Jus ask Naz to point out his cook. Did you meet Naz's new woman? She's that real hot shit. She's a keeper if you ask me. And making him crazy money and he ain't feelin' her. I want you to meet her and tell me what you think. She was the realtor on this place and I'm telling you she hooked me up. Did the same thin. when Naz bought his but like I said he aint feeling her for some reason?"

"You ain't givin' him time to grieve and get Monica out of his system. You know he has to be devastated. You know Naz ain't never really connected with no female other than as friends. It was different with Monica. She knocked his ass out. It was the first knockout of his career. My nigga was in love. He got to be hurtin' a whole lot more than he lettin' onto."

445

"You bout ready to walk down there?"

"Yeah, you strapped?"

"Man, you ain't in New York. We goin' to Naz's house."

"Alright. I ain't the one gonna be caught slippin'."

"Damn Trip don't you ever relax?"

"In this business you relax and you're dead. Ignorance ain't just located in New York. They've got ignorant, sheisty, motherfuckers down here jealous cause you got on shit they could never hope to wear unless they rob you for yours. And when they come I'll be ready for them."

"You put it like that and I'd better grab mine. You go on. I'll be along shortly."

Moments later, Murph arrived and never one for having a great deal of tact and in lieu of his enormous appetite

446

he went in search of Jo the cook. He figured since she was a chef they'd have much to talk about as he fashioned himself one as well.

Murph was even more surprised that Jo was warm, down-to-earth and cute in her own sort of way. He liked to think of her as pleasantly plump and Naz was only too happy to see the two hit it off. For now, she would at least be out of his hair.

Kree found herself sucked into one of Trip's power meetings on the redistribution of New York's five boroughs where everyone was happy with their share. When she walked away it was almost as if she'd attended a Harvard seminar and being introduced to Machiavelli for the first time. She found it truly enlightening. She saw these men from a new perspective. Given the right environment and tutelage and any one of them may have been a CEO for one of

Forbe's Five Hundred Companies. Chips just hadn't fallen in their favor. And yet they had succeeded in their respective fields despite the odds. Kree was impressed and promised herself she would sit down with Trip, Priest, Tony Rich and a few of the other New York bosses whose philosophies on business and life in general had impressed her. These were all Naz's counterparts, none more than twenty-three or twentyfour years old and many, if not most were skirting the edges of being millionaires. The investment potential was undeniable. And there was no better advertisement than Naz and Trip having already purchsed beach front properties from her.

The following day Bea had the two tour buses ride by her beachfront properties handing out her business cards to anyone interested on their way to Montego Bay. Everyone seemed sad to leave the island festivities but no one more than Murph who had fallen hard and quickly for Jo and her cooking prowess. And it was Murph who became Kree next customer purchasing a modest beach front bungalow for he and Jo.

All in all, it was a joyous occasion. My Negroes from New York promised to reciprocate within the next few weeks and we all looked forward to it. Bea was especially curious. It seemed to send a chill so close to someone who had more than likely taken another's life. Most people would have been cordial and kept it moving but it was the whole thug culture that she was in awe of. The mentality. The way they saw the world. It was all so intriguing to her.

"Heard Murph purchased the bungalow at the beginning of the point."

"Yep."

"I should have signed a contract to get a percentage for my referrals ," Naz said staring Kree in the eyes.

"Oh, stop crying you know I've got you. Get a couple more of your friends to buy homes here and we can call it Gangsters Paradise," Kree grinned.

"You can't get over that can you?"

"No, it's just hard for me to believe that in 2018 brown men still carry guns to have to protect themselves from other brown men. It's just hard for me to believe that we haven't progressed any farther than that."

"Let's be careful not to be stereotypical and lump everyone into the same category. I live there in the jungle in the heart and soul of the violence and madness. It's a different culture. It's a cuture that demands you protect yourself at all times. For many of my friends that showed up their mentality is to protect themselves at all times and never get caught slippin' where you ain't strapped. Where I'm from tha could very well mean the death of you. I've never been involved but have seen more than I'd like to even think about. You've got to realize that Trip and I grew up in the same building and he began slingin' right outside our building since he was ten or eleven. Always had twelve or thirteen people working for him and was stackin' real paper even then. So, I got a first-hand view. I think the only reason I didn't turn out like Trip e between us is that I had a father that kept me under his wing and pointed me in another direction. He was a stickler for having a sound mind, and body. So, he stressed education and sports. He pushed, and I excelled. That's the only difference between Trip and myself. But that's what that culture breeds. It's almost a miracle if you escape it.

My father was very active in the community. He started the largest well-known gym in Harlem. But his biggest thing was getting the kids off the street and into the gym."

"And how did that work for him?"

"He used to always say that if he saved one kid from the streets his life as a success. He ended up saving hundreds. When he passed away I was expected to continue doing his work in the community. You know the philosophy about giving back."

"Same thing we talked about earlier this week."

"Yes, but to be honest with you all I wanted to do was escape the madness."

"Do you still feel the same way?"

"Absoutely, well, to an extent I do. I'm tired of boxing. But I've come to realize after talking to you and my sister that I have a job to do and have a chance to impact and influence people so whether I am tired or not doesn't matter. I just have to get myself in shape mentally for the onslaught that's about to come."

"And we both know you're stronger than anything they try to throw your way."

"I'm glad to know you have such confidence in me pretty lady."

"What did you say when you won the championship? 'I'm on top of the world ma.' And now that you're on top of the world you're going to change it. When do you start training for your mandatory defense?"

"I'm thinking Trip should be getting me that information any day now. Soon as the commission let's him know but I would say three months."

"Okay, Naz what I want you to do on your time off is to do a sort of a fact-finding trip through some of the most afflicted areas of our coumtry and I want you to talk to the people and see how they're living. Then when you return I want to know what about their living conditions bothered you the most. Then we can sit down and see how we can realistically change these situations so that

these people, our neighbors can achieve a better quality

of life.   Take Mr. Medina and someone else that will

help you see things and put them in perspective."

"I like the idea. I've never really been anywhere

outside of my neighborhood." Naz nodded. "I really

would like to see how my people are living or surviving

out here."

"I think it will be an eyeopener. I want it filmed and if

it's anyway close to what I think will transpire we'll have

a documentary at the very least. We can call it

'The Other America'."

"I like that. When do we leave?"

"Just as soon as you'd like," Kree said handing him a

manila envelope.

"What's this?"

"Your itinerary. The cities, the stops, the duration. It's all there baby."

"So, you already knew I was going to do this?"

"I didn't have anything to lose but a few ideas and I always have plenty of those. I know you're good people with a heart and a conscience, so I knew that if given the podium and a chance to help others you wouldn't, couldn't just turn your back and walk away. You just ain't built that way."

Naz had no reply.

'Dallas, Houston, L. A. He hadn't even heard of a lot of the cities on the list. Yes, this would be a good trip. She had a knack of pointing things out that he hadn't noticed. In short, she was insightful and had a broader more abstract way of thinking that he needed to help him broaden his horizons. But she had to work. The only other person I knew that would take the trip

seriously was Sin. So, I asked her if she were

interested. She thought it was a marvelous idea and

was all in. But against Kree's better thinker I decided

to take Trip.

It was Sunday. We were to leave on Wednesday and

Kree spent every minute in my company.

"I can come see you if you get lonely. Just call me. I

love you Naz," she said loud enough for both Trip and

Cynthia to hear before kissing him on the cheek and

rushing out of the airport.

"And I thought you told me you and her were history,"

"She ain't nothin' but a play thing for Naz. He ain't really

thinkin' about her but I'll tell you one thing. She ain't

playin' when it comes to you and you'd better be

cognizant of the fact that she controls your money.

You'd actually be smart to marry her. You'd better learn to love her."

"That's real talk bruh. And she rampin' up bundles every day. You may have to say fuck love and take one for the team. You could do worse bruh."

There was the boarding call and it couldn't have come at a better time. Why was everyone rushing for him to get married. Her he was only twenty-two. He was the welterweight champion of the world. Those were two reasons that he should not even consider marriage in his opinion but everyone he knew that was close or in his inner circle all said the same thing when it came to Kree. They'd never even mentioned marriage when it came to Monica. Perhaps everyone was seeking a security blanket to rest my head during my grieving process. Maybe I just wasn't seeing Kree in light of Monica's death. Perhaps Kree was the reason. I didn't know. I'd consider all of these things on this trip but right now I'm going to close my eyes.

New York never seemed to change aside from getting faster. I was surprised to find out though on my return that there had been places I never had a mind to go to or reason to right here in the city. We went to Fort Greene in Brooklyn and spoke to a few of the residents about the housing conditions and what they most needed before shooting over to East New York once named as the murder capital of the country. It was a community of Blacks and Hispanics devastated by the influx of drugs and what was left were the bear remnants that had once been a thriving community. We then went to the Fort Apache section of the Bronx. I was familiar with this neighborhood as I had once dated this girl from up there. And the only reason we broke up was that it was too dangerous going up there. I wasn't exactly sure I wanted to go up there now with a reporter and camera man that both looked like they were more ready for Princeton than the Fort Apache part of the Bronx.

"I love you both. But you two stay on the bus this round." Trip said. "This one's strictly for Naz and me?"

"Okay. But may I ask why?" Renee the pretty, young journalist asked.

"This is Fort Apache and they'll be able to spot you and size you up with the quickness. Once they see you're lames it's basically open season. Naz and I look like we fit even though a true bad boy will know we're from uptown and not the Bronx."

"I can't tell. Are you sure you're not making more to this than there is?"

It was Naz who responded this time.

"Stay on the bus," was all he said before heading off into the darkness. Trip was soon at his side.

"Man, I mean she's a sweet little girl. I even thought about taking her up to the room."

"I was pretty sure you had the way she was sweatin' you back in Fort Greene."

"I considered it but I didn't want to be considered a pedophile."

"What are you talking about. She told me she's twenty-seven bruh."

"Chronologically. But if you talk to her she's all bright eyed and bushy tailed. She's all idealistic and wants to save the world because she's still innocent. When I talk to her I feel like I 'm talking to my two-year-old niece. She didn't grow up like we did. She's innocent. She don't know what time it is. She Black but she come from a different world. If I went up in that bitch that would be all she wrote. You feel me. She's innocent. It would be like taking candy from a baby. Real talk. She can't even conceive of who I really am. My daddy once told me when speaking of women that you don't always step in every hole you see. Probably the best advice the nigga ever gave me but yeah that girl will get us killed up here."

Trip nor I were comfortable and got the hell out of there before the word that two niggas were up there asking questions like social workers but dressed like Harlem niggas.

We all stayed at mama's that night and awoke at eight to board the bus that would take us to Newark first then to Camden, Trenton and Philly before heading west.

461

By the time Naz was finished with those four cities it was clearly visible that he was shaken.

"Man did you see how those people were living. I mean ain't nobody s'poze to be living under conditions like that. Roaches and rats everywhere. Man did you see the size of that motherfucker that went underneath the table in the living room?"

"How you gonna miss something the size of that monster. I thought it was a cat at first," Trio replied.

"I don't know why they don't do that," Sin said as we headed for the bus.

"What's that baby girl?"

"A cat. Why doesn't she just get a cat?"

"Shit the size of them motherfucker rats I can guarantee that they'd fuck up a good-sized cat," Trip laughed.

"You see I had my pistol loaded," Trip said continuing to laugh.

"Ain't the point. Who's the landlord? The woman said she complained and got no results," Naz screamed clearly agitated.

The reporter and cameraman who were within air shot turned to Naz.

"We have all of her information and the landlord's name and number. That's a city owned building for low income families. A phone call or two and we should have Ms. Warren's problem fixed. We all have several pictures of our little friend for proof."

"I can't believe they actually allow people to live this way and under these conditions. I'm sure the caseworker lives in a fairly nice home without rats and roaches running around like they're trying out for the four forty relay. So, if they walk in and see people

463

living under these conditions why isn't this reported and that building condemned.?" Naz asked innocently enough.

"You heard tenants say that all the apartments are in virtually the same condition," Cynthia chimed in. "All to a man said that they had rats."

"And that alone is reason enough to tear down those buildings and begin investment into some affordable low-income housing that the inhabitants can eventually own," Naz said speaking to the Camden news crew that assembled to see the newly crowned champ.

"So, champ what brings you to Camden?" one young white reporter asked.

"I'm pretty sure I've got a pretty accurate view of how the more affluent live in America from the media but often time we lose track of how the other half lives and, so I thought I'd get a bird's eye view. And for some reason I was sent here to Camden, New Jersey. I've seen but I am not here to expose or to comment on the conditions I've seen. I am only here to see how I may lend a hand in some way to alleviate the problem and make a few families quality of life just that much better," I said.

All seemed satisfied with this explanation and we packed up and left. The young Black female reporter was as astute as they came and after only fifteen minutes she had the word from the Deputy Mayor that he would look into the conditions that Ms. Warren and others were living under. She'd wait 'til the end of the week to call Ms. Warren to see if the city was active and moving on the building. She was good and was compiling a portfolio for the documentary on Naz and his feel-good campaign to fix the world. All Naz saw though was an awful lot of pain and suffering and Lord knows if Trip and Cynthia hadn't been there to ease his

own suffering Naz would have been a broke man.

At first, he wanted to know why he couldn't help but

after two weeks on the road he knew that the problem

couldn't be fixed without a helping hand here and there.

No, if all he had seen could be put together it required

FEMA. This was widespread devastation.

Sitting in New York he could never have imagined.

The richest country in the world and people were still

living in what amounted to squalor. There were so

many people suffering, just trying to make ends meet

on a daily basis and all too often falling short on the

basics like food to feed their children. He could only

imagine what Mexico must be like if they're rushing to

get here.

By the time he reached St. Louis a change could be seen

in all three but not so much as in Nazar. He was

ecoming bitter, somewhat meaner, older, more mature,

more reserved and if nothing else more insightful. He knew his work couldn't be limited to a gym or two.

In the end, he was conducting the interviews with the children and their most pressing wants and concerns. And all too often he heard the same thing.

"Sometimes I don't wish for nothing but for them to stop shootin' so much around here. Like you always be duckin' cause these fools all the time be shootin' and tryna kill each other."

This hurt Naz the most. Money and new homes wouldn't change the mentality. No longer did Naz go to sleep with little on his mind but he was committed to finding a solution to those problems and atrocities that he could somehow amend.

"Hey Kree".

"*Damn baby!* You don't know how good it is to hear your voice. How are you?"

"I'm good. I usually hear from you once or twice a week so when I didn't hear from you I wasn't sure if something was on your mind or you just didn't want to be bothered so I called Cynthia and she said that it was taking its toll on you. And you were doing your best to just hang in there and see it through. So I'm wondering why you didn't call me."

"Yeah, it hasn't been easy that's for sure. There's mad poverty out here and people are doing everything just trying to eat and for way too many it's just not enough. It's bad Kree. And the sad part about it is I can't do anything to help. I see it and when I'm introduced as the welterweight champ they know I have money and they look at me with hope in their eyes and I have nothing to give them. It's a damn shame that this should even be in a country as weathy as ours."

468

"Be patient young man. See the anguish, the pain, the suffering. Embrace it. When you go to dinners with senators, congressman and those big donors and you show the slide show of 'The Other America' with you speaking with all the passion and compassion of someone actually having been there they will feel compelled to open their checkbooks. Our foundation can then go about bringing in federal grants and other contributors that will enable us to alleviate some of those atrocities you've been seeing firsthand. And what you're feeling right through here will subside knowing that you are helping to alleviate the problem."

"Well, we're at the end of the road. We're in L.A for a week. It's the weekend. Why don't you fly out for the weekend?"

"Let me think about that. I'll call you back in an hour."

"What? Are you telling me that you have to break a date to come and see me?"

"Something like that," Kree said matter-of-factly,

"Sorry I asked now."

"Truth hurts."

"I'll talk to you."

"Ciao."

The day had been more than a little eventful when two gang members agreed that as long as they were living they would remain loyal to their sets and would like nothing better than to blow each other's head off with each gang member lifting his shirt to show he was equipped to make that happen.

Naz did his best to try to explain that they were so much better than that. That they were men. They were the leaders. You're fathers. But in the end, and when Naz had finished all they were convinced of was that the other was a hoe ass nigga that didn't deserve to live.

Trip lit a cigar as Naz walked over.

"I want you to know that I applaud you bruh. I was listening to you politicking with those young cats but they on some ol' crazy around the way shit I can't even relate to. How is this your turf? How you protecting some shit that you don't even own? And these niggas is killin' each other over city blocks with no money involved but because of the color they choose to wear.

I didn't leave the conversation. I wanted to see where you going to lead these niggas but when they gonna pull up and show their toolies in a public place I said let me go over here and get behind this marble column should these simple niggas get to shooting."

"Boys was just showin' out. Neither one wanted to die today. You could see that."

"Lord knows you got some good eyesight. I've had a different experience with guns. But any way are you glad your fact-finding mission is over?"

"C'mon man."

"Was rough on you wasn't it?"

"You don't know man. There was many a night I upped and left the hotel and just walked and cried rea tears."

"I didn't walk but I'm sure those were probably the same nights I shed a few tears as well. Those po' white folks in Appalachia did me in."

"You. I don't know how many hours I spent in that train's bathroom long after we left West Virginia. I never thought I'd ever cry over some white folks."

"We human, ain't we?"

"Baby girl didn't hide hers. Cynthia cried from West Virginia right on in to D. C. I think what really got her was that little girl going to the pail for some rain water to drink and just falling down when she found it empty. That was sad to watch.

Now the two little boys going to school dirty and them fighting over a pair of socks was a hoot to me. Talk about some comical shit. I don't think you were there for that one. These two little boys were having an out and out slugfest at seven thirty in the morning because they could only find two socks between the two of them. But their mother being a resourceful mother gave each of them one sock apiece and sent them off to school. That shit tickled me. But most of the shit I saw on this fact-finding journey only went so far as to confirm many of my suspicions about Black folks in America. Gave me a better perspective though. We are like the lost tribe of Israel. Each with its own separate agenda. We're not a unified front and therefore we pose no viable threat," Trip said. "I enjoyed the trip though don't get me wrong Naz. I'm glad you invited me to go. Found it very informative knowing that there's still so much racism. A lot of its institutionalized and will take a long time to erase but there's still a lot we can do to improve the quality of life for many of those people out there suffering. You feel me? It was sad, an eye-opener but we ain't got no time to hang our heads. We got too much work to do along with your title defense. We gonna need every dime with the work we got to do. You know Naz for the first time in my life I feel like I have a purpose in my life."

"I feel you bruh. That trip changed my life. I didn't know how good I had it or had bad others had it. Sometimes it was hard to watch but I know I have no choice but to try and fix things. I really believe that between you, me and Kree should be able to make some changes for the good of a whole lotta people."

"You really think so?"

"We'll see what Kree has in mind when we get back on the island tomorrow. She's been in constant contact with Renee working on the documentary, but she hasn't gotten our perspective and insight on what needs to be done."

"You really think we can make a difference Naz?"

"I have no idea but if this woman sent me out on this little fact-finding venture I'm pretty sure she had ulterior motives. She wants us to come back with a call to action.

She'll run by us how we should proceed next and that will be it." Trip laughed.

"So, we're nothing more than pawns in the game?"

"No, In Kree's eyes we're strong Black men without the knowledge to see or proceed in the larger world. You know how you were telling me Renee was twentyeight but just a kid to you. It's the same thing with

Kree. She knows we have money, but she also knows we're on another level when it comes to what we do with our money or how to invest it. And so we've let her handle our financial dealings and ain't never done anything but win." Naz said grinning and slapping Trip five.

"And we been winning big too. Anybody ever say anything to or about Kree and I might just have to body them," Trip laughed slapping Naz five again for good measure.

"Kree ain't hard to figure out though. I think she's like every other woman I know. She's treacherous and has ulterior motives for everything she does. Yo, bruh. Check it out. Follow me down this road for a minute. Peep this. You know the way she took you on the beachfront tour showing you all them pretty houses with everything about them in a shiny gold envelope, so you wouldn't forget on the way back to her office. There was no mistake about what house you wanted to buy by the time you got back. All she had was show you. She didn't really have to say a word. The houses sold themselves. All she had to was show 'em. Don't you see? She did the very same thing here. And what you may not know realize is that Kree has this whole Mother Theresa thing working secretly where. You see despite the way she is baiting us and drawing us in she is at heart a very giving and loving soul. She has grandiose plans on saving the world.

She expects us to come back screaming about all the injustices and poverty that's affecting us as a people and then together we're to pool our funds and go on this modern-day crusade."

"Yeah, that's pretty much what's up my nigga. Smart woman. She sold me. I'm down. We can start by unifying—you know bruh—just the three of us at first. You can use your platform as champ and get others to join us. We might just be able to make a difference bruh."

The two met with Kree later that week. After hugging each other the three met down and rehashed the trip, the problems and each with their own solution. But all agreed they'd kick the whole Tomorrow's the Future Foundation off with a thousand dollar a plate fundraising dinner. The documentary which had been

sent to Bea piecemeal from the very beginning of the

trip was now complete and was professionally done.

But then what would have anyone expected from Kree?

She was definitely wifey material, Naz thought, for

someone.

The documentary was sensational and when Naz

glanced over at Kree he couldn't help but notice her

crying freely. Trip did not try to hide his tears. And

between the three of us a bond was formed that day.

When it was over Kree turned to the two gentlemen

who sat before her.

"You two ready to take your show on the road following

the fight? What we can do is have the initial fundraiser

within the next month at my parent's estate.

Don't worry about the cost. I just want you to do the

introduction, Trip. Nazar I'm going to make sure you

have the most gut-wrenching speech following the

documentary that those wealthy do-gooders will bank

roll our whole concept. You're going to have them

eating out of your hands and feeding you at the same

time."

"Well, let's get this party started. Just tell me what you

want me to do," Trip said decidedly excited to be doing

his part to make the world a better place.

"All I need you to do is put out the word among your

friends with money. I'm looking for those that will be

down with a good cause that ain't stingy and will want

to participate."

"That shouldn't be hard to do. I know some pretty

good brothers that may be looking for something right

along these lines."

"They lookin' for a tax shelter is what they're lookin'

for. Somewhere to hide all that dirty money," Naz said

laughing.

"Charitable deductions can be used as write-offs. It's true," Kree said.

"And every one of Trip's boys knows it too," Naz laughed. "They been waiting for something like this. Probably just sitting there waiting on something just like this. You gonna elevate Trip to the status of king when this gets out. But please tell me how that's not money laundering?"

"Shut up Naz. Ignore his obnoxious ass Kree. Now what were you saying you needed me to do Kree?" Naz was laughing out loud by this point.

"You remember the conversation we had in the Bronx when we refused to let Renee get off the bus."

"What about it?" Trip asked hesitantly praying that Naz wouldn't blow the damn thing.

"Someone once said the innocence of youth is a beautiful thing," Naz said.

Kree knew that the references were meant for her but chose to ignore them for now. At the end of the meeting she concluded with.

"And I'll make sure our legal team looks into the possibility of any charitable contributions and the idea of money laundering as that is not my area of expertise just as the area of financial investing may not be another person's area of expertise or forte," she said shooting a quick glance in Naz's direction. "I don't know when you two begin training but I'm flying up to New York tomorrow to handle some business. You two are welcome to join me."

"I haven't gotten any word on when your mandatory title defense is, so you might as well go," Trip said looking at Naz. "I have to go up and try to play peacemaker between Murph and Dez since he's decided to resurface.

"Kree could you schedule me for a flight as well? I just have to check on mama and Sin and make sure they have everything they need."

"That's already been taken care of. And someone named Maine tried to contact you to let you know that he's having the biggest birthday bash New York has ever seen and he'd be honored if you two would attend. I think you should not only attend his party but be seen in and around every hot spot in the city. We need you to be a household name. What we need to do is keep your picture in the tabloids and market you champ. Anyway, I'll take care of it. Two weeks too long?"

"No. That's fine."

"Then we'll leave in the morning."

"Love you dear," Nazar said as he rose from the chair kissing Kree on the cheek. Trip followed suit. The two men left the office and got in the new Black Mercedes.

As Naz pulled off Trip acknowledged that he now understood Naz's hesitance when it came to Kree.

"Kree's been sheltered huh?"

"I tried to tell you. You couldn't find a nice, sweeter person and as you heard her tell me she's a financial genius, but she has her shortcomings and that shortcoming is that she's too damn nice. She's innocent. I mean I think if we were to link up I wouldn't want for anything but hell who wants that? I want a woman with some sass. You know what I'm saying? I need a challenge not a younger sister? I guess I feel about her way the you felt about Renee."

"With one difference. I never slept with ol' girl."

"C'mon bruh. Look at her. Girl is too fine."

"Yeah, and she's in love with you and you have no intentions of giving her what she wants. She's busting her ass not only because she loves you but also to make you a commodity which in turns is making you filthy.

And what does she get for her efforts?"

"She gets a hefty commission on every dollar she brings in. She went from being wealthy to being filthy."

"And if she's been wealthy her whole life what does money matter? She hasn't changed, and her eyes are on you not the money. But keep fucking around and diggin' her like you did today and one day you gonna wake up broke and holding your own dick. Feel me bruh. I know you young and ain't tryna be married and tied down but sometimes you have to realize where you are in your life. Some men can live ten lifetimes and never run into a Kree."

"I feel you, bruh but can we change the subject,"

"Just don't want you to sleep on your blessings."

Now if there's one thing you must know about Kree it's that she loves the nightlife. So, when she recommended Naz get out there in the spotlight it was a license for her as well and one that she readily welcomed. And I suppose after sitting in boardrooms pushing a product endorsement that could very well be for twenty-five or thirty million she was entitled to letting her hair down and unwind from time-to-time. Kree loved New York and had friends that kept her up on the latest happenings and by the time she arrived she was pushing Naz.

"Come on baby the car's s'pozed to be here in less than ten minutes and you haven't even taken your shower yet."

"I'm tired Kree. Baby can't we at least stay in the first night here?"

"We're only here for two weeks."

"Only two weeks? I was born and raised here baby."

"Come on sweetie pie. It'll be fun."

"Baby..."

"Come on old man," she said grabbing his tee-shirt and pulling it over his head.

"Damn, baby!"

An hour later, Naz was glad he'd gone. The club was hot. Naz knew the DJ from uptown when he used to do house parties. And then there was Cathy who he'd gone to high school with and had a crush on. He's wondered what had happened to her.

"I'm an investment broker for Wells & Fargo."

"I knew in high school you were destined for big things."

"Look who's talking. Everywhere I go I see your picture. Got Milk? You have become quite the name for yourself. I can't even picture you knocking someone out. You were always so shy and timid," She said smiling. She still had whatever it was that used to make Naz freeze up and he suddenly found himself at a loss for words.

"It wasn't that I was shy or timid. It was you. I thought you were the prettiest girl in the school and would just freeze up when you were around. I had the biggest crush on you."

"Wow! That' amazing! She said grinning broadly.

"Why do you say that?"

"Because I had a crush on you but was too shy to say or do anything about it."

"Stop playing."

"Well, I liked the way you made me feel back then even though I wasn't able to speak about it."

"We used to sneak quick glances and smile at each other when we'd get caught. Everyone knew we liked each other."

"Nothing's changed on my part. Put my number in your phone so we can see how it would have played out."

"By all means. I'm curious to know as well. I may call you before you get home."

"You could do better than that. Why don't you meet me at the house for a nightcap at say one?"

"Sounds like a plan to me." Naz said smiling as she made her way off into the crowd. Naz wanted to follow but thought better as he felt Kree's eyes staring through him. Had she been there the whole time?

"Friend of yours?"

"Yes. Went to school with her."

"Pretty girl," Kree commented.

"No doubt," Naz replied his mind cloudy from the transaction between he and his elementary school crush.

He was staying with Kree. They'd come together. How was he just going to split and meet Cathy for a late night? At that moment Naz wanted nothing more than to get away for the night, go to a party, meet some new people, do something different. Hell no. He couldn't be married. He was too reckless. He bored far too easily. And now New York was no longer just his livelihood. It was his oyster to be played with, toyed with, explored.

Yes, for the first time in his life he could enjoy the real New York with all of its exclusive night life, its Broadway plays and finer restaurants. Yes, for the first time in his life he could afford the finer things in life. If Monica's death taught him anything it was to live each day to its fullest for tomorrow was promised to no man.

The two had a few drinks and along with some of Kree's friends and relatives the night turned out to be a rather lively occasion.

An hour after they were in the door and Kree was sound asleep Naz made sure he had his key and eased the door shut. Downstairs he grabbed a cab, gave the cabbie the address and was on hisway. Naz was surprised to find Cathy's building on the upper East Side where you could still walk late at night without fear of being robbed or mugged.

"Evening sir. May I help you?"

"Yes, I'm looking for a Ms. Catherine Harmon," Naz was surprised at how easily her last name had come.

"Ah yes. Ms. Harmon. Let me ring her and tell her you're on your way up. And you are?"

"Mr. Nazar Muhammad."

"That name sounds awfully familiar. Where have I seen that name before? Oh, yes, Ms. Harmon there is a Mr. Muhammad here to see you. Yes ma'am."

"Sixteenth floor. Apartment 1602. I've seen that name before."

"Check the sports pages," Nazar said grinning at the paunchy little door man.

"Hey Naz," Cathy said pretending to kiss him on both cheeks.

The apartment was gorgeous with a breathtaking view overlooking the East River.

"So, do you like?" she said pirouetting to show Naz everything.

"I like," he said making sure his eyes never left her.

"So, tell me what's been happening with you? I try to keep up with you and your career as much as I can but you don't know what to believe when you open the papers these days."

"Well, now that you have access to me you don't have to rely on the tabloids. You can ask me firsthand. But let's not ask all at one time. Ask me in a way so that I can get to know you again at the same time."

"Sounds good to me. Hennessey?"

"Whatever you're having is fine."

"So, now that you're a famous boxer and the hottest bachelor on the scene I guess the ladies must be knockin' down the door."

"Not until you came knockin' down the door," Naz laughed.

"Oh, no you didn't. You haven't changed one bit. Still have that smart mouth I see."

"No. On the real though. I'm just out here floundering literally like a fish out of water. I have a publicity team whose aim it is to have a picture of me on everyone's refrigerator and in everyone's bathroom right next to the Tidy Bowl man. Those pictures with me posing

494

with every single woman in New York is all for
publicity.

I'm single and alone because I'm still in the grips of my
manager, coach and fiancée passing away earlier this
year."

"Yes, I saw that. I'm sorry. She was a cute, little
something. So, you're still in the midst of coming to
grips with it."

"I have little or no other choice. Life goes on. But
anyway, to answer your question about the ladies. I
had to ask myself before coming back to New York if I
really feel like getting back into the dating scene. But
before I had a chance to answer who's the first person I
run into?"

"No other than the one and only Cathy Harmon. Hello.
I think your thirst to get back into the dating scene may
have come to a rather sudden endthanks to me." The

sultry young woman said placing her hand on Naz's thigh. "This is something I should have done back in the day. I won't let the chance slip away again," she said putting her drink down and leaning over and kissing Naz long and hard.

"So, where are you living?" she said attempting to compose herself now.

"Well, mommy and Sin still have the apartment uptown. I bought the two of them a house down in Jamaica. That's where they are now."

"I believe I asked you where you were living."

"I bought myself a home in Jamaica right outside of Negril. It's peaceful and quiet. I like it. Gives me a place where I can get away from it all and think when New York becomes too hectic."

"I imagine that's important when you're in the spotlight as much as you are."

"You just don't know. If I had my druthers, I'd stay there year-round and never come back."

"And what's to stop you from doing just that. From what I've read you're the champ now. You're supposed to be the one calling the shots."

"It would seem so. Doesn't work like that though. Once you become the champ you have a greater responsibility than just to yourself. You have a responsibility to the community in which we live and serve. So, you see once I get out of the ring that's where the real fight begins."

"That's quite commendable Nazar. I would have never imagined that that shy, little, boy from C.E.S 73X would grow into a world champ and an earth shaker."

Naz went on to tell her about the trip and the foundation's plans and promised to send her an invite and some more literature. Who knows? Maybe she could introduce some of her very influential Wall Street friends and they could all come and make a weekend of it.

She promised she would spread the word and after one Hennessey too many Naz remembered Trip's father's words about not stepping in every hole you see and forced himself to get up and leave as badly as he wanted to stay.

Cathy was no longer the skinny, little, light-skinned girl with the two Pippi Longstocking pigtails. She had grown into a rather buxom young woman thick in all the right places and hung just the way Naz liked. But no, not the way Kree had stared him down. He didn't know why he felt any type of guilt. He and Kree wre just kicking it. There was nothing exclusive about their relationship. She may have wanted there to be but they had never talked about it other than she leaving and saying she couldn't do it anymore before crawling back into his arms a week or so later.

Still, if he did decide to kick it with Cathy or anyone else it was only right that he talk to Kree and clear the air first. Again, he did not know why he felt this sudden allegiance to Kree and didn't like it. It was almost as if she were haunting him. Why it was just this morning that he'd been lectured by Trip on her apropos of nothing. And it was beginning to be a regular thing. If it weren't Sin warning him about his money, then it was Trip telling him not to sleep on the regular. And here was this bright, beautiful redbone standing there his for the taking and he couldn't act because of a guilty conscious. *Damn!* Even mama who never interfered in his personal life told him that she hoped I was gonna do right by Kree. There was no question she was a hit in any circle to everyone but him. To him Kree amounted to no more than a friend and confidante. The last part bothered him. Daddy used to say there was no such thing as a female and a friend. And when a woman goes as far as giving you her treasure trove of goodies it's time to start pricing rings.

That's what daddy believed. Once you committed to having sex with a woman then you were committed one hundred. It was time to buy the ring and the car seat.

What he needed was to get out more, meet more women, expand his horizons, enjoy his youth. He'd talk to Kree first thing in the morning and define the lines.

"You want some breakfast baby?"

"No. I'm good. I have to tell you I enjoyed myself last night. I'm glad you made me go."

"You met an old classmate that you used to be stuck on and she was glad to see you as well. You should have seen yourself after she left. You were on cloud nine the rest of the night."

"Stop it."

"Did you meet her later to catch up on old times?"

"Actually, I did one better. You know she's an investment broker for Wells Fargo."

"You don't play, do you? You go after the thoroughbreds."

"Anyway, I told her about the foundation and invited she and three of her friends down on an all-expense three-day vacation. Her donation alone should cover the trip."

"Novel idea. I have to add that to the game plan. Nice enticement especially this time of the year. You realize we could actually be sitting on the beach sippin' Pinas right now instead of going out into this wintry wonderland." Naz laughed.

"I believe this was your idea. Let's go to New York in January."

"So, were there any sparks?" "What

are you talking about?"

"Between you and ol' girl?"

"Oh, you're back to Cathy. No. I don't think so. At least not on my part. Was just good seeing someone from the old neighborhood make good. I guess it's been a good ten years since I've seen her, but you know I'm glad you asked me about that. This is really the first time I've been out without being blinded by the thought of Monica and…"

"And what happens when that certain one turns your head. What about Kree? You do what you have to do Nazar. Some of us don't have to go out and remake the wheel. The one we presently have works fine. Others have to search and dig to find what's standing right before them. So, I'll wait until you search and dig. I'll still be here."

Naz could do little more than smile.

"You remind me of my father. He was good for preaching how persistence overcomes resistance," Nazar laughed.

"You don't think I know you Naz. Any good general always has a strategy. But before he even thinks about plotting a strategy he has to get to know his opponent. So, he studies him and learns him. Then he can plan his strategy according to the tendencies he's discovered."

"And what have you discovered in my case?"

"Nothing unusual. Men are simple. You see men are simply little boys that get bigger. Same mindset in a man's frame. You see you have been sheltered Naz and when your father was gone you had a woman who governed your life in a similar fashion. So, and even though they have passed away and you loved them dearly their passing allows you a freedom you have never known and not only were you given your freedom you were given your freedom along with more money than you ever dreamed of. So, even though you've already met your wife you're not going to let some broad slow you down with that relationship crap at this point in your life. You want to look good, in your new Black whip swinging around the way with the fellas. You gotta make sure your whip is clean, so you can swing over to Branch Brook Park and look at the pretty girls on Saturday afternoon. How am I doing? And fine as that bitch is running her mouth in front of me I gots ta stay strong or I'll be running around with one kid in my arm and one on y leg and who wants that shit right now. But damn that pussy is TADOW. That shit is to die for. Maybe I can hit her up when the pace slows down. Might have to marry the bitch. And don't let her go out here and decide to date. I'll kill the bitch.

Ain't that how it goes Naz?"

"Pretty much" Naz said smiling. "I bought you a ring you know? Was trying to give it to you one nigh but you were too busy going out with your girls?"

"Huh uh? Are you serious? I was trying to figure that night out. Why it was so important that I stop by and then when I got there you told me to go ahead."

"Yeah. I had Jo fix veal parm and had a bottle of wine chillin' but you showed up with a car full of howling females and short lived my plans for a romantic evening."

"And so, what happened? Was it a one-shot deal? You don't ask again? What kind of shit is that?" Naz smiled.

"No. It's everything you just said about me sowing my wild oats is all."

"Oh. And this is a solo mission which must mean you 're interested in what's out there as far as the opposite sex. And I am supposed to sit and wait until you finish hoeing yourself out."

"No. That's what I've been trying to tell you. I don't like your strategy of persistence overcoming resistance.

Let me go. We're already tied together at the hip. We

will always be in each other's lives, but I don't want us

to be romantically involved right through here and I

don't want you to wait on me. I'm different. I can't call

it, but that trip did something to me. I feel differently

about life now. I realized just how fragile life is. And

all the money in the world can't help you if you can't

get a good doctor to recognize you or when you're old

and there's no one to look after you. I've learned not to

slow down or look back for anyone. Life is too short,

too damn precious and I'm gonna run it 'til the wheels

fall off. I'm not sure if this next journey is one I'd like

to take anyone with me on. I have no idea where this is

all gonna end up but like I said I don't want anyone to

be responsible for anyone."

"But baby the risk would be all on me."

"No, Kree."

That's was all we ever said concerning the matter and Kree went her way and I mine. Two or three weeks later I got a call from Ms. Kree.

"Oh, so cause we ain't sexin' we ain't friends? What's up with you, nigga? You can't pick up the phone and call a girl?"

"Nothin' intentional baby. Funny I was just looking at some of your pictures from the party."

"And?"

"What can I say?"

"That you made one huge mistake and that you need me in your life."

"And I see that as a very real possibility when I come to a landing but I'm still trying to get it together baby. I can say I do see some progress. I'm working out again and that's always therapeutic. Have a fight in less than

four months. Some Ukranian fighter. You know the

type. Hard hitter. Tough guy. One of them that you hit

so hard you break your hand on his head and he's still

coming forward like you ain't hit him at all. I hate

fights like this. These are the kind that test both your

skills and your heart. You have to go in there a

complete fighter."

"And you will. Have you been practicing your

speech?"

"I've got it down pat."

He did too. The first time he read it he broke down

reliving the tortured stories of the people he met in his

travels. He saw the rats and the roaches, the family with

frozen pipes and no heat huddled around a potbellied

stove for heat. Then there was the man using the

cardboard boxes as blankets to ward off the whistling,

wind and rain rushing in from under the underpass he called home. Except for a minor change here and there he was ready. There were several passages that still choked him up, but he was smooth, passionate and eloquent in his recital. Monica would have been proud of her man giving this speech to this crowd in his black tux. She always saw more for him.

Training now consisted mostly of cardio vascular and Naz never minded running. When he finished his run, he would glance over the speech once more making sure he hadn't forgotten anything or left anything out. Convinced that he hadn't he closed his eyes.

The days flew by and the next thing he knew he was sitting backstage to the ballroom which held five hundred but must have held at least seven hundred on this night. Attired in their finest garb, these were the Black people with money. Kree made sure there was a senior rep from Pepsi and our other companies ready to donate.

Naz was chomping at the bit as he watched the film along with the crowd many of whom were sobbing openly. By the time he took the stage there was not a dry eye in the building.

"And I conclude by saying, 'Not in America'. We people of influence can no longer stand by and watch our children and our seniors suffer. We the people must stand up and make a difference. Giving to Tomorrow's the Future will help get the ball rolling. Ladies and gentlemen, I thank you for your time and have a good evening. Dinner is being served in the second dining room to the left. For those staying on there are people handing out the addresses of where you will be staying. Your bags and other belongings have already been delivered to your rooms. If you have any other questions, there is a number on the outset of each pack. Call that and someone will be glad to help you.

There are several very nice bars as you walk up the

beach. I tend to prefer Boston's myself but feel free to

patronize the one you feel most at home at. If I don't

see you enjoy your night and thank you again for

supporting Tomorrow's the Future."

Kree and Trip were on top of him before he could get

off the stage.

"Beautiful baby! You were absolutely beautiful baby!

Wasn't a dry eye in the building by the time you got

done," Trip said embracing Naz tightly.

"You did the damn thing, Naz. I am so proud of you. I

think you may have a second career looming and you

don't even know it."

Naz grinned and hugged both of his friends simultaneously.

"The question is are they opening their wallets and checkbooks?" Naz asked.

"Look at the line by the door. I'd say they're opening up. We can look at the numbers tomorrow. C'mon. Let's go take part in the festivities," Kree said grabbing both men by the hand.

"My crowd's all heading to your crib baby. You know Murph's probably already there," Trip said. "You know Murph's following his nose. You know I really think he's going to marry Jo for no other reason than he loves her cooking," Trip laughed.

It was at this point that we noticed a woman approaching quickly from a cross the dining room. She was elegant. That was for damn sure. Dressed in all black Naz had to glance twice.

"Hello. I told you I was coming," the woman said handing Naz a check.

"Cathy meet my good friends Trip and Kree."

"Nice to meet you both. Is there someplace we can talk in private," she said redirecting her gaze to Naz.

"Sure, why don't you meet me at the house in say an hour. I'll text you the address."

Putting her hand on his and staring him straight in the eye she pleaded.

"Can you make it sooner Naz. It's kind of a pressing matter."

"How's thirty minutes sound."

"So, much better," the woman said sending a shivering glare in Kree's direction before walking away.

"OMG! Did you see that Trip?"

"I saw her. I don't why bitches like to start shit." Trip said.

"And the only thing pressing is her trying to get out of that tight ass dress. That's that investment broker we saw at the club last week isn't it? I knew that hungry ass bitch would come here. That gold diggin' bitch aint doin' nothin' but lookin' for someone to leech onto. You meet with her Naz. You have all of ten minutes to address her pressing matter. Do you understand?"

"I thought we had this conversation Kree."

"Ten minutes Naz. You ain't out of that house in ten minutes I'm comin' in for that little nappy headed heifer. And don't even think about locking the door." Trip dropped his head. Naz, who had never seen Kree upset was shocked by her response. Caught off guard by this latest tirade he smiled. Kree was like an animal who'd marked her territory and wasn't about to let this woman come in here and just take what she'd worked so hard for. And then there was the part of Naz that objected to her trying to possess him when they had just talked about this. And then he smiled again realizing that logic came easily but love, passion, and emotions are what he was being introduced to tonight.

"Chill Kree. Didn't we just talk about this?"

"Ten minutes and I'm coming in. Don't play with me Naz. You do, and you'll lose. I want her on her way."

Trip just hung his head smiling. He'd forewarned Naz about just this sort of thing.

An embarrassed Naz walked slowly up to the house. Trip and Kree stood on the beach.

"Come on sista," Trip said grabbing Kree's arm and leading her to the lawn chairs before digging into his pocket and pulling up on a gold-plated cigarette case. Rummaging through e pulled up on a blunt and handed it to Kree.

"Here sis. Might help ease your nerves. But if you don't mind me saying, Naz would never disrespect you. And whether he knows it or not he loves you. Trust me you have nothing to fear." Trip said as he lit the blunt for Kree.

"I apologize for making a scene."

"Why don't you wait a few minutes? She looks like the type that may try to challenge his weltererweight belt and try to take it forcibly. You may have to go in there and set her ass straight," Trip laughed.

"Oh, hush Trip. You know I wouldn't lower myself to that level."

"Real talk sista and you know I love the nigga more than I love myself, but you have every right to go in there and rip the weave right off that little yalla bitch."

"You really don't like her, do you?"

517

"Ain't got nothin' to do with her. You feel me fam? It ain't got nothin' to do with her. It's just the fact that you've put in the work, proved yourself and it's time he recognized. It's all about appreciation and loyalty. And he owes you that. I know because I owe you."

"I like the way you think. C'mon Trip," Kree said passing Trip the blunt and heading towards the house. Once there Trip smiled as Kree took a deep breath before reaching for the door.

"Hold on," Trip said reaching into his waist band. "You need this. I've found that it quells any arguments or objections." Trip smiled.

"Put that thing away," Kree said shooting an angry glance at Trip. "C'mon."

Kree knocked before walking in.

The two, Naz and the woman known as Catherine stood in the middle of the floor toasting something or another with Jo and Murphy.

"Oh, Ms. Kree. You're right on time. Have you met Ms. Cathy? She just pledged fifty thousand dollars to the foundation."

"Isn't that wonderful? The foundation is sorely in need and appreciates your donation Miss?"

"Harmon. Catharine Harmon. And you are? I have such a hard time remembering names."

"Kree. Kree Edmunds."

"Oh, you're the realtor that Naz has told me all about. I absolutely love the house. Perhaps you can show me your listings."

"Perhaps. Give me your number and I'll give you a call before you leave the island," Kree said trying to be as cordial as she could under the circumstances.

Trip who was sitting behind the woman kept shaking his head 'no' and lifting his shirt exposing the gun and prodding her to take it. Jo and Murph had a difficult time holding a straight face.

"Naz we're supposed to be at Boston's by eight," Kree said.

"Oh, is that where everyone's meeting? Do you mind if I tag along?" Cathy said grabbing and holding on to Naz's arm. Again, Trip lifted his shirt exposing the 9MM Glock. Bea was almost ready to take it. The nerve of this woman.

At Boston's Cathy stuck close to Naz. Despite Kree's being there Cathy was all over Naz. It was obvious that

Naz was uncomfortable with the situation and excused himself and pulled Trip to him.

"What's up with your girl, Naz? Ain't she from uptown?"

"Yeah. You remember Cathy Harmon from elementary?"

"Get out of here. Little, skinny, Cathy?"

"The very same."

"Damn she filled out right nicely. Turned into a right, fine woman."

"Didn't she though?"

"Yeah bruh but you may have to pass on that. I don't care how fine she is."

"Kree?"

"Kree."

"Kinda figured that. You know we just had a talk about this shit."

"Might want to have that talk again. She's ready to do get medieval on your girl."

"What do you suggest?"

"I told you how I felt about the whole situation all along. You're playing a dangerous game Naz. The woman's in love with you and has total control of your assets. Like I said you're playing a dangerous game. If nothing else you should tie the knot out of loyalty and appreciation. Present a united front. That's how I'm feeling about this whole situation bruh. But you play with her and she's gonna hurt you bruh. What do they say about a woman's wrath?"

"I feel you. But what can I do? Cathy flew down here to hand me a check for fifty thousand."

"Who you talkin' to my nigga? Cathy came down here and handed you a check for fifty chips. Along with trying to rock you to sleep she figures she's investing in a potential gold mine. That's what she's thinking. Kree created that gold mine. You feel me bruh? Now you want her to sit by while some other woman tries to eat away at her investment? You're crazy as hell, bruh."

"But wouldn't that be kinda foul to take her fifty and then shoo her off the island after inviting her?"

"We all fuck up from time-to-time but it's okay if you catch it and stop the bleeding in time. What you don't need to do is compound it. I blow fifty g's shooting craps on the block. And you have a lot more chips stacked than I ever will. So, just chalk it up to a lesson learned but I'm going to tell you one last time. Don't fuck over Kree."

"So, what you're saying is to get rid of Cathy?"

"You mean to tell me she's still here? She's trouble.
Get rid of her with the quickness. If your meal ticket
doesn't want her around, then she's got to go before
any one gets hurt. I don't want to be part of the
collateral damage. She's got to go bro. *Pronto!*"

I knew Trip was looking out for both of our interests,
but I saw no way to ask her to leave. I knew she was
expecting me to spend my time with her but with Kree
and Trip both wanting her gone I saw no way to make it
work. In the end, I would just have to be upfront and
tell her.

I excused myself and grabbed Kree by the arm.

"I need to talk to you."

"Talk to me Naz."

"I'm going to ask Catharine to leave. If she makes you feel uncomfortable then she needs to leave. I'm just wondering if she needs to go tonight or if you were seriously considering showing her your homes."

"That bitch cannot come down here and live. I don't want her on my island. New York is too close. I want her out of here."

"You don't sound exactly sure to me. I need you to be absolutely sure about this." Naz smiled.

"Get rid of her Naz," Kree said. There was no humor in her voice.

"It's done and I'm sorry if you were made to feel uncomfortable," he said pulling him to her and hugging her tightly.

Cathy saw the two as she walked up.

"Listen you two. I just got a call from my baby's nanny. Seems he's cranky and feverish. Seems they're always coming down with something when you make plans to do anything. But anyway, I'm on the next thing out of here. Thank you so much for the invite and perhaps I can see your homes on another occasion Kree.

Call me when you're in the city Naz and keep me abreast on the foundation. Maybe we can do lunch sometime." she said shaking both their hands before heading to the limo parked a few feet away.

"Didn't know she had a child," Naz commented as he watched her walk away.

"She didn't either. I don't think she had any idea what she was walking into when you invited her here. I think she has a better understanding now."

"Still, think you should hae followed my advice Kree," Trip said walking up and lifting his shirt once more.

"Boy, it's nice to know I can count on you to give good rational advice to a distraught woman. We could have all been dead."

"Ah come on bruh I was teasing. Besides you know I would never give it to Kree. And you should know Kree ain't built that way. I think ol' girl clearly got the vibe that she wasn't wanted though." "Ya think?" Kree added.

"Anybody got any numbers on how we did tonight?" Trip asked pouring another glass of Hennessey.

"Let me call and see what I can find out now," Kree said stepping outside to hear better.

"Man, if I had known how fine ol' girl was I would have run interference. I could have taken Kree to the wine distributor to get some more wine and you could have taken ol' girl to my place."

"I had all intentions of spending a day or two with

Cathy, but it just didn't feel right besides I couldn't do that

knowing how Kree feels about me. You know we have our

own little history."

"Glad you're finally coming to your senses bruh.

Listen bruh. I've got to go up top tomorrow and see if

I can get these brothas to stop killin' each other."

"Murph and Dez?"

"Yeah. I keep trying to tell them that it's all about the

money, but they got this feud going. Now how you

gonna make money if you can't sell your product. I

keep tryna tell them brothas. And both of 'em mad

'cause ain't no money flowing. Seems simple to me.

Concentrate on making money not killing each other.

Stupid motherfuckers."

"You wanted me to fly up with you. You don't exactly come across as a neutral party."

"You would do that for me?"

"Murph is fam and may be the best one of us. I love him just like I love you and Noah. By the way, is there any word on Noah?"

"He's cool. Been stickin' close to the crib. Murph is making sure he eats and has his medicine. Murph bought him a television and chained it down in the living room. Say he has this pretty little girl that comes and sees him two or three times a week. No one knows who she is, but they tell me she ain't bad lookin'."

"And she likes Noah's crazy ass? I gotta meet this girl."

"Me too. Let's make it a point to run up in there. He'll be tickled to see you anyway. Have you seen him since you won the belt?"

"No. I went to look for him a couple of times, but you know how it is when he don't wanna be found."

"Yeah, well believe it or not some of the fellas saw him runnin' a couple of days ago. Said he ran for a couple of days. He keep runnin' and I'll have him at an NBA tryout before he knows what hit him."

"I don't doubt anything you say bruh," Naz laughed. "Where did Kree go?"

"Said she was going to check the numbers."

"Speak of the devil," Trip said. "How did we do?"

"The early numbers are one point seven in donations alone. Once the numbers come in from dinner we should clear two mil."

"Is that good?" Naz asked.

"That's the thing. I have no clue. I'll have to sit down with some people that know more about this whole fund raiser thing than I do. I do know that with the overhead and general cost we need a lot more of these speaking engagements Naz."

"No. what you need to do is go back and research the whole charity aspect and see how institutions like the Boys & Girls Club elicits donations and model the foundation on them. You're not gonna kill me while you sit back at the office."

"Whoa! Slow down cowboy. What was that all about, soldier?"

"You're manipulative Kree. You have objectives that you want to meet and that's great, but you are not going to use me as your gopher to run here and there whenever you get the whim."

"Stop actin' like you're new to all of this. Who else is going to go out there? Me? Trip? No one's coming out to see us. They're coming out to see you champ. You're the only one that can do it."

"She's right Naz."

"You are not going to run me like there's no tomorrow. I don't care what you two agree."

"Come on bruh. Let's not be hasty. Let's wait and see what the numbers tell us, and we look at all the alternatives. Is that cool?"

"Yeah. I suppose that's cool. Listen you two. I apologize. I'm exhausted is all. I'm headed in. You two have a good night."

It would have been nice to have spent the night with Kree but with his petulanct behavior he knew she wasn't having that. Naz packed his bag for the trip and called it a night.

At six the next morning Naz heard his phone.

"Morning fam. You need to be up if you're not up already. Plane leaves at eight. Want me to pick you up at seven?"

"No, I'm good. I'll meet you at the airport."

Naz hung up, showered and thought about calling Kree and saying goodbye then thought about it again and dismissed the thought. It seemed like only minutes before they were touching down at LaGuardia. It was early evening before they arrived uptown at the only other home he'd ever known.

The two had grabbed lunch at Sylvia's and spent the day shopping and received a warm homecoming when they arrived on the block.

"I've got a little business to handle. I shouldn't be too long," Naz said before hugging Trip.

"Be safe, bruh."

There was no question as to where Naz was going and Trip knew it. Twenty minutes later Naz pulled up in front of Cathy's building.

"Hello, Ms. Harmon."

"Evening Mr. Muhammad," she said smiling before taking him in her arms and kissing him deeply, passionately. "Want to stay here and share a bottle of wine or do you want to go out?"

"I've been ripping and running all day. I'm a little tired to be honest with you."

"Not too tired I hope. I have plans for you."

"Oh, really?"

"Yes. But let me run something by you first."

Cathy returned with a glass of Hennessey and a large manila envelope. Handing him the glass she proceeded to open the envelope.

"Thought I'd grab this chance to speak to you about some investment opportunities we're currently sponsoring."

Naz needed to hear no more. Kree had been right all along. A quick drink, a kiss to show she was there for the taking before selling herself in the bedroom and then closing the deal. Naz promptly stood up before draining his glass, leaning over, kissing her on the forehead and leaving. He could hear her calling as he closed the door behind himself but there was nothing more to say.

The temperature had dropped somewhat since he'd arrived, but it was still nice and he walked a bit before hailing a cab. It was still early, and he had yet to see Murph so he walked up into the cut where he was welcomed home with much warmth and congratulated on his championship run. He couldn't believe how man people were milling around waiting to be served. No wonder Dez was on the warpath.

"What's up with the crowd, Murph?"

"I slashed the prices. Still bringing in the same money. Just increased the crowd."

"Looks like Time Square up here and the police don't say nothing?"

"They're paid. They don't bother us unless someone gets to acting stupid. We usually handle that though. So, no we don't have any problems from the police."

"This must be killing Dez."

"We're picking up more and more of his worker's everyday. They say they ain't eatin'. You know Trip cut him off from the connect when I got shot."

"No wonder he's upset. You gotta allow the nigga to eat Murph. C'mon man. You gotta make some concessions Murph. Everyone was eating. Hook him back up with the connect."

"You gotta talk to Trip about that Naz. That's out of my hands."

"You seen him?"

"I'm pretty sure he's upstairs at your place chillin'."

"Alright Murph. I'm headed in. I'm beat. Stop by when ou get off so we can talk some more."

"I will if I get a chance."

"Be safe."

"Already."

Naz climbed the three flights only to find Trip sound asleep and soon followed in his footsteps.

The next morning it was Trip who woke him up.

"Rough night?"

"Nah, man. Actually, it was an early night. I was downstairs talking to Murph last night for a good while. He tells me you cut Dez off from the connect."

"I didn't cut Dez off from anything. The connect was mine. I did him a favor by supplying him with the best product at the cheapest prices. But you can't shoot one of my fam and expect for me to continue to hook you up. Ya feel me bruh?"

"I do but ya gotta expect the man to feel some kind of way after spending five years buying from you and then you have Murph replace you, make him a boss and hook him up with the connect."

"You right but he wasn't angry about that. He brought the madness because Murph whooped his ass. You don't come 'round here shooting up the place and endangering innocent people who ain't got nothin' to do with your personal beef with Murph."

"You're right, bruh but in order to make the peace ya gotta give him something so the shootings stop. Are you willing to at least hook him back up with the connect to stop the bloodshed?"

"I don't know bruh. I ain't really feeling that motherfucker. Never had."

"Ya gotta give him something Trip if you want this madness to stop," Naz pleaded. "It's the only way you're going to stop him from taking potshots at Murph."

"I hear ya. But Murph controls the connect. Same arrangement as before. He's not to meet the connect but we will supply him. You can take that to the meet. You can speak on my behalf but I ain't really got nothin' to say to the motherfucker. And now that I think about it do you think it's smart that I should even be there?"

"That's your call bruh. I don't know your relationship."

A knock came at the door.

"Morning. Car's here Naz."

"Car?" Naz asked.

"Yeah. Today you're a boss. You gotta roll the way we bosses roll, "Trip said smiling.

"You're not going, bruh," Murph said looking at Trip.

"Nah, Murph. I think Naz would stand a better chance procuring the peace without me."

Thirty minutes later Naz arrived at Juniors where Dez sat with two bodyguards, one on either side of him. Seeing Naz by himself Dez drew a big smile.

"Champ! How ya doing my nigga?" he said hugging Naz tightly. "Where's your man?"

"They decided not to come. They thought I'd have a better chance of making the peace."

"They're right," Dez added before going on to telling Naz the situation. When it was over Dez hesitantly accepted the deal. There would be no more shootings and the boundaries were drawn so the two didn't step on each other's toes. If however, something did go awry. Dez was supposed to sit down at the table before endangering innocents. Dez agreed. When the meeting was over the two talked about Monica's death and left better acquainted than they had been.

Naz had one thing left to do before he left the city. He and Trip had already agreed on scooping Noah up and taking him back to Jamaica but in the two days and with feelers out they were unable to locate Noah and so they headed back without him. Murh promised to put him on a plane just as soon as he showed up.

Naz headed back home and back to training. He had less than two weeks to go when a disheveled Noah showed up.

"What's up my nigga?" Noah shouted seeing his boyfriend friend.

"You're what's up Blackman. How've you been doing?"

"Same ol'. Same ol' But I feel good. I've been trying to kick and been running. I feel pretty good. Figured I'd come down and workout with you. What did pops used to say about a strong mind and body? And you got down with me after pops died and then went on to be world champ. Maybe I can do that to and pick up where I left off playing ball. Even if I don't I've at least kicked. You feel me?"

"I do bruh. C'mon in and let me show you around," Naz said hugging his friend again. "Go

543

upstairs and look in my closet and get fly so I can show you the island.

Naz and Noah spent the remainder of the day shopping and reminiscing before going to see Trip and then mamas for dinner. That night and for the first time Noah talked to Naz.

"Man! And to think I could have been living like this if I had made better choices and had someone to guide me."

"It's never too late but if you're going to roll with me you'd better get some sleep. I'm up and running at five."

"Gotcha bruh."

Up with the crack of dawn Naz was surprised to find Noah and Jo in deep conversation on the best ingredients for homemade soup and after telling Jo how he had grown up with Murph that was it a bond had been formed. Breakfast consisted of no more than a half a grapefruit, a slice of toast with no butter or jelly and a cup of black coffee.

"And you say that's your cook? Bruh, last night she gave me a sandwich and some chips and this morning it's a half a grapefruit. What the hell kind of cook doesn't cook? I mean c'mon bruh."

"Murph likes her."

"Murph's in New York, bruh. And Murph would fall in love with anyone that had could boil Ramon noodles. What's that motherfucker know about fine cuisine?"

"C'mon man. We got another half mile to go. Let's finish up strong."

Noah despite the anguish of Naz's training regime made it through the hardest part of the day and even went a few rounds sparring with the local talent.

"New prospect?" Mr. Medna asked. "Kids got raw talent. You should bring on and let me work with him."

Naz smiled. Noah had God given talent and even though he hadn't been in a gym for years that talent showed through.

"It's time we took a look at our opponent. I had one of my boys pull as many tapes of this kid Lomanchenko as we could find but let me tell you to have thirty fights there isn't much to see. We were only able to find three of his most recent fights but that may be enough. Anyway we need to start watching them tonight? Do you have an hour later?"

"Sure. Of course, I have time. How's about eight sound? I'll have Jo fix you dinner."

Over dinner Noah, Naz and Mr. Medina watched tapes of the young bull-headed Ukrainian who walked through his opponents with no defense. Leading with his head he took some unbelieveable shots but never stopped coming forward.

"I don't know how you'd fight a fighter like that. He keeps his hands at his waist and ain't worried about you hitting him," Noah ventured. "I guess the only way you beat someone like that is to just box him and outpoint him. And Lord knows you can't stay in front of him. If he tags you with one of those bombs its lights outs."

"Noah's right. Stay in front of him and you can chalk this one up. You've got to stay on your toes and dance. Keep your distance and keep your jab in his face.

It may not hurt him but it'll keep him off balance. Our strategy for this fight is going to be slightly different. We are not going to look to get this guy out of there. We just want to box him. That's where we have the clear advantage. He's a slugger and as you know a good boxer will always beat a good slugger. And on Saturday you're going to make that theory ring true."

"I gotcha."

"I hope so son. To my knowledge you haven't fought anybody of this guy's caliber. He reminds me a little of Duran with his hands of stone. I mean this kid's lethal carrying as much power in his right as in his left.

Your job is to stay beyond his reach. If he gets close, we just wanna tie him up. You feel me son? We're gonna work on tying him up and your movement tomorrow but I want you to watch the tapes. See if you can pick up any flaws or tendencies that may be to your advantage."

After the old man was gone Naz invited Noah into the study where he poured he and his old friend a glass of Hennessey.

"C'mon Naz. You're in training! When did you start drinkin' anyway? Man, pops would roll over in his grave if he could see you now but let me talk to you about something on the serious side. Can I ask who set this fight up for you?"

"Trip? Oh my God! Trip is the original O.G. That nigga believes in money before loyalty. You feel me. No wonder the gym and training camp don't feel right."

Noah was what you might call a poor man's Lou Duva. He knew boxing.

"What are you talking about Noah?"

"C'mon man. You've been around your pop's long enough to know this ain't even got the feel of a real training camp. I went to a couple of your sparring sessions when they told me that Mia was actually in your corner and her training camps were non-stop, intense, disciplined and well regimented. You couldn't help but be in the best shape of your life after one of her training camps. But this is like vacation at Atlantis in the virgin

Islands or where ever the fuck it is. Man, ain't no fire here. And you need that fire to get you to fire on all cylinders or else you wind up fighting to your opponent's level. You know what I'm saying is true Naz. Man who knows you better than I do?"

"Trip said the same thing. And I got the same feeling but ever since Monica passed I can't tell.

Everything seems different now. Between her passing and that trip I took it just seems everything's changed."

"Everything has changed and nothing's changed bruh. The trip and Monica just sped up your maturity. You're good, bruh. You and I are a lot alike in that regard. We're both trying to pick up the pieces and put our lives back together. And it's funny but you got dough and I couldn't rub two nickles together and even if we did have all the money in the world it wouldn't matter. It couldn't fix what ails us."

"You are correct my good brother but if we keep pushing who know what the good Lord has waiting for us around the next curve. You just gotta be strong and keep the faith right through here. You feel me? Let's run."

The two men stayed in close company just as they had when they were boys. The two sat now and had a drink here and there read when they were tired of listening to music and watching television. Their physical regime was horribly tormenting, but each went through the rigors and knew they were the better for it. Noah was beginning to look chiseled and one day slipped away from everybody. Thinking the worst Naz and Trip scoured most of Negril. Kree sent one of her men who knew the backstreets and alley ways of Montego Bay and

Negril. After hours of searching a smile hone on Trip's face.

"I know where that little grimy ho is. You see bruh you have to look at the glass as being half full instead of being so pessimistic and thinking the worst. Make a right at the light Naz. Now drive down to the end of the strret where the courts are. I bet you any amount of money since he's back in shape he's at the courts. Isn't that where he used to live before he got hooked,"

"Hope you're right."

"Just pull up. Yep, there he is. Just park Naz. Damn if he don't look like hs old self. You think God put me here to save both of you in the same life and make myself extremely rich in the process," Trip laughed. "He do look good, though don't he? I could at least see about getting him a contract overseas."

"C'mon Trip I ain't got but a week before the fight. I need to be in the gym. I need to put in that work." "Hold up Naz. Let me run and get this fool."

"No. Trip. He ain't doing nothin' wrong. I don't want him to think I'm spyin' on him. You know that's his first love. He was going to eventually find a game.

I'm glad to see it but he ain't done nothin' wrong. He found his way here. Let him find his way home."

The week before the fight flew by and before I knew it was the eve of the fight and it seemed half the world was in mama's kitchen. Things had certainly changed. This used to be quiet, family time when we'd all reflect on his blessings and pray for neither man to endure any serious hurt. This was a time for serious inflective thought. This too had changed. And on fight night a stretch limo awaited me downstairs outside my parents' home. The last two fights I'd taken the subway.

It was all so different now.

Even in the ring I somehow felt different. I prayed to God and asked that he have Monica guide me through this fight. I prayed for a clean fight where neither he nor I is maimed or harmed. And then just like every other fight I went to work stinging him with hard jabs to which he would reply 'Come on' at the top of his lungs. I knew right then and there that what separated Lomanchenko from every other fighter I'd ever fought was that he was crazy. That was what made him an exceptional fighter. He had somehow made his mind and body believe that he could not be hurt. And because he willed it it was. I peppered him with every punch in my arsenal and he just kept coming forward lunging with wild left hooks I could read a mile away. It was an interesting fight. There was one round where he didn't lay a glove on me. I was dancing, moving, stickin' him with a jab and I was gone. In the ninth I don't know what happened, but my legs felt like lead and I couldn't really dance like I wanted to, so I tied him up for most of the round and fought him off the ropes when the ref warned me for holding. I couldn't afford to lose a point but if he caught me with one of those hay makers with me on the ropes it was good night. And don't you know he caught me with one of those haymakers while I had my back on the ropes. I went down hard. And if I could have gotten it together I would have told him that there was no need to count. I was not nor had any intention of getting up.

If anything I wanted someone who knew about head trauma to put everything back in its proper place and make the pain subside. When they saw it safe to sit me up everyone congratulated me on a well fought fight with the by-line Shit happens or You just got caught. Happens to the best, baby.

I thought about what Noah had said that this wasn't anything but a preview to the second one I would win setting up a third tie-breaker. I really hadn't given this any thought until Trip didn't mention putting anything on it.

556

"Have I ever lied to you my nigga. Why would I tell you and discourage you when you were putting work in? But no I didn't bet on you for this time. I didn't bet on you for two reasons, bruh. And let me tell you this it was never because I didn't have faith in you my brother. I didn't bet on you for two reasons and no disrespect, but Mia wasn't in there. She could tell me straight up that it wouldn't even be close and that was all I needed to hear. Then when she started putting her ends in there I knew it was a no-brainer. And I know that the master is working with you now, but I didn't get the sense that he was in it the way he had been when his daughter was in the corner. And I didn't get a good feel with your whole training camp regime. It just didn't feel right." "Thanks for being straight up, bruh."

"What you think I'm gonna tell you? What? I'm gonna lie to my nigga?" Trip said throwing a quick jab that Naz parried and blocked out of instinct. "You'll be fine bruh. Might have been the best thing that happened to you. Brings you back to earth. It'll help bring that fire and hunger back. Now you can start at ground zero, reassess your career and get back to that dirty, grimy, gym that made you. You need to stay right here in the city for the next fight. Jamaica's and that easy living's making you soft, bruh. Oh, and by the way, where is your phone? Kree's been trying to get in touch with you for the the last day and a half."

"It's right here." Naz said holding his phone up so Trip could see.

"Well, why aren't you answering?"

"I don't want to be bothered. I've disappointed just about everybody and you know my endorsements are dpendent on my winning. Won't be any more

endorsements off of that performance."

"Man you crazy. That girl ain't thinking about that shit. She loves you. She's calling to check on you. She needs to hear you tell her you're okay. That's all she needs to hear. And she needs to hear it from your mouth."

"Ask her to give me some time, bruh?"

"I can do that. What are your plans?"

"Plans? I don't have any. Just gonna relax— you know—chill for awhile and try to get my life together."

"Don't spend too much time. What I suggest is you take a couple of weeks to relax then jump back in there and get on tour for the foundation."

"Think they'll still come out to see a loser?"

"Man, folks don't come out caring whether you won or not. They come out to see a celebrity. And

Kree has a lot do with making you a celebrity. Working for the foundation and you'll always be a winner, bruh. Kree tells me that we already have low income-houses going up in Camden. Remember the woman with the rats?"

"How could I forget?"

"She's already in her house. Go to the website and see."

"That's beautiful. And you're going to put that loss behind you and start your real calling. Helping niggas in need. Do you realize that you make the same amount of money throwing a charity dinner as you do stepping in the ring without the six month training camp.
When boxing's over you're going to find that this is your true vocation. I guarantee you that you're going to love it especially with your good-doer personality"

"Listen Trip I was wondering if you could fix me up a package, break me off something for right through here and send the rest to Jamaica."

"Tell you what, bruh. I'll make you up a package and you do what you want with it."

"Preciate that, bruh."

"You like that shit don'tcha my nigga?"

"Helps me get through the rough spots.'

"You right. Just respect it. Take the motherfucker but don't let it take you. But then why am I telling you? You've done this before and won a championship. I'll have one of the fellas bring it to you. I'm headed back in the morning. Stay up and be safe mybrother. I love you man."

"Love you more," Naz said hugging his brother.

"Where you going to be?"

"Probably at Noah's crib. Been helping him fix it up."

"Don't put too much money in it. If he slips he'll sell all of that shit. And keep on the dl. I like what I'm seeing from him right through here. He's been working out and running every day. I'm trying to get him a workout and an invitation to the Knick's training camp in September.   I think he has a good chance of making the team."

"I gotcha."

Trip went to stay with some woman he'd been seeing for a month or so now. Noone knew who she was. She must have been some kind of special though for Trip not to bring her around. There was no one home when I arrived at Noah's. I'd ordered a bed and some other furniture and some other accessories like dishes and silverware and went about putting things in the proper place. He knew Noah would be impressed. When finished he threw on some Coltrane and sat back and closed his eyes. He felt the punch, felt his head bounce off the canvas and the bell ring. He wanted to get up, but his legs and body would not respond. He heard the ref count him out and still he could not move. He wondered if he was paralyzed. He woke up as he had the last few nights soaked in a cold, damp sweat. Had the knock at the door awakened him?

"Yo, what's up Blood?" the young man said hugging Naz tightly.

"Same ol'. Same ol'."

"What you 'bout to do Naz? You gonna start slingin' this shit?"

"C'mon man. You know that ain't me. That ain't me."

"I was just sayin' with that kind of weight."

"Ain't nothin' but Trip trippin'. You know how to hit a nigga off?"

"Yeah. I fuck wit' it a lil' bit?"

"Then hook a brotha up. And get you some but I gotta ask you to leave 'cause Noah's clean and I don't think it would be a good thing for him to see, I'm going to go in there turn up the music and lay it down as soon as you hit me up. But like I said get you some to tide you over my nigga. You feel me."

"Good lookin' out my nigga."

"You know how we roll. Fam forever."

Naz closed his eyes while Blood cooked enough for them both before tying Naz off and hit him right smack dab in the center of that bulging vein. When the blood had rushed halfway up the hypodermic Blood squeezed slowly but forcefully and watched as Naz's body eased into the soft leather couch and became one with it. Sitting up he took Blood's knife and cut the kilo in half dropped in a plastic bag and handed it to the young man.

"You ain't serious Naz? That's half a key my brother on the strength. Soon as I flip it I'll bring you yours. Already my nigga?"

"You don't owe me shit Blood. That's your come up. It's on me. And I'll let Murph know I gave it to you because you were struggling tryna eat out here in these streets. He'll understand but once you finish that their package you gonna have to find some other place to post up."

"Damn man I don't know what to say. Love ya man. Should you ever need anything, bruh. I'm here for you," Blood said leaving.

Naz could feel the warm rush as he straightened up the mess and threw the heroin in his backpack in the closet.

Lying down on the bed he gave in to the warmth and comfort the dope gave him and eased into the melodic sounds of Coltrane. Pops had turned him on at first. He wasn't turned on to him at first. He thought he was a little too out there but then he found that controlled more traditional Coltrane when he came across Ballads. That was his Coltrane and he played it for everybody. It was a good piece to introduce if you hadn't listened to Coltrane. It was cool with a good beat and a nice melody. And it was what he liked to listen to when he was in his zone which was now. Funny thing was he'd listened to Ballads over a thousand times and each time he would pick up something new and applaud Coltrane again. The dope gave him the opportunity to revisit a happier place and he saw both pops and Monica smiling. At least they were happy. He even saw Cathy as a shy, innocent, skinny, knock-kneed eleven year old. He liked her better when she was trying to steal a glance back in Ms. Oakley's class. Now here she was like the rest of the leeches out there. 'Naz I'm gonna give you some but first before you must pass go and collect two hundred dollars and by the way I need you to look at these investments potentials'. Yeah, I liked her better in elementary he thought to himself. He was in a coma like state now, wrapped in his own securities full of nice dreams when he heard when Noah come in. There were two voices. The other a female. Noah came in to check on me to make sure I was alright but I feigned sleep and he closed the door behind him, but it mattered little. I still heard her and couldn't help but hear her prodding Noah.

"I understand, and I am so happy for you baby. I wish I could get straight and I am in no way suggesting or trying to influence you baby. I'm just asking you if you can help me get a lil' something to put me to sleep, baby. I know you been hanging out with your boy Naz and he hooked you up."

"Sorry I can't bae. My man's Naz gave me moncy because I was straight to do some things around here. You know fix the place up. If I know my mans he probably gave it o me because I was straight. I can't fuck that up even for you babe. That's my brother. I can't betray him."

"Ah. Babe. I'm hurtin'. You gots to hook a sista up. Let me get a twenty baby and I'll come back and take real good care of you."

"Here. Here's a twenty but I'm gonna tell you what once you take this twenty forget you knew my name. Don't you ever come back here. You heard me." "Ahh babe don't say it like that. You almost sound like you mean it. See you in a little while," she said reaching up to kiss an angry Noah who pushed her away and out of the apartment.

Naz smiled. His boy Noah was back.

The sudden knock at the door aroused Naz. The affects of the dope were beginning to wear off and he needed another bump but there was no one but Noah to administer it and he couldn't ask him although he'd see it enough times to do it himself by now.

"Hey bruh."

"What's up Noah? Where've you been all day?"

"Down West 4th hoopin' with the big boys. I think I'm just about ready."

"To go pro?"

"Yeah. Either here or overseas."

"Well, congratulations my brotha. By the way who was ol' girl?"

"Just some junkie I used to run with. She helped me pull off a couple of capers but she ain't really feelin' the new me."

"Sometimes you've got to get the poison out of your life. Some people can end up being toxic, like a cancer and you've got to get rid of it before it infects you."

"I feel you, bruh. You know I've been here all of a couple of days and the competition's better here, but I don't want to be here any more bruh. It's like I know I can't shake my past but damn I don't have to confront it every day either. I mean when I was in Negril no one knew me. It was like I was brand new. It's like I was born again. I had a chance to start over. I didn't bump into fiends like that one."

"Just let me know when you're ready to go, bruh. I'm ready to go whenever you are. I was feeling just the way you are and that's why I left the first chance I got."

"Okay. Give me a couple of days to wrap some things up."

"Just let me know."

"Oh, and Naz I appreciate the way you hooked the place up. You're a good brotha."

"No worries,"

"I'm a lay it down. Wake me up if you're running in the morning. Night," Noah said before leaving. That night he did something he hadn't done since he was a kid. Noah got down on his knees and thanked God.

Naz had no intentions of running. It was the same week as the fight and Noah knew the routine. There was no physical anything after a fight just plenty of r&r. Naz wasn't even sure if he was going to wash. Turning on the television he eased back on the couch content to watch old reruns of Martin.

"I'm out baby," Noah said hugging his boy before heading out the door ball in hand.

"Already, bruh. Don't take all them cats money."

"Ain't even lookin' for no run. Just working on my handle and post up game today."

"Okay. I feel you. Do you, bruh."

572

"Gotta give myself the best shot I can so I can get me a little house down there with you, Murph and Trip. What? You thought you were just going to leave me here?"

"Nah, bruh. You know whether you have the ends or not we gotcha."

"I know that. My niggas have always been down for me. Couldn't ask for a better family. My real family never cared about me the way you brothas do."

"Always have always will now get up outta here with all that sentimental shit."

"How you handlin' the loss?"

"I can't with you runnin' your mouth, bruh. Now would you go I need to think."

"I'm out. You're a sore loser Naz. I never knew that."

"That's 'cause I never lost, bruh."

"How 'bout that? The Mighty Naz cannot handle losing," Noah laughed before closing the door behind him.

"Fuck you, Noah," Naz screamed throwing a pillow at the door. "You idiot."

Naz picked up the phone no soone than he saw Noah hit the street.

"What up my nigga. Where you at?"

"Downstairs. What's up Blackman."

"I need you to hit me off."

"On my way."

"Morning."

"Morning. I just saw Noah. That nigga's serious. I do believe he gonna make it too. He wants it so bad. I'm thinking that he came about it in his own time but he wants to join his friends down in the islands and he knows he still has the talent that they'll pay him handsomely."

"I hope you're right."

Naz heard the front door close but wasn't sure if someone was coming or going. He was zooming in and out of the spectrum. He faded in and out of hues of blues and purples tasted the words of Sade and smelled the sounds of Will Downing. He heard Malcolm speaking only to him and then there was Martin. He walked hand in hand through Washington Square Park with Monica and raced his daddy to the corner when he was eight before falling off to sleep a smile tattooed on his face. "He awoke to the sounds and smells of the blues and wondered if life weren't just one shade of blues melting into another. And then there was the nerve wracking sound of pots and pans clanking together in the kitchen. Noah as he remembered was a fairly good cook. In fact, Noah was pretty good at anything he chose to do."

"What's up bruh? Don't tell me you've been sitting here watching television all day?"

"Yes sir."

"A therapist might say you're suffering a bout of depression after your first and most recent loss. How would you rate that assessment?"

"Pretty damn accurate. You didn't meet Kree did you?"

"Nah you kept tellin' me we had to meet but we ran out of time."

"In any case, I was talking to her about retiring after I won the belt and she couldn't even conceive of such a thing. But what she couldn't understand was that after twelve years being on top of the game I'm burnt out. I mean I know I have the skills to beat most fighters these days, but I've lost the heart—you know—the eye of the tiger. That's why I lost that fight because I didn't have the heart to take it from him. The desire's gone. I really don't want to fight anymore."

"You don't even want to win back what's rightfully yours?"

"No, bruh. I don't even want to do that. Don't you see? I lost 'cause I didn't want to do this anymore. Neither my head nor heart was in the fight. And you can't win like that."

"Then you know what you gotta do."

"Yeah, I know what I want to do but I have so many obligations and responsibilities hanging over my head. I have so many people counting on me."

"And, when haven't you? That's just your nature, Naz. You're like the pied piper. You always have been. You were always the leader of the pack of bad boys. It was funny that the good wholesome kid with the impeccable reputation was the leader of a pack of hardcore juvenile delinquents. No one could ever figure it out,"

"Wasn't the leader of anything. Was just hanging out with some of my boys is all."

"And no matter what we were doing whether it was being an athlete or trying to be a boss in the drug business we all patterned ourselves after you with your discipline and resolve. And all of us have been very successful at whatever it is we endeavored to do. Now you're talking about quitting. Man, I'm not sure if you know it or not but these cats are still looking at you for direction. Is this really how you want to leave things, bruh? That ain't the Naz I know. No, the Naz I know would never walk away a beaten man. If anything, my Naz was always a winner. At least go out a winner, bruh."

"What you don't know was I was down for the count when my ol' man died but Monica got me up and back in the game. It wasn't for me though. I didn't want to fight at that point. I was done. She was the motivation.

I fought so she'd be proud. But when she passed well that was the final blow as far as I was concerned. This time I was out for sure. I had no motivation left but Kree and Trip decided that now I fight for something greater. I now fought to keep my name out there so I could affect some type of change, but I can't do it anymore bruh. I'm just tired and burn't out."

"So, go ahead and retire, bruh. What did pops always say? Self-preservation is the first law of nature.

Chill, my nigga. At this point in your career and as much as you've accomplished over the last twelve or thirteen years you deserve that. Fuck what anyone says. Let them sit by and wait on you to come out of retirement or take your place in the ring. It's your call, baby," Noah said shooting right jabs at a grinning Naz.

"Man, go ahead with that Noah," Naz said doing his best to cover up. "You know Mr. Medina mentioned working with you. Just think of that, bruh. There's the actual very real possibility of of you becoming a legitimate two sport athlete. You can really concentrate now. It ain't like high school with Missy Brown always chasing after you. You can focus now."

"Mr. Medina? I'm not sure so sure if I liked the way he worked with you on your last fight. But seriously, I could if I had your heart but I aint never liked going anywhere I know a niggas is tryna purposely disfigure me. That's your thing. That ain't never been me. I fuck wit it but when them niggas got serious money on the line with the intent—like I said— to disfigure or do harm to me that's when I tend to get ghost. That shit's crazy if you ask me."

"Funny thing is I'm startin' to agree with you," Naz and Noah both laughed.

The days continued in much the same way with Naz staying in and Blood visiting regularly to tie Naz off. Occasionally, Naz would venture out sometimes for a short run other times time just to get an update from Murph on the local happenings. Naz had let his phone go off a month ago. He'd called mom and Sin but had purposely avoided contacting Trip and Kree.

"They calling me every day, Naz. That's your fam, Naz. Call them and let them know you're alright. They're worried about you, bruh. Kree said if she doesn't hear from you by tomorrow then she and Trip are coming up to see what the fuck is up. Now if you don't want to be bothered right through here shoot them a text sayin' you're fine and came to New York to get away and you'll be home soon."

"I don't even have a phone Murph. I let it go off. Think that may have been a hint," Naz grumbled.

"They love ya' man. I know you're down 'cause you lost, bruh but that's all apart of life but this is the true challenge. Can you get up pick up the pieces and start all over again? That's the true test. We all fall down."

"Ain't even thinking about that. I just want to relax and chill. I don't want to think about boxing or anything else right through here. That's what people feel to realize. I might just need to breathe. Instead everyone wants to tell me what I should be doing when there's no need to be doing anything."

"I gotcha. You might need to tell your extended family down in Negril. They don't know any of this and are worried about you."

"I'll let them know. Let me see your phone, Murph."

"Here use this one," Murph's said pulling out three.

"What up fam?"

"Damn Naz you had me worried. Ain't nobody heard from you. Your numbers been disconnected, and I know what I left you. You had me scared man."

"Shit. I gave half of that shit to Blood. He's always been a good brotha. And ever since I known him he been trying to help out at home. I don't know how many brothers and sisters he got but that nigga could start a football team just with his brothers and sisiters. And he was always trying to feed 'em and take care of 'em. That's all he did."

"I think there were either eight or nine of them and Blood had three or four of them slinging. His crew is made up of his brothers and sisters."

"Yeah, I checked with Murph before I gave him the half a brick,'

"Have you seen him since. Yeah, but I can't get a grip on how he's living just know he's dressing a lot better."

"Make it a point and go around to his crib and make sure they're all eating and not just Blood. They should all be nice off half a key. You feel me?"

"I'll do that tonight around dinner time. What's up with Kree?"

"Nothin'. Doin' her thing. Movin' the foundation forward. Guaranteein' you a win in the rematch and telling potential endorsers that you are 'resilient' and will knock Lomanchenko out in the rematch."

"And how are they responding?"

"They are enamored by her but are waiting until her prognosis rings true before investing or having you endorse their product. Nike's got a hundred million dollars waiting when you defeat him, and do you know what type of monies that will feed the foundation. I think she's excited. She can't wait to tell you."

"Okay. Let me give her a call Trip."

"When you coming home?"

585

"Waiting for Noah to tie up some loose ends. Maybe the end of this week."

"He's not using, is he?"

"No. He doesn't even know it's here. All he's been doin' is workin' out and ballin'. He and I run together every now and then but yeah, he's on the right track. Talkin' about goin' overseas and play for a few years."

"Beautiful. I'm going to hold him to that. You going to call Kree?"

"Nah, but I'd appreciate it if you told he her I was okay and will give her a call as soon as I work some things out."

"I'll do that and take your time working things out just be careful with your meds."

"I gotcha. One."

Naz used the phone to check the funds on his card and found that he was down to only a hundred and fifty that wouldn't even be enough to feed the two men for the next week. Perhaps he would have to call Kree after all.

"Why haven't I heard from you Naz? People that love each other argue and disagree and then if they're mature they communicate until they work out a win or a compromise but what they don't do is let an argument or disagreement end their love affair and friendship stupid. Or are you just that fuckin' cold that you can just stop talking to me for the rest of your life. Is that it you cold, ass, mothrfucker? Why should I have to call your mother or sister to see if you're alive?"

"I don't know either other than to tell you that I need some time to think. I've disappointed a lot of people and I just need some time to think and put things in perspective."

"Baby you did your best. You lost. So what. Life goes on. What's next? I'll tell you what's next. I miss you and now that I've heard your voice I've just got to see you so expect me either late tonight or tomorrow morning. Talk to you later sweetie."

Naz gathered the few belongings he had and walked the block and a half back to his apartment where he took a shower and threw on some of that Anderson Paak to set the mood. He knew Kree would somehow find herself uptown in Harlem tonight and so he found the Nike sweatsuit he'd packed away for a special occasion threw it on with his gold chain and after sniffing a few lines and having a glass of Hennessey he leaned back and let the Hennessey take effect. That was until he heard her voice calling him. At first, he thought he was a dreaming and then he realized she was actually here. He knew she was coming. Why was he surprised? Kree traveled countries like niggas crossed streets. And if it was something that she had her sights set on she always moved with haste and tonight she wanted her man.

Naz had kept Kree off his mind as much as possible and seldom thought about her but it hadn't been easy as he Still remained quite fond of her. She was fine as fuck and the shit in bed. And she loved him. That's what made it hard to push her out of his thoughts. But their lives were so intertwined he hardly worried about ever seeing her.

"Hey baby. Ooh, you look even better than when I last saw you. Anyone else here," Kree smiled.

"Nah baby. It's just me."

"Good. It's not necessary that you utter anothether word tonight sweetie."

It was early afternoon before they woke up. Kree was up first and ran to the local bodega to grab a grapefruit and a couple of coffees. When breakfast was over they made love again. She made him want for her again but before he could let her know she was dressed and out the door. Some meeting or something. She said she'd be back by earlier evening. Suddenly he felt his stomach turn. Reaching for the garbage can he felt his mouth fill. *'Damn'*. At first, he thought it was the breakfast then realized the heroin every morning had finally taken hold and was now a part of his daily routine and he was late. Naz called Blood. Minutes later his boy showed up.

"I stopped by Noah's and he told me you were here," Blood recalled. "I was on my way here when you called."

"Good lookin' out, Blood. My girl flew up. I figured we needed some privacy, so I came home."

"I feel you. You gonna let me meet her?"

"She went out to take care of some business, but I will. Let me ask you something, Blood? I woke up and threw up this morning."

"When was this?"

"A minute or so before I called you."

"When's your next fight Naz?"

"I'm not sure. Why do you ask?"

"Because you might wanna pass on this shit for the next few days or so. What is happening is you missed your usual dosage and it just let you know that it was time. Your body's calling for it. It's teling you that need it. You're body's hooked. Leave that shit alone or you'll never box again."

"Are you serious, bruh?"

"Dead serious, bruh. Leave that shit alone. You're no longer in control. It's taking over. I can't do it anymore. Trip, Noah, or Murph find out that I'm the one that been hitting you off and they'll kill me, bruh."

"I feel you, Blood and I appreciate all you've done for me."

"Man don't thank me for that. If anything were to happen to you I 'd never forgive yourself."

"You're fine, bruh. Come on. Let's take a walk. How's your fam?"

"They're good. Thanks to you."

"Let's go. I've been meaning to shout at Tasha."

"She'd love that, bruh. She's always looked up to you as sort of an older brother. She's put together a scrapbook of all your fights. Man, for you to just show

up would mean the world to her."

"Then let's go, bruh."

Minutes later they arrived at the three storied

brownstone. Two dorrs down it looked like a

homecoming of sorts as a small crew gathered.

"What's going on Blood?"

"Nothing out of the ordinary. Just a blessing. I

could slash prices because of the price I got it for,"

Blood smiled.

"Is that right?" Naz smiled.

"Hold up. Let me run to the spot and get her,"

he said as he headed to the corner. "The doors open.

Go ahead in."

Naz mad his way inside. The house was

immaculate and had been recently refurbished. Naz now thirsty opened the refrigerator and finding it packed grabbed a diet soda just as he heard the front door open.

Seeing Naz the girl screamed.

"Nazar! Oh my God! How long's it been?" she said before running and jumping into his arms.

"Hey Tasha," Naz said grinning. Tasha was four or five years years younger than Naz but had always tagged along behind him as a kid and tried to emulate everything Naz did and had even tried boxing just to be close and near to him. And after getting caught up and giving her his number and promising to stay in touch made his departure much to the teenager's chagrin.

Instead of heading back to the house. Naz jogged the ten blocks or so up to Dez's spot and was greeted warmly. Thanks to Naz they were back in business and eating again.

"What's up, bruh? Never did get a chance to thank you for what you did. I appreciate you," Dez said.
"What can I do for you today Blackman?"

"I need for you to hit me off."

"No problem."

Two and a half hours later Naz made his way back downtown to the crib and not too soon as Kree walked in moments later.

"You okay baby?"

"I don't know. I've been feeling a little under the
weather today."

"I wasn't too much for you last night, did I?"

"No. You were beautiful, baby," Naz said taking her into his arms and hugging her tightly.

"You know I had to come up and stoke the fires for you sweetheart. With all these beautiful women in New York. I said you'd better go and make sure your man still has his sights set on you."

"Come on Kree, you know I only have eyes for you."

"Then why don't we fly home together and let me cater to your every need?"

"I wish I could Bea but I still have some things to tidy up. It shouldn't take me long. No more than a week or so."

The two made love several times that day before Kree had to go. Naz was surprised to find the woman

596

tearful on her departure. But once gone Naz retreated to his comfort level and soon found himself back at Noah's.

Down to his last hundred dollars Naz had forgotten to ask Kree to deposit more money in his checking and considered calling and asking for more but didn't want to arouse any more suspicion and so thought better of af asking. Once at Noah's Naz felt something awry in the household.

"You okay, bruh?"

"Yeah, I'm good. Why do you ask?"

"Because there's never been anything between us. Remember when you were fourteen or fifteen and everyone had gotten their first piece af poonanny and you still hadn't and so you made it up under the bridge at Hunt's Point after you saved up all your allowance and lunch money."

"Yeah, yeah, yeah," Noah said a smile trying to creep in.

"So, you went under the bridge on that Friday and paid for one of those girls. Saturday you were screaming and yellin' about how your dick was on fire but being that it was Saturday and there was nothing open. Well, you could have gone to Harlem Hospital but as everyone knows Friday and Saturday they ain't going to see you so you, but you had no choice. Friday and Saturday is
Harlem Hospital night and if you wasn't shot or stabbed they weren't going to see you so you screamed and cried until Trip gave you something to tide you over 'til Monday. Anyway…"

"I know what happened Naz. If you remember I was there."

"Just let me finish, bruh."

"You know sometimes I just think you just like to hear yourself talk Naz."

"Anyway, on that Monday me, Trip and Murph took you to the hospital and they gave you some antibiotics and painkillers and a stern warning about going up to Hunt's Point and messin' with them ho's. We all joked and laughed about it but just as soon as you'd saved up enough you were back up their again. And everybody knows what happened. When I asked you why you would go up their again knowing what the results would be you said it was so good that you had to go back. I never told anyone because it was something we shared. We never held anything from each other but now I feel like yoou're holding back. Come on Noah.

That ain't how we roll."

"Oh, it's not? Then why did I find this under your bed when I was straightenening up?" Noah said holding up the orange and clear hypodermic needle.

Nazar dropped his head before speaking. Clearly caught and embarrassed Naz looked hard at his oldest and perhaps dearest friend before speaking.

"Man, do you know how many people love you and want to see you make good on your recovery? I was not going to be the one that was responsible for you falling off. I'm sorry man but I wasn't going to be the one," Naz said before getting up and rushing to the bathroom where he left it all.

"That bad huh?" Noah said on his return.

"Just started yesterday."

"You know what that means don't you?"

"Yeah, Blood told me yesterday."

"Blood?"

"Yeah, he was the only one I knew I could ask without it getting back to you and Trip and Murph."

"You right about that, bruh. If any of us had known, we would have beaten yo' ass welterweight belt or not. Where are you getting from anyway?"

"Trip gave me a brick for me to ship back to Negril."

"And?"

"I gave half to Blood who seems to be struggling tryin' to eat and feed his fam."

"Gave? Have you lost your mind Naz? Okay.

Forget the dumb shit, bruh. Where's the rest of it?"

Naz pointed to the black backpack by his feet.

"Oh my God! This is a junkie's paradise," Noah smiled as Naz began wretching again. "You know this monster got a hold on you when it tells you it's time for your dose."

"Yeah, so I've been told."

"Roll your sleeve up."

Naz did as instructed and was leaning back in a matter of minutes soaking up the sweet sounds of Sade and all was right with the world. Naz could hear Noah talking to him but by now everything was just a cacophony of sound. By the time, Naz came around he found Noah sitting there needle dangling from his own arm a smile on his face that said all was right with his world as well.

CPSIA information can be obtained
at www.ICGtesting.com
Printed in the USA
LVHW031637300919
632705LV00010B/634/P